SUDDEN PLEASURES

The Pleasure Channel, Book Three

BERTRICE SMALL

Sudden Pleasures

Copyright © 2007, 2021 Bertrice Small
All rights reserved.
This edition published 2021

Cover design by Cynthia Lucas

ISBN: 978-1-68068-285-4

The characters and events portrayed in this book are fictitious. Any similarity to real persons, living or dead, is coincidental and not intended by the author.

No part of this book may be reproduced or stored in a retrieval system, or transmitted in any form or by any means, electronic, mechanical, photocopying, recording or otherwise, without express written permission of the publisher.

This book is published on behalf of the author's estate by the Ethan Ellenberg Literary Agency.

Books by Bertrice Small

Leslie Family Saga (Cyra Hafisa)
    The Kadin
    Love Wild and Fair
The Border Chronicles
    A Dangerous Love
    The Border Lord's Bride
    The Captive Heart
    The Border Lord and Lady
    The Border Vixen
    Bond of Passion
O'Malley Family Saga
    Skye O'Malley
    All the Sweet Tomorrows
    This Heart of Mine
    A Love For All Time
    Lost Love Found
    Wild Jasmine
Wyndham Family Saga
    Blaze Wyndham
    Love, Remember Me
Skye's Legacy
    Darling Jasmine
    Bedazzled
    Besieged
    Intrigued
    Just Beyond Tomorrow
    Vixens

Friarsgate Inheritance
- Rosamund
- Until You
- Phillippa
- The Last Heiress

The Pleasure Channel
- Private Pleasures
- Forbidden Pleasures
- Sudden Pleasures
- Dangerous Pleasures
- Passionate Pleasures
- Guilty Pleasures

World of Hetar
- Lara
- A Distant Tomorrow
- The Twilight Lord
- The Sorceress of Belmair
- The Shadow Queen
- Crown of Destiny

The Silk Merchant's Daughters
- Bianca
- Francesca
- Lucianna
- Serena

Single Titles
- Adora
- Unconquered
- Beloved
- Enchantress Mine
- The Spitfire
- A Moment in Time
- To Love Again
- The Love Slave

Hellion
Betrayed
Deceived
The Innocent
A Memory of Love
The Duchess
The Dragon Lord's Daughters

Anthology Stories
"Ecstasy" in Captivated
"Mastering Lady Lucinda" in Fascinated
"The Awakening" in Delighted
"Zuleika and the Barbarian" in I Love Rogues

Dedication

*To my editor, Kara Cesare, who said I could when
I was sure I couldn't.
This one's for you, sweetie, with my grateful thanks.*

Table of Contents

Chapter One 1
Chapter Two. 29
Chapter Three 60
Chapter Four 86
Chapter Five. 114
Chapter Six. 142
Chapter Seven 169
Chapter Eight. 198
Chapter Nine 225
Chapter Ten 253

Epilogue. 287
About the Author. 289
About the Publisher. 291

Chapter One

Screwed! She was royally, totally, and completely screwed. And all because that charming old man who had been her grandfather came from a generation that still believed in happily ever after. Ashley Cordelia Kimbrough, the richest woman in Egret Pointe, could have told you that there was absolutely no such thing as happily ever after.

"You can't find any way around his will?" she asked her attorneys for what was probably the hundredth time. "Nothing?"

Rick Johnson and Joe Pietro d'Angelo shook their heads at her.

"You've still got eighteen months," Rick said. "A lot can happen in eighteen months, Ash. There's still plenty of time."

"Yeah," Joe chimed in. "And it would have been a lot worse if we hadn't found out about Derek. If you'd married him, it would have cost you a lot of money, Ash. A lot of money. I would have thought a guy like that would have been smarter, but maybe it's just been luck that kept him one step ahead of the law. But once he started howling about the prenup, bells started going off around here."

Ashley sighed. "Thank God you two checked him out, but everyone seemed to think he was the perfect match for me. But then, what wasn't to like? He was tall, blond, athletic, well-spoken. He was a great dresser, and seemed to be well-fixed himself. Who knew that Derek Douglas Carruthers was wanted in Georgia and South Carolina for fraud? And that his real name was Elmer Oswald Leonard?"

"Let's not forget he is also wanted in Thailand, Italy, and Turkey," Joe reminded her dryly. "This guy was a con man extraordinaire, Ash. He's left a long trail of broken hearts and empty bank accounts in his wake."

"So now I'm back to square one," Ashley said. "You know, guys, I'm starting to be known around Egret Pointe as the Bad-luck Bride. It's more than embarrassing."

"Oh, come on, Ash," Rick said. "These things happen. Weddings get called off at the last minute all the time. No big deal."

"This is the third wedding I've planned," Ashley said, "that's been called off at the last minute. The first one was the year after grandfather died. I was twenty-four, and really should have known better, but I didn't, did I?"

"None of us knew that Carson would run off with the best man two days before the wedding," Joe said. "Usually it's the maid of honor the groom runs off with, isn't it?" He struggled to hold back the smile that was threatening to burst forth. In retrospect it really had been a comical situation.

Ashley laughed. "I thought it was so romantic that he was saving himself for our wedding night," she said. "Carson was really the nicest of them all, you know. I see him every now and again in the city. He finds these wonderful new young designers for me all the time. It's like he's trying to make it up to me. He's still with Peter, and they're very happy. They're even talking about adopting a baby."

"You've got a good heart, Ash," Joe remarked.

"Yeah, sure, but I've also got lousy taste in men. May I remind you of my second attempt at marriage? Chandler Wayne. Former quarterback for a pro team, and all man, all the time. I made damned certain he wasn't another Carson, and he wasn't. Not too inventive in the sack, but very enthusiastic," Ashley said, enjoying the fact that her two attorneys were embarrassed by her frankness, especially as both of them remembered that it had made the tabloids when Chandler had died during a bout of autoerotic sex while in Vegas with his six groomsmen for a weeklong bachelor party.

Both lawyers had been married for a long time. Both had children who were grown and out of the house, or still in college. Both were obviously content, although Ashley knew that their wives were frequent visitors to The Channel. And very few women who visited The Channel did so for sightseeing purposes only. Most women visiting The Channel did so to satisfy their sexual fantasies. Ashley certainly did. Without it she would have gone crazy after all the Sturm und Drang in her life.

Her parents had been drowned in a boating accident when she was fourteen. She and her brother made their home after that with Grandfather Kimbrough at Kimbrough Hall. Their maternal grandparents were deceased, and there were no other relatives. Her brother had graduated from West Point, and as a second lieutenant been killed in Desert Storm at the age of twenty-three. Ashley was in her freshman year of college that year. She hadn't wanted to go to college because she had an idea to open a specialty shop in Egret Pointe. But Edward Kimbrough had insisted, promising to back her venture when she graduated.

With that incentive dangling before her like a golden carrot, Ashley managed to graduate in three years' time with a degree in business. It had meant no dating, no vacations, no life. But she had done it, and true to his word her grandfather had financed the elegant lingerie shop that Ashley named Lacy Nothings. He hadn't thought much of the idea, he told her candidly, but Ashley knew her market. Egret Pointe was no longer a dull small town. When grandfather had built Ansley at Egret Pointe, his first upscale development, everything had changed. The village, while maintaining its small-town charm, had become more sophisticated.

Lacy Nothings had been a big hit, and a welcome addition to local shopping. And as its reputation spread, women from nearby towns came to the Egret Pointe store to purchase the alluring undergarments and night garments that the shop sold. Many were original designs. Many were handmade. And everything was of the absolute best quality. And then she had done her first catalog, and the orders began pouring in from all over the United States and Canada.

"Who would have thunk women would pay so much money for so little?" her grandfather had said, surprised, but actually pleased that Ashley had spotted both a trend and a need, and locked onto it. He hadn't always agreed with her, for Edward Kimbrough was a conservative man, but he had been Ashley's biggest booster.

And now Ashley was in the process of opening two new stores: one in an upmarket neighborhood in the city, and another in a similarly good location in a wealthy suburb. But everything was being threatened by this stupid clause in her grandfather's will: Ashley Cordelia Kimbrough had to marry by the time she was thirty-five or she would lose everything. Her home. The millions of dollars her grandfather had left her. And her investments, including Lacy Nothings, because her stores were originally a part of

Edward Livingston Kimbrough's investments, and the monies she was using to open the new stores were part of the estate. They were hers to use only until she was thirty-five. If at that point she didn't have a husband, then Ashley would lose it all to SSEXL, the Society Seeking Extraterrestrial Life. Not that her grandfather had believed in life on other planets. No. He had done it to please his stupid girlfriend, who couldn't be satisfied that she would get a million on Edward's death. So he had added the clause to please Lila. He had certainly never expected that his granddaughter would strike out three times trying to get a man to the altar. A gay fiancé; a sex-addicted fiancé, and a con man.

"My luck with men just sucks," Ashley said gloomily. "What the hell am I going to do, guys, if we can't break the will? Can we prove that Lila took advantage of him? Used her wiles to cajole him into the clause so her cuckoo organization would profit?"

"Not a chance," Rick replied. "Edward was not senile or delusional at all. He was in full charge of himself when he added that clause, Ash. I'm sorry. There is no way around this. You'll have to get married in the next eighteen months, or you'll lose it all."

Tiffany Pietro d'Angelo, Joe's wife, had been sitting in on the meeting. She had become his legal assistant a few years ago, when their children had left for college. "The trouble with lawyers," Tiffany said softly, "is that you don't think outside the box."

"You have a suggestion?" Ashley asked hopefully.

Tiffany nodded. "What about an old-fashioned arranged marriage?"

"An arranged marriage? What's that?" Ashley wanted to know.

"You're crazy," Joe said to his wife.

"No, I'm not," Tiffany replied. "What, you think in the twenty-first century things like arranged marriages no longer exist? Well, they do. And that would seem to be Ashley's only way out. Are you seriously proposing she turn up her toes and let SSEXL have everything? Let Lila Peabody, the old bitch, get it all? No way!"

"Somebody please tell me exactly what an arranged marriage is?" Ashley said.

"It's an old-fashioned way of matching people up by religion, economic background, ethnic similarities, that kind of thing," Joe said.

"It's a legitimate possibility," Rick said thoughtfully, "but where are we going to find a match for Ashley, Tiff?"

"Yeah, Tiff!" Joe echoed sarcastically.

Tiffany Pietro d'Angelo was a slender, petite woman with champagne blond hair. No one had realized how very smart she was until she had gone into her husband's office ostensibly to help out after their last child had gone to college. But Tiffany had been listening to Joe for over thirty years, and once in the office she had learned quickly. Now she turned her blue eyes to look at the two partners. "Your cousin, Joe. He has a client with the same problem as Ashley." Now she focused on Ashley. "Joe's cousin Raymond is a lawyer in the city. Some big fancy firm with three or four WASPy names. We had dinner with him and his wife, Rose, last week. He's got a client whose father put a similar clause in his will. The guy has got to marry soon or he loses everything." She looked back at her husband. "Remember now, *stupido?*"

Joe clapped his hand to his head. "Tiff, baby! You're right! I should call him immediately and find out exactly what his client's problem is. Then we go from there."

"You're suggesting that you arrange a marriage for me with a total stranger?" Ashley asked. "No. I don't think so."

"Listen, Ashley," Tiffany said quietly, "no one is suggesting we set a date and you two meet for the first time at the altar. This isn't India. Let Joe check it out with his cousin.

If there is a possibility that you two might be a match, we'll arrange a meeting in our offices here. If you and the guy hit it off, then we can run with it from there. Hey, it takes all the fuss and muss out of looking for a guy. We'll have his background, because he's Ray's client. And he has to have a few bucks or his father wouldn't have put in such a clause trying to protect him and the family money. It could be an ideal setup for you."

"Then if he's rich and relatively acceptable, why hasn't he found his own wife?" Ashley wanted to know. "Sounds very fishy to me. What if the guy is weird or a perv?"

"Ray will know," Tiffany said soothingly.

Ashley sat silent for several long moments while they waited for her to say something. Finally she spoke. "Okay, check it out, Joe. And when you have all the facts—and I mean *all* of them—come back to me with them. I'll make my decision then." She stood up. "I've got to get back to the shop. I have a special shipment coming in today for Emily Devlin. Pure silk, lace made by nuns in a convent in Madeira, the whole thing hand-sewn. Her husband ordered it for her as a surprise for after the baby is born."

"That man is a treasure," Tiffany remarked. Then she got up too. "I'll see you out," she said, "and Joe, get on the phone now with Ray."

The two women walked arm in arm into the office's reception area.

"An arranged marriage sounds like it might be a good idea, Tiff," Ashley said. "Thanks for being so on-the-ball and thinking of it."

"Don't think badly of the boys for not coming up with a solution," Tiffany answered her. "This is a thorny problem you've got, sweetie. They're guys. They think practical." Then she grinned. "And this is definitely a night for The Channel, huh?"

"I can never thank you enough for introducing me to it," Ashley said, returning the grin. "After the debacle with Carson I really needed a serious diversion. Everyone is always telling me how calm and levelheaded I am. Well, that's because I take my means out in The Channel." She chuckled. "And someone's cute butt is going to get strapped pink and hot tonight, I can assure you."

"Glad I could help," Tiffany replied, surprised at what she had just heard. She would never have considered that Ashley was into domination, but then, she had learned long ago never to judge a book by its cover. "Have fun," she said as she ushered Ashley out the door of the office. "See you at the club."

Ashley waved a diffident hand as she hurried down the stairs. Outside the June afternoon was a glorious one. Watching the light traffic she walked across Main Street to her own shop. "Did the Devlin order come in?" she asked Nina, her assistant, as she entered the store.

"Yep, just while you were gone. I didn't open it. I thought you would want to do that," Nina said with a smile. "But I have to admit I'm dying to see it. It's in the back."

"Have we been busy?" Ashley wanted to know.

"Sure we have," Nina replied. "Bridal season, and they all want sexy underwear."

Ashley smiled and went into her office, where Nina had placed the small package. Carefully she tore off the paper wrapping. Then she opened the box and lifted the exquisite silk-and-lace nightgown from the tissue wrapping. It was the palest pink, with the most delicate lace Ashley had ever seen. Carson had discovered the lace while vacationing with Peter on the island of Madeira, ferreted out its source, and brought the information to her. She had paid the nuns for a year's supply of their lace, and put it with her seamstress to use on certain garments. Part of her shop's success was being able to offer unique, one-of-a-kind items. The nightgown in her hands was certainly beautiful.

"Nina, come and look," she called out, and her assistant hurried in.

"God, it's beautiful!" Nina said. "She's going to love it, but I wonder if he knows it will be Christmas before she can wear it. I mean, it isn't something you put on when you're nursing. Breast milk would really stain such delicate silk, and she'll nurse exclusively for six months, like they all do now."

"It's the thought that counts," Ashley said softly. "And he thought of it. Now, why can't I find a guy like that?"

"You want to talk about it?" Nina asked sympathetically. She was a motherly but fashionable woman in her early fifties.

"What's to talk about?" Ashley said gloomily. "Three weddings planned. Three weddings canceled. Three florists, three caterers, three bands, all paid for and canceled. Three wedding gowns and twelve attendants' dresses, all paid for and then donated to the hospital's secondhand shop. And let us not forget the hundreds of wedding gifts that have all had to be packed up and returned with a handwritten note of regret. 'Dear Mr. and Mrs. Van Buren: I'm so sorry to tell you that the wedding has had to be canceled because the groom turned out to be gay, dead, a con man. I am returning your beautiful and most thoughtful wedding gift via Federal Express. Fondly, Ashley Cordelia Kimbrough, who has sucky taste in men.'"

Nina couldn't help it: She laughed. "Oh, honey," she said. "I'm sorry."

"I'm sorrier," Ashley replied. "But it really is getting to be rather comical, isn't it? I wonder if 'three strikes and you're out' applies to situations like this?"

"I think you just haven't met the right man," Nina, a widow, said cheerfully.

"I've got eighteen months," Ashley said softly, "or I really will be out. Out on the street. Damn! I will not lose everything to an organization called SSEXL, even if I have to marry a monkey in the zoo!"

"Speaking of monkeys, Lila Peabody came in today to pick up her new bras," Nina murmured. "That boob job she got looks great. And at her age, too. She said she was just seventy."

"Seventy-five," Ashley corrected. "Perky boobs, and a face like a leather satchel. She has the money. Why she didn't do the face too, I don't know. I suppose it's because her skin is so damaged from her constant tanning."

"Rumor has it she has a new beau," Nina said.

"I heard. Old Paul Hilton," Ashley replied.

"No fool like an old fool," Nina remarked.

"Do you ever think of remarrying?" Ashley asked her assistant.

"No. I don't want to break another one in, thanks. Besides, who needs a man when you have The Channel, my dear? I can't thank you enough for introducing me to it. I can have sex anytime, and any way I want it, and at four a.m. I'm back in my own bed. It's just too perfect."

Ashley laughed. "TMI," she told Nina, who just chuckled.

"Do you want me to call Mr. Devlin and tell him his order is in?" Nina asked.

"Yes, please," Ashley said.

The rest of the afternoon passed without incident. Two more brides-to-be came in to purchase items for their trousseaux. One of them was a girl Ashley remembered being the little sister of a schoolmate. She almost winced when the girl glowingly told Nina that Ashley and her sister used to babysit her when they were in their teens. Then Ashley made the mistake of asking after the girl's older sister.

"Oh, Claire's been married over ten years now, and has three kids," came the reply. "Can I tell her that you said hi?"

Ashley nodded, smiling, but catching Nina's sympathetic gaze. *Bloody hell!* she thought. *Why is it that everybody but me can find a husband? I'm not looking for anything unusual. I want a nice guy with a good sense of humor with whom I can talk and share things. Is that so hard?* Obviously it was. Being rich was both a blessing and a curse.

At five p.m. on the dot she closed up Lacy Nothings for the day and bade Nina good night. Then, going around back, she got into her silver Solstice and drove home.

"Good evening, Miss Ashley," Byrnes, her butler, said as she entered the house. "Shall I tell Mrs. B. dinner at the usual time?"

"Yes, but I'll want to eat out on the porch tonight, Byrnes," Ashley told him.

"Very good, miss," the butler replied with a bow, and went off to the kitchens to speak with his wife, who was Kimbrough Hall's cook.

Ashley went up to her bedroom suite. After stripping off her clothes she walked naked into her large bathroom. Opening one side of the double glass doors to her shower, she programmed it and turned the water on before stepping into it. A dozen water jets spurted forth from the marble enclosure as she turned herself about to get thoroughly wet. Reaching for a cake of olive oil soap a friend had brought her from Italy last year, she washed herself quickly. She didn't want to be late for dinner, because Mrs. Byrnes usually did some sort of steak dish midweek, and dinner was served at six p.m. on the dot. She would want a little time for a glass of wine before she ate.

Turning off the shower after she was well rinsed, Ashley stepped from the glass-and-marble surround and reached for a towel. The towel was warm from the heating rack. Once dried, she looked at herself critically in the full-length mirror. She wasn't one of those tiny size-zero or size-two little girls. She was the average size of the American woman: size fourteen. But there wasn't an ounce of fat on her body, her legs were long, and her breasts were high and softly rounded. Everything was in proportion, she thought smugly, even if she couldn't be called dainty. That was one reason she had opened Lacy Nothings: so that every women from size two to size twenty-two could have sexy underwear and night wear.

Pulling on a pair of soft, fleecy pale gray pants and a light pink cotton tee, Ashley padded downstairs in her bare feet and headed for the screened porch that overlooked the bay. Byrnes was waiting for her with a glass of red wine. Ashley took it from him and sniffed. "North Fork viticulture," she said, and the butler nodded. She took a sip of the wine, swishing it about her mouth, breathing the fragrance. "Bedell Cellars Main Road Red," she decided, and looked to him for confirmation.

"Very good, Miss Ashley," Byrnes said with a small smile.

"Mrs. B. is cooking me a filet, isn't she?"

"Yes, miss. Shall I tell her to put it on now, or do you wish to wait?" the butler asked.

"Now, please, I'm starving!" Ashley told him. "It's been a long day, and Grandfather's will cannot be broken."

"Mr. Kimbrough was a very careful and thorough man, Miss Ashley," Byrnes observed, and then he hurried off to the kitchen.

Ashley chuckled as she sipped her wine and gazed out over the bay. Byrnes knew her late grandfather probably better than anyone. He had grown up at Kimbrough Hall, as his father had been the previous butler. And he knew all about the clause that had been added to her grandfather's will at Lila's behest. Byrnes had not liked Lila Peabody, but he would have thought it presumptuous to voice an opinion on the matter. But Ashley had heard him speaking to his wife on the subject one day, and the butler had not spoken well of her grandfather's last girlfriend, stating most bluntly that Lila was no lady. Ashley smiled to herself as she remembered the butler's disapproving tone. But, of course, he was right: Lila Peabody had not been a lady, which had amused Ashley's grandfather.

Hearing Byrnes rolling in the dinner cart, Ashley seated herself at the little table that had been set up for her. Byrnes placed to her left a small salad plate of endive dressed lightly with a raspberry vinaigrette. Next came the dinner plate, which held a very rare piece of filet mignon, three small potato puffs, and several slender stalks of asparagus with a splash of Hollandaise sauce. The butler stood in attendance while Ashley ate in silence. When she had finished he cleared the dinner and salad plates from the table, replacing them with a dish of freshly hulled local strawberries dusted with sugar, and a tiny pitcher of thick cream.

"The berries were picked this afternoon, Miss Ashley. The strawberry patch is quite bountiful this year," Byrnes said. "Mrs. B. will be making jam and freezing some whole berries for the winter."

"They're delicious, and still warm with the sun," Ashley noted.

"Are there plans for this evening, Miss Ashley?" the butler wanted to know.

"No, I'll be going up to my quarters after I've finished," Ashley told him.

"If you don't mind my mentioning it, Ghostly and Graybar could use a good run on the beach, Miss Ashley."

"I have been neglecting them, haven't I?" Ashley said. "It won't be dark for a while. I'll take them out. Thanks, Byrnes." Finished with her dinner, she stood up. "Are they in the kitchen with Mrs. B.?"

"Yes, Miss Ashley, Shall I bring them up?" the butler asked her.

"No, I'll go and fetch them myself. I want to thank Mrs. B. for such a wonderful dinner. The potato puffs were marvelous, even if I do try to stay away from those hard carbs," Ashley said with a smile. She hurried down to the kitchen, where she found her two greyhounds sprawled beneath Mrs. B.'s large wooden kitchen table. "The puffs were heaven," she told the cook. "Thanks, even if I shouldn't have them."

"Nonsense!" Mrs. B. said with a smile. She was a small, round woman with fading strawberry blond hair that she wore in a bun. She was a perfect contrast to her tall, thin husband. "You're too thin, Miss Ashley, as it is."

Ashley laughed. "Bless you!" she said. Then she whistled to the two dogs, who roused themselves and ambled over to her. Ashley took their leads from a hook on the wall where they were hung, fastened them about the dogs' collars, and led them out of the house through the kitchen gardens. Once on her private beach she released Ghostly and Graybar, and let them run as she strolled along.

The sun was getting lower and lower on the horizon when she finally decided to turn back. Whistling for the two dogs, she turned about. She wanted to get well settled before she turned on The Channel. They had done some upgrades in the last year. Now you could simply subscribe to it the way you would any other premium channel. And the remote had a terrific new feature on it: You could have two fantasies ready to go if you wanted, and Ashley did.

In both of her fantasies she was a Roman noblewoman, the lady Cordelia, but the fantasies had slightly different themes. In fantasy A the noble Cordelia possessed a Celtic sex slave named Quinn, whom she used and abused to their mutual pleasure. In fantasy B, Cordelia, visiting her properties in northern Gaul, was kidnapped by a northern barbarian named Rurik, who made her his sex slave, to be deliciously used and only sometimes abused.

Ashley debated about which fantasy she wanted tonight, but she was still feeling cranky about her visit to the offices of Johnson and Pietro d'Angelo today. She felt so damned helpless about the situation in which she was caught. She had no choice in the matter: If she didn't find a husband she would lose everything, and she didn't want to lose everything. She liked her comfortable lifestyle. She loved the mechanics of her business. And if she had to take a husband to keep it all, she damned well would.

"A," she said aloud. "Tonight I need to be completely in charge, even if it's only my fantasy." Arriving back at the house she let the dogs back into the kitchen. Their beds, when they weren't sleeping with her, were in an unused pantry. "Good night, boys," she said, patting the silky heads. The kitchen, she noted, was vacant. Everything was in its place, but it was empty. Mrs. B. had already retired to the apartment where she and Byrnes lived above the kitchen wing of the house. Back in the open foyer of the house she encountered her butler locking up.

"Will you be needing me again tonight, Miss Ashley?" he asked politely.

"No, thank you. Run along, Byrnes. I'm heading upstairs myself," Ashley said as she mounted the stairs. "Good night."

"Good night, Miss Ashley," the butler replied.

Ashley entered her bedroom suite just as the clock on the mantel of the fireplace in her bedroom was striking eight o'clock. Her bed was already turned down, something Byrnes did every night without fail, as Ashley didn't feel the need for a private maid. Stripping out of her pants and tee, she climbed naked into her bed. Picking up the remote, she pointed it at the wall above the fireplace mantel and pressed a button. Immediately the wall slid back, revealing a large flat-screen television. Ashley pushed a second button and the television came to life.

"Good evening, and welcome to The Channel, where your fantasies become your reality," a silky voice purred. "Please press button A or button B, followed by the enter button. Thank you, and enjoy your evening." The screen darkened.

Ashley pressed button A, then the enter button. She experienced a slight sensation as if her insides were being drawn out, and then she was there, in the bedchamber of her villa, standing naked before a silver mirror. "Where is Quinn?" she demanded of her slave woman. "Why is he not here? The day has been long and trying. He should be here! Find him and bring him to me immediately!"

The slave woman scurried off. Ashley viewed her naked body in the mirror. Her hair in her fantasy was long and luxurious. It fell down her back to her waistline. In reality she had short hair, styled in a gamine look. Her nipples were rouged to make them more prominent. She could hardly wait to get her hands on Quinn tonight. She needed to punish him as she was being punished.

The male sex slave came into the bedchamber. He stood six feet, five inches tall. He was totally naked, for he was not allowed to cover himself except in cold or wet weather, and only if his mistress permitted it. His body was perfection, with everything in proportion and nicely muscular. He was devoid of any hair except on his head, and it was bright red-gold. His eyes were bright blue, but before his mistress he kept them lowered unless commanded to raise them. His genitalia were huge, even at rest. They were bound in leather lacings. He knelt before her, his head down.

Ashley slowly licked her lips. "You are not ready for me," she said in a hard, deadly voice. She raised his head up with one finger of her hand, but his eyes remained unfocused, not looking at her. "Why are you not ready for me? Have you not been told you must be ready for me at all times, Quinn?"

"Yes, mistress," he replied low.

"Yet you choose to disobey," Ashley murmured. Her hand ruffled through his thick hair. "Oh, it is a bad slave, it is. You are bad, are you not, Quinn?"

"Yes, mistress," he agreed in a toneless voice.

"Then you must be punished, Quinn," Ashley said. "I will not be disobeyed and defied by a slave. Your bottom must be burnished until it glows and your cock is standing tall and ready for me. Prepare yourself at once!"

The tall slave stood and went quickly to a cupboard, then drew out several items. One was a device consisting of a bar set between two sturdy marble columns. The bar was wrapped first in thick lambskin, which was then covered in silk. The bar could be raised or lowered to accommodate height. From either end of the bar hung short gold chains with gilded leather manacles. Quinn rolled the contrivance into the center of the chamber. He adjusted the bar to fit his height. Returning to the cupboard, he brought forth a leather strap some eight inches wide and an inch in thickness, which was attached to an ivory handle. Bringing it to his mistress, he handed it to her, eyes still lowered, tensing when the fingers of her other hand wrapped themselves firmly about his balls.

"You will quickly get hard for me, won't you, Quinn?" she whispered in his ear, her tongue licking at him.

"Yes, mistress," he replied softly, reaching up to pinch one prominent nipple.

In return she squeezed his balls tightly. Not hard enough to cause him pain, but hard enough to remind him that she was in charge here. "Make yourself ready, then, Quinn," Ashley told him.

He bent himself over the padded bar and fastened the gilded leather manacles about his big wrists. His mistress tilted the bar so that his buttocks were elevated and most prominently displayed. Then he spread his legs slightly apart. She came around to stand directly in front of him. She thrust her mons directly into his face, and his tongue immediately pushed into her slit and sought her clitoris. Her hiss of indrawn breath told him that he had found his target.

"I did not say you could lick me, Quinn. You really are a very badly behaved slave tonight. That clever tongue of yours will not deter me from whipping you." She stepped back just slightly and held out the leather strap to him. "Kiss it, and thank me for what I am about to do," she said softly.

He kissed the strap—a slow, deep kiss. "I would rather this be your succulent lips, mistress, but thank you for the correction you will give me."

Ashley smiled and moved around behind the slave. Raising her arm, she brought it down with all her strength upon his deliciously wicked butt. For the next few minutes the only sound in the room was the strap smacking Quinn's ass, but then, as the color of his buttocks began to glow pink and then a fine burnished red, Quinn groaned. This admission of her superiority let a flood of pleasure fill her. "Are you getting hard, Quinn?" she demanded of him. "I want you as hard as rock." The strap bit into his succulent flesh several more times.

"I am hard, mistress. So hard I will keep you writhing with pleasure for the next several hours if you will but let me," Quinn told her. The leather about his cock hurt him.

"Are you certain you can keep your promise to me?" Ashley asked him. "If you do not I shall devise an even more painful punishment, Quinn."

"See for yourself, mistress," he invited her.

Lowering her arm and setting the strap aside, she moved around before him and bent down. The straps on the slave's penis were near to bursting. She undid them, freeing him of the tight leather. The penis swelled a bit more. "Perhaps you are ready, or near to it," Ashley allowed. "A few more strokes and you will be near. Then I will finish you off with my mouth before I let you fuck me," she told him. Picking up the strap, she laid five more blows upon him. Then, setting the tawse aside, she moved to the bedside, where a basket of toys was waiting. Choosing a finger-thick piece of marble with a silver loop handle at its end, she dipped it into a bowl of sweet oil.

He howled in outrage as she slowly pushed it into his anus. *"No!"*

Ashley laughed. "You do not tell me what to do, slave. I tell you, and it amuses me to bugger your ass while I suck your cock. We will see if you are as strong as you claim you are. If you come then I will give you as a toy to the other men slaves. If you can hold your juices until you are inside me, I will reward you with a wool garment you may wear in icy weather even without my permission." Sitting down before him, she studied his enormous penis thoughtfully. Then, leaning forward, she took the tip of him in her mouth and sucked hard. He was so big she knew she could not even devour half of him, so she concentrated upon his sensitive tip, her tongue encircling it, nipping at the tender flesh with her little teeth.

Quinn groaned, struggling to keep himself from releasing his passions. Had he been able to he would have put his fist into her dark hair to hold her firm and shoved his penis down her throat, making her milk him dry. But his arms were bound, and the sensation of the little dildo in his ass was frustration beyond all. The thought of putting her under him in a few minutes and fucking her until she was senseless helped him to control himself. That and her promise of a warm garment he might wear whenever he was cold. Sometimes the damp coming off the River Tiber in the winter was almost painful when it worked itself into his bones. Gritting his teeth, he concentrated more on the shameful sensation between his buttocks instead of the delightful sensation of her skillful mouth. Finally she released her hold on him, laughing.

"You are strong, Quinn," she told him. Standing up, she first withdrew the little dildo from between the cheeks of his ass, and then she released him from his manacles.

He stood tall, towering over her. "Am I forgiven, mistress?" he asked her softly.

Ashley ran her hand up his broad, smooth chest. "You are forgiven," she said. "Now put everything away, and then you may take me to bed, Quinn."

He quickly obeyed, and when he turned about he found her already sprawled upon the great bed on its raised dais. He joined her to lie upon his back. Then, lifting her up, he lowered her slowly onto his thick, hard penis, drawing her down, down, down, until she had fully sheathed him.

"You may look at me," she told him, and his blue eyes locked onto her green ones as she began to ride him.

Reaching up, he took her breasts in his hands, playing with them, kneading them, leaning forward to at first lick, and then suckle the nipples. He smiled as her eyes closed and she moaned softly. "The mistress is skilled at riding," he said.

"I learned at an early age from an uncle," she told him, her eyes still shut.

"And did he possess the weapon I wield for you, mistress?" Quinn asked daringly.

Ashley laughed, and her eyes opened to meet his. "You are unique in your attributes, Quinn," she told him. "Most deliciously unique."

He wrapped his arms about her and, sitting up, forced her to be still. His mouth closed over hers, his tongue snaking into her mouth to play with her tongue. Her breasts were mashed against his chest, and he actually felt her heart jump when he rolled her over to put her beneath him. "Wrap your legs about me, mistress," he growled in her ear. "You have had a most trying day, I can see, and you need to be well fucked before you sleep tonight. I am your slave, and I am ready to service you."

"Yesss!" Ashley hissed. She did want to be fucked. Fucked hard, so that all the frustration of the day would melt away. "Fuck me, Quinn!" she ordered him. "Service your mistress, and service her well!"

He began to move on her, at first with long, slow strokes of his long, thick penis. He pushed hungrily into her, making her whimper with her need for his hardness. He stopped after a few minutes and let her feel the throbbing from his member as it lay buried within her tight vagina. Her legs were tight about him as she opened herself as wide as she could to his passions. His big body towered over her. He held her arms pinioned over her head.

"Make me come!" she demanded of him.

The rhythm increased until his penis, wet with her juices, was flashing back and forth within her. Reaching out, he began to tease at her clitoris, rubbing and then pinching it. She squealed, and then he felt her hidden walls beginning to contract against his thick peg of flesh. The clitoris beneath the ball of his thumb grew swollen, and then her lust exploded, and she screamed with the torrent of pleasure that began to overwhelm her. When some minutes later she came to herself once more, she was pleased to find he was still hard, and still within her.

"The gods!" she exclaimed. "You are truly very proficient with that weapon of yours, Quinn."

"You are pleased with me, mistress?" he asked her softly.

"You have been a good slave," she said. "But the night is young yet, and I am still hungry," Ashley told him. "You will have to work hard to earn your wool garment."

"If the mistress is hungry, then the mistress must be satisfied until she is no longer hungry," Quinn said. Then he began to move on her once again.

If there was one thing Ashley loved about The Channel, it was the tireless men—and her ability to enjoy several orgasms in a single visit. She had five that evening, and awoke the following morning replete and more relaxed than she had been in several weeks. Automatically she closed off the television screen and set the remote aside. Outside of her windows it was already growing light, but a glance at her bedside clock showed it was just five fifteen in the morning. But then, it was June. The birds were already making morning noise in the trees around the house and the ivy climbing up the side of the building. She stretched, and then, rolling over, Ashley went back to sleep.

She awoke to the sound of a knock on her bedchamber door.

"It's eight o'clock, Miss Ashley," Byrnes's voice said through the door. "I've set your breakfast out on your terrace."

"Thank you," Ashley called out to let the butler know she was awake. Getting up, she ran into her shower and refreshed herself with a quick warm-to-cold rinse. Then, toweling off, she slid on a pair of pale green silk bikini pants, and wrapped a matching silk robe about herself as she moved from her bedroom out into her sitting room and then onto the stone balcony overlooking the sparkling waters of the bay.

Seating herself at the little round café table, she gobbled down a bowl of strawberries and cream. The berries had obviously just been picked, as they were still warm with the sun, as last night's fruit had been. The plate beneath the silver dome contained her usual breakfast: one scrambled egg, three strips of bacon, and half of a whole-wheat English muffin with butter. And iced tea, since Ashley occasionally had the odd habit of preferring Crystal Light iced tea to coffee with breakfast. Mrs. B. kept a large container of it in the fridge for her.

Her breakfast finished, she picked up the telephone and called Tiffany Pietro d'Angelo before she left for the office. "Hey, Tiff! Ashley. Any word for me on Prince Charming?"

Tiffany laughed. "Ray was out of town taking a deposition in D.C. yesterday. Joe didn't want to discuss it with his assistant. He should be back to the city this morning. How about if I call you when we get something from him?"

"Okay," Ashley said. She was disappointed. She had hoped for something this morning. "Tiff, are you sure this is okay?"

"It could be a perfect solution for you, Ashley."

"But if this guy is normal, how come he isn't already married?" Ashley wanted to know again. It was such a radical idea, an arranged union. "What if he has two heads?"

"Well, if he does, let's hope they're both handsome and have wicked tongues," Tiffany said mischievously.

"You are terrible." Ashley giggled. "Okay, I'll admit to being nervous. I just wish I knew a little bit more. I mean, if I have to go out on my own again, I better get moving pretty fast. Eighteen months will go like wildfire, Tiff."

"Look," Tiffany said, "it's Thursday. We should have something late today or tomorrow to tell you. Now I gotta run, sweetie. I open the office in the morning. Have a good day."

Tiffany put the phone down and turned to her husband. "Joe, first thing, you phone Ray. Ashley is very nervous, and she needs to know something about this guy. And frankly, I'm dying of curiosity too."

"I'll call him. I'll call him," her husband said. "How about I call him now? He'll be commuting, and his cell is always on."

"He'll be on the subway," Tiffany protested. "He won't be able to hear a thing."

"Subway? Ray Pietro d'Angelo? Not since he was thirty, babe. He has a car service pick him at his apartment every morning." Joe picked up his own cell and began to dial.

"Ray? Joe. You know that client you were telling us about the other night at dinner?... Yeah, the guy who needs to get married. I've got the same situation with a client... Ashley Kimbrough, owner of Lacy Nothings... Yeah, the gift Tiffany brought Rose came from there. She's pretty, thirty-three, rich, successful, and has to get married by thirty-five or she loses everything to some cockamamie group called the Society Seeking Extraterrestrial Life... Yeah, SSEXL." Joe listened a few moments, and then he laughed. "Nah, her grandfather put a clause in the will to satisfy his crazy girlfriend who's into that crap. Now tell me a little more about your client." He listened for several minutes, finally saying, "Sounds to me like he'd be perfect for my client, Ray. They're both self-made with regard to their businesses, and dedicated to what they do. They're careful with money. Different religions, but not overly religious. This could be a win-win thing. Talk to your client, and let's set up a meeting as soon as possible. Your guy has only nine months left before he hits the big four-oh... Yeah, okay. I'll talk to you later today, buddy. Hi to Rose." Joe Pietro d'Angelo closed his cell and turned to his wife. "Ray says hi to you," he said.

"And?" Tiffany asked.

"And what?" he teased her.

"Joe, I'm gonna kill you," she threatened. "Gimme the details!"

"The guy has to get a wife before he's forty or, like Ashley, he loses everything. Crazy thing is, he's the one who made his father's firm so profitable, but the family is very old-school. When the old man died he gave a quarter mil to each of his six daughters; set his wife up in style; and then the bulk of it went to the son. With a catch, of course: If the son doesn't marry by forty it all gets sold and divided among the women. The sisters are even now looking for a buyer for the business," Joe said.

"Nice girls," Tiffany remarked. "Filled with sisterly love. So how come the brother is turning forty and isn't married? Is he gay?"

"No. Just a workaholic. There's never been time for him to get into a relationship that could thrive. If he isn't working, he's flying all over the world drumming up work for his business. He loves what he does, and Ray says he does it very well."

"Does what well?" Tiffany wanted to know.

"Oh, I didn't tell you? He's Restorations and Replications, R&R. You've heard of them, Tiffany. They're the fancy antique restorers, and they also design furniture that looks like it's antique for all that new money that wants to look old and respectable," Joe told his wife. "His father had a good restoration business going, but it was the son who saw the need for new antiques. And it's all American-made, although he has brought expert artisans over from Europe and Ireland to teach his employees the old tricks of the trade. He's one smart guy. Just like Ashley, he saw a need and stepped in to fill it. It's made him a multimillionaire. He won't lose it for lack of a wife."

"He could get one of those mail-order brides, couldn't he?" Tiffany said.

"Nah, not his style. With the people he associates with in his business, he'll want someone who is educated, can speak intelligently with his clients, and will be a terrific hostess. And Kimbrough Hall would be a wonderful place for him to entertain. We both know that Ashley isn't going to give up her home for anyone, and besides, he'd be nuts not to want to live there. It's a perfect venue for a guy in his field."

"So now all we have to do is get Ashley to agree," Tiffany said.

"No, first Ray speaks with his client, and then if the man is agreeable we set up a meeting with our client. They might not even like each other, Tiff, and they have to at least like each other to make this work," Joe said to his wife.

"How could any man not like Ashley?" she replied. "She's gorgeous."

"A lot of men have liked her, but for all the wrong reasons," Joe reminded her. "At least with this guy we start with an even playing field. She's rich; he's rich. So we know he's not after her money. Still, I'm going to run a check on him just to be certain. We can't be too careful, and Ashley has got to be protected."

"When will you talk to Ray again?" Tiffany wanted to know.

"This afternoon," Joe replied. "Don't call Ashley."

"Why not?" Tiffany wanted to know.

"Because until Ray's client says he is willing to meet her we have nothing. I don't want her getting her hopes up, only to dash them. She's had enough sorrow these last few years. She doesn't need to be rejected by someone who hasn't even met her."

"You're right," Tiffany agreed. "Poor kid. Losing her grandfather and her brother, having three weddings called off. It's a lot to bear. It's a wonder she's so normal and nice, isn't it?" And then Tiffany remembered Ashley's remark yesterday afternoon about someone's cute butt getting whipped. She almost giggled as she considered what kind of fantasies Ashley must have on The Channel. But hell, if a little naughty spanking took the edge off of her nerves, so what? That was the beauty of The Channel: Nothing was real. She turned to her husband. "You playing cards tonight with your group?"

"Yeah. We'll have dinner at the club and play there," Joe told her. "You don't mind being alone, do you?"

"Of course not," Tiffany said with a smile, and she patted his shoulder. "You need your nights out." *And I need The Channel,* she was already thinking. Tonight she was going to let the young sultan spank her, and then he would fuck her brains out. No. She didn't mind Joe's card playing after work at all. She welcomed it!

Chapter Two

Ryan Finbar Mulcahy winked at the receptionist in the foyer of Alexander, Stoddard, and Kingsley as she told him to go right into Mr. Pietro d'Angelo's office. He heard her giggle behind him, and he grinned. She was petite and blond and cute. Just the kind of girl he'd marry if she weren't so damned young. Was she even twenty? he wondered. And he winced, realizing that the receptionist was probably young enough to be his daughter. He had nine months to go until he was forty. It was a sobering thought.

"What's up, Ray?" he asked as he lowered his long frame into a chair opposite the desk. "What's so urgent that you have to drag me from work?"

"Your mother called me a few weeks ago," Ray began. "She and Frankie don't like what your other sisters are doing. You know they've lined up a buyer for R&R, don't you? What the hell is the matter with them, Ryan? Wasn't what your dad left them enough? Unfortunately there's no way around your dad's will."

"What did Ma want?" the younger man asked.

"To arrange a marriage for you," Ray said, watching to see what Ryan's reaction to this news would be.

"So she did it, did she?" Ryan Finbar Mulcahy laughed. "She's been threatening to sic a matchmaker on me for a year now. She says she and Dad were matched and made a go of it. There's no reason I can't. And Frankie's in on it too? What a sweetie that baby sister of mine is," he said.

"I found a possibility," Ray continued, and swallowed a chuckle at the look of surprise on his client's face. "She's got the same problem you have—a will that says she's got to marry or lose it all. You've got enough in common to at least meet. I want to arrange it."

"Look, Ray, if I can't drum up enough money to buy the business from the estate, then I'll start all over again, and screw my sisters," Ryan said stubbornly. "Five spoiled little bitches. Only one of them worth anything is Frankie."

"Don't be a fool," Ray replied. "R&R has a reputation. You willing to give that reputation away to someone else? Especially a son of a bitch like Jerry Klein? Right now he's the high bidder, and he's going to stay the high bidder because he wants R&R. And all you have to do to save your ass is get married."

"I don't like being told what to do," Ryan answered irritably.

"Funny thing—neither does my cousin Joe's client. But unless she gets married by the time she's thirty-five she loses everything she's worked for, because her grandfather thought a woman had to be married to be happy and safe," Ray said candidly. "You see? Already you've got similarities."

"She's thirty-five?"

"She's thirty-three."

"Why isn't she married? Fat? Ugly? Warts?"

"She's been engaged three times, and each time it's fallen through," Ray remarked.

"Difficult, huh? A diva."

"No, unlucky. She's smart in business, but not in men. They wanted her money," Ray said. It was the easiest explanation to offer right now.

"Is she pretty?" Ryan asked.

"I wouldn't know. I've never met her. She lives in a small town called Egret Pointe about a hundred miles from the city," Ray said.

"What kind of business?" Ryan wanted to know.

"She has a lingerie shop," was the answer.

"Doesn't sound like big business to me."

Ray chuckled. "It's upmarket, many one-of-a-kind things. She started small; then came the catalog, and now she's opening two new stores—one here in town, and the other in an elegant suburban mall. It's called Lacy Nothings."

"Geez, Frankie buys stuff from that catalog. It's as expensive as hell, and since there's very little of it I don't know why," Ryan said.

Ray laughed. "My cousin—he's her lawyer—says she's a very nice girl. What could it hurt to meet her? She's got no illusions about any arrangement that you two would make. Joe says her house is gorgeous and filled with antiques. It would be a great place to entertain, and she would be a terrific hostess. She'd know how to speak to your fancy-shmancy clients, Ryan. Her grandfather was probably one of your father's clients."

"Has Miss Lingerie Shop got a name?" Ryan asked. The truth was, his interest was piqued. The girl Ray was describing was young enough to be a mother, and he did want kids; and she probably had people running her business for her, so she could be a wife and mother. She had her own money. Her own house. And she needed to get married in order to keep them. Actually it could be a perfect solution to his problems too.

"Her name is Ashley Kimbrough," Ray said.

"Pretty name," Ryan allowed. "So when do you want to set up this meeting?"

Ray smiled. "Let me talk to Joe. You're not due to fly off anywhere soon, are you? I know your schedule is pretty frantic these days."

"I'll make time, and no, I'm not going anywhere at the moment," Ryan said. "Why don't we make our first meeting in Egret Pointe. Miss Lingerie—Ashley—would probably be a bit more comfortable there than here," he suggested.

"Thoughtful," Ray teased him. "Shows your sensitive side."

"Bite me!" Ryan shot back, and then he unfolded himself from the chair. "If that's it, I gotta go. Bill me for the time."

"Bite *me!*" Ray laughed. "You're going to get a big fat bill from ASK when this is all over, buddy. I may even get the senior partners to start up a new department. Matchmaking for Millionaires." And he laughed harder as he waved Ryan from his office. Then, clicking his intercom button, he said, "Nancy, get me Joe in Egret Pointe." And a minute or two later his assistant signaled him, and he picked up the phone. "Joe, Ray. We're coming shopping. Any one day better for you than another?"

Joe Pietro d'Angelo masked a deep sigh. "Where do you want to meet?" he said.

"Ryan wants to come out to Egret Pointe," Ray answered him. "He thought it might be easier on Ashley. Nice, huh?"

"Yeah, very nice," Joe acknowledged. "We could make it Friday, and you and Rose could stay the weekend with Tiff and me."

"Sure, why not? I can get Ryan back without having to go into town myself," Ray said. "Yeah, Friday. Eleven a.m. okay with you?"

"Hang on, and let me call Ashley," Joe replied. He pulled his cell from his pocket and dialed Lacy Nothings.

"Morning, Nina. Would you put Ashley on, please? You still there, Ray?"

"I'm here," his cousin's voice responded.

"Ash, listen, my cousin and his client would like to meet here in our offices on Friday at eleven. That okay with you?"

"So soon? Gee, Joe, this guy must really be desperate," Ashley said.

"No more so than you, honey. Bring a sandwich and eat with Tiff and me in an hour. I'll fill you in, okay? Eleven Friday, then?"

"Why not?" Ashley said. "Best to get it over with. See you in an hour."

Joe flipped the cell shut and turned back to his office phone. "Okay, we're on, buddy. I'll see you Friday." Hanging up the phone, he buzzed his wife in her cubicle and waited for her to come in, and when she did he said, "We've got a first meeting Friday."

Tiffany clapped her hands together. "That's just terrific, Joe." And throwing her arms around his neck she gave him a quick kiss. "Now," she said, stepping back, "tell me all about the guy. Is he tall, dark, and handsome? Does he have family? What's his name? Give! I want to know everything."

"Ashley is coming over to have lunch with us," Joe said. "I'll tell you both everything I know then, and not before," he told her.

Tiffany shrugged her shoulders. "I'm not happy," she said glowering.

He grinned. "Go get a chocolate bar," he teased her.

"I'm going to need a quarter-pound box of Godiva to bring my mood back up," she grumbled. "Or maybe a bag of truffles." Tiffany considered. But she waited because there was no other choice until noon, when Ashley arrived carrying a carton of Columbo Light Key Lime Pie yogurt, and a little silver spoon. "You keep a silver spoon in your desk?" Tiffany said, impressed. "Now that is cool."

They were in the little conference room of the firm. It had big windows that overlooked Main Street with its big trees lining it. Rick had come in to listen and, spreading their lunches on the big table, which was an elegant old door covered with a glass top, they all now turned to Joe, who was thoroughly enjoying a meatball hero from the local pizza place.

"Nobody makes sauce like Angelo," he said, licking his lips.

Ashley dipped her spoon into the pale green yogurt.

"Yeah," Rick agreed. "He got the recipe from his grandmother in Rome."

Tiffany fished a crouton from her salad and ate it. "Talk," she said.

Joe took another bit of his hero and then, grinning, put it down, looking at Ashley. "His name is Ryan Finbar Mulcahy. He owns an outfit called R&R—Restorations and Replications, Inc. His father started the business and did nicely. Ryan graduated college and took over the company to build it into a multimillion-dollar establishment. But it was still the old man's company. When he died a couple of years ago the old man left each of his daughters a quarter mil, and the wife the house and a good income. Everything else went to Ryan on the proviso that he be married by the time he was forty. He'll be forty next spring, and he hasn't even come close to getting married," Joe said.

"What's the problem?" Ashley wanted to know.

"The guy is a workaholic," Joe said. "His old man was the craftsman, the artisan. Ryan knows what good is, but his head is more for the business. It was his idea to add the reproductions branch of the business. There's a lot of money out there today, and new money wants to look like old money. But there are only so many antiques to go around. So R&R designs seventeenth – and eighteenth-century repros that look every bit as good as the real thing. The business is booming. And Ryan hasn't had a moment to get a relationship going with any woman. But if he isn't married by forty, he's out, the business is sold, and his sisters get the benefit of the sale."

"What if he doesn't like me?" Ashley asked.

"What if you don't like him?" Joe countered. "Look, Ash, life is at best a crapshoot. You toss the dice and hope you don't hit snake eyes. You've hit snake eyes three times now. I think it past time for you to make craps. Ray is bringing him out tomorrow for an initial meeting. No promises. No obligations. You're just both going to take a look at each other to make certain you're human."

"Let's Google him," Tiffany said.

"Of course!" Ashley agreed. "Now that we know his name and his business name we can look him up."

"In my cubicle," Tiffany replied, standing up from the conference table. "Come on, Ash. Enjoy your lunch, boys!" She hurried out with Ashley following with her yogurt.

"What do you think?" Rick Johnson asked his partner.

"I think we've got a shot," Joe responded, "if they click."

"An arranged marriage. It sounds so cut-and-dried. So loveless," Rick said. "I thought people had to fall in love to get married. What are they going to do about the sex, I wonder?"

"That's one matter they'll have to negotiate themselves," Joe said, grinning. "We can set up the prenups with Ray, but the rest of it is going to be up to them."

"What do you think he's like, this Mulcahy guy? Is he really so busy he can't make time to go courting?" Rick wondered.

"Want to check out what the girls have found?" Joe said as he picked up the second half of his hero.

"And let them know we're as nosy as they are? I think not," Rick said. "I'll wait 'til I get home to Google him. Carla's filling in tonight at the hospital for one of the night nurses. She won't be home until around eleven thirty. God, I hope she likes him. We gotta get Ash settled, and soon. Old Kimbrough will come out of his grave if we let his wealth go to SSEXL."

"Then he shouldn't have been such a smart-ass and added that clause to the will. I told him not to do it," Joe grumbled. "Mulcahy is probably all right. Have you ever seen an ugly Irishman, Rick?"

"Yeah, as a matter of fact I have," Rick replied. He cocked his head to one side. "Did you just hear a 'woo-woo' from Tiff's cubicle?"

"Oh, my God!" Tiffany Pietro d'Angelo stared at the computer screen. "Well, he ain't ugly," she said. "You're going to have beautiful babies, honey."

But Ashley wasn't really looking at the face on the screen. She had given it a quick passing glance to ascertain whether he was normal-looking, and then she had moved on to his biography. He had gone to Catholic school first, done his undergrad work at one of the state universities, then gotten a second degree from the Wharton School of Business. *Smart*, Ashley thought. The state school was cheap, and good for a bachelor's. It was the grad school that had to be the best, and it was.

"Will you look at that face!" Tiffany enthused.

"He's nice-looking," Ashley said, "but I'm more interested in his background."

"Nice-looking?" Tiffany said, surprised. "He's a god."

"Look at how fast he brought his father's business from just a restoration house making a nice bottom line to a restoration and reproduction business with an incredible bottom line. Boy, I would love to do that myself for Lacy Nothings. Think he would give me some advice, Tiff?"

"I don't believe you," Tiffany said, exasperated. "Here is this gorgeous man whom you will probably marry, and all you're interested in is his business acumen?"

"Tiff, *if*—and it's a big if—Mr. Mulcahy and I decide to marry, it's just a business arrangement. We've both been the recipients of bequests that will screw us out of our inheritance unless we get married. I've got lousy luck picking men, and he's too busy to properly look for a wife. And time is running out on both of us."

"Marriage isn't a business," Tiffany said, not certain whether she should be shocked.

"Sure it is," Ashley told her.

"What about love?" Tiffany asked.

"What about it? Three times I thought I was in love. I obviously don't know what love is, and any man willing to marry to keep his money doesn't know either. Love will not be part of the equation here."

"Sex?" Tiffany said weakly.

"I've got all the sex I can handle on The Channel with Quinn and Rurik," Ashley said. "Tiff, this isn't happily ever after. It isn't personal. It's business. If he wants to have a girlfriend it's fine with me, as long as it's discreet."

"My God!" Tiffany said. "What have I done?"

Ashley laughed and patted Tiffany's hand. "You've probably saved me from a fate worse than death—poverty! Now, I've gotta go. Nina has a dental appointment at one fifteen, and I'll need to be in the shop. Brandy doesn't come in until after school."

Tiffany Pietro d'Angelo watched her go, and then walked back into the conference room, where her husband and his partner were just finishing their lunches. "This is terrible," she said, plunking herself into a chair.

"What's terrible?" Joe asked.

"Ashley said any arrangement made will be business, no sex, and he can have a girlfriend if he's discreet," Tiffany said.

Rick snickered.

"Good," Joe replied. "I'm glad Ashley understands, and doesn't have any silly romantic ideas in her head about Mulcahy."

Tiffany looked at her husband as if he had just returned from the moon.

"Is the guy hot?" Rick wanted to know with a grin.

"Yes, he's hot," Tiffany snapped. "Joseph Anthony Pietro d'Angelo, where has your heart gotten to, and don't you see how awful this will be for Ashley if she isn't loved by her husband? And what about kids? What the hell good is all that money going to do either of them without kids to share it with or help out?"

Joe reached across the table, took his wife's hand, and kissed it. "My own little romantic," he said with a smile. "Listen, honey, Ashley and Mulcahy have a problem, and getting married will solve that problem for them. If they like each other, maybe something good will come of it. But for now it's just business. An arrangement like this can't be anything else but business."

"I think this is so sad. When I suggested it I wasn't considering the reality of it all," Tiffany responded with a deep sigh.

"What would be sad would be if these two hardworking people lost everything because some damned fools added dumb clauses to their wills in order to get their own way even after death," Rick remarked. "I don't know about Mulcahy's father, but why the hell Edward Kimbrough thought Ashley couldn't survive without a big, strong man to keep her safe I'll never know. She is one competent girl."

"Yeah," Joe agreed.

Tiffany got up from the conference table and looked at both of them with a jaundiced eye. "Well," she said, "at least you guys understand that women are capable of managing alone if we have to or choose to, or whatever. Now I've got to think about what I'm going to wear tomorrow."

The two men laughed as she left them.

When she had gone Rick Johnson looked at his partner. "Do you think they'll like each other?" he wondered.

"They have to," Joe said. "I don't see that either of them has a choice except to give up everything they've gotten or worked for, and that's just plain crazy."

The following morning the two partners stood in the conference room window looking down at the silver-gray limousine that had just pulled up in front of their building. Joe had already told Rick that his cousin had never learned to drive, and used a car service on a regular basis. Normally he would have arrived in a Town Car, but as his wife would also be with them he would want a bigger vehicle. The driver jumped out and ran around the car to open the door. Two men stepped out.

"That's Ray," Joe said, pointing to the shorter of the two men. "He's older than me by a couple of years. He was always good to me when I was a kid."

"That why you went into law?" Rick asked.

"Yeah, I guess it was. I've always admired him. He's a senior partner at ASK. When Joshua Alexander retired a couple of years ago he handpicked Ray for his place. But Alexander's name remains on the letterhead," Joe explained.

"Where's the limo going?" Rick asked. The two men had disappeared into the building, and it was pulling away from the curb.

"Out to the house. I made Tiffany stay home. I didn't want heR&Rose hovering while we were trying to make a deal. Where's Ashley? She should be here by now," Joe said as the intercom buzzed, announcing their two visitors, who were then ushered into the conference room.

"And Nina's here from Lacy Nothings," the receptionist said. "She needs to see you, Mr. P. Shall I send her in too?"

"Yeah," Joe told her. What the hell was going on? If Ashley was going to try to pull out of this he would no longer represent her. Hell! He'd represent SSEXL. "Ray!" he greeted his cousin, and the two men embraced warmly. "Sit down. You know my partner, Rick Johnson. Just give me a minute, will you?" He turned to Nina. "Where is she?" he asked.

"She's going to be late. Madeira called, and I don't speak Spanish," Nina said. "It shouldn't be any more than ten minutes." Then she turned and hurried out.

"Sorry about that," Joe said. "Ashley is going to be a few minutes late, and she sends her apologies. She had to take an overseas call. Could I offer everyone some coffee? Water?"

Judy, the firm's receptionist, stood waiting, and hurried out when she had been given orders for four coffees.

"Ryan," Ray Pietro d'Angelo said, "this is my cousin, Joe Pietro d'Angelo."

The men shook hands and chatted over the coffee that Judy had returned with for them. And then the intercom buzzed again, and Judy said, "Miss Kimbrough is here. I'm sending her in, sir."

The conference door opened and Ashley came in, breathless from running from her shop. She was wearing white silk slacks and a red tee. "I am so sorry," she apologized. "Did Nina tell you? Sister Marie Consuelo called from Madeira."

"She couldn't call back?" Joe asked. .

"No, she couldn't," Ashley said. "There is no phone at the convent. I pay the tavern keeper in the village a yearly fee to allow her to call me when my order is ready and has been picked up by FedEx. They're a pretty cloistered order, Joe, and she can't keep running down the hill from the convent all the time. Then I have to have the bank transfer the funds I owe them immediately. The convent isn't a wealthy one with a rich *patrona*. I want to make certain they have their money by the next day, and in order to do that I have to call the bank before noon." She turned and looked at the men in the room. Then, walking over to Ryan Mulcahy, she held out her hand. "I'm Ashley Kimbrough, and since your companion looks like Joe, you must be Mr. Mulcahy."

He was dazzled by her bright green eyes. She wasn't at all what he had expected. Shaking her hand, he said, "My dad was Mr. Mulcahy. I'm Ryan, Miss Kimbrough."

"I'm Ashley," she responded, and then they sat down. If she hadn't sat down, Ashley thought, she would have fallen down. He was nothing at all like she had expected. The picture she had briefly glimpsed on Google didn't do him justice. For openers, no one had told her he would be six feet, five inches tall. Or that he would look like an Italian model. The brown eyes that had locked onto hers momentarily were like liquid chocolate beneath their dark, bushy eyebrows. His face was long, with a long, narrow, aquiline nose and high cheekbones. His mouth. Oh, God, his mouth! It was full and lush. It begged to be kissed. And then she pulled herself up. This was business, and she was already half in lust. This was what always got her in trouble. She drew a deep breath. "I suppose we should get started, gentlemen."

She was all business, and it really turned him on, Ryan thought as he inspected Ashley from beneath half-lowered eyelids. But it shouldn't turn him on, damn it! She was nothing at all like the kind of girl he wanted to marry. To begin with she was big. Not fat by any means, but big. She had to stand at least five feet, eight inches tall. She was a brunette with pale skin like ivory porcelain, not the petite peaches-and-cream blonde he had always imagined he would marry. But those green eyes! *Mamma mia!*

"Well, there's no secret why we are all here today," Joe began. "But let's put our cards on the table. Ashley Cordelia Kimbrough is her grandfather's only heir. The bulk of his estate is hers, but only if she marries by her thirty-fifth birthday, which is in December 2009. Unfortunately her business is part of the estate, and she will lose it if she cannot comply with the terms of Edward Kimbrough's will. She has made Lacy Nothings so successful that she could not afford to buy back her own business if she lost it, and there are at least two companies who have expressed interest in having it if she were interested in selling. They do not, of course, know Ashley's tenuous position. Ray?"

"Ryan Finbar Mulcahy has a similar problem. Although he made the business the financial success it is today, his father's will states that if he isn't married by the time he is forty—and that happens next spring—everything gets sold, and the proceeds parceled out to his sisters. His father was very generous in his will to those sisters, but they're already looking for a buyer for R&R. The value of the business is as much in Ryan's reputation as it is in the physical business itself. He could not outbid anyone else. Joe?"

"So," Joe said, "since both of these people have to marry to retain what is really theirs, it seems only logical that they marry each other. It would be a business arrangement with a prenuptial agreement signed by both parties. The marriage would have to last at least two years, and then each would leave the marriage with what they brought into it. In other words, no one gets hurt. But I think before we go any further we should hear from Ryan and Ashley." He turned to them. "What do you two think?"

"I think Ashley and I need to speak alone for a while," Ryan said.

"Yes, we need to get to know a little bit more about each other before we make any decisions," Ashley agreed. "Even if this isn't a real marriage in the strictest sense, Ryan and I have to see if we can be together without grating on each other's nerves."

"Good!" Joe said. "I've ordered lunch in for you two. We'll come together again at two thirty and see how it's gone and what you think." He stood up. "Ray, Rick, come on. I made reservations for the three of us at the inn." Joe walked out in the company of the other two men, closing the conference room door behind him.

"He's a decisive guy," Ryan remarked with a small smile. "A lot like Ray."

"I hadn't planned to be away from the shop for so long," Ashley said.

"What do you get from a convent in Madeira?" he asked her.

"Lace," she answered him. "Exquisite handmade lace. My first ex-fiancé found it for me when he and his partner were traveling in Europe."

"You're still friends with a guy you were once engaged to?" Ryan asked, surprised.

Ashley giggled. She couldn't help it. "Carson is gay," she told him. "I was young and didn't realize it, and he had asked me to marry him. He says he was in his 'I can beat this' stage of denial over his homosexuality. But he couldn't. He ran off with the best man a couple of days before the wedding. I thought it was so sweet that he wanted to wait until we were married to have sex." And she giggled again.

He grinned at her. In retrospect it was pretty funny, and she was certainly being a good sport about it. It said a lot about her character that she could laugh at herself. "I've heard you had a couple of other fiancés," he noted.

"Yep, number two was Chandler Wayne."

"The pro quarterback for the Chicago Razorbacks?" he asked.

"One and the same," she responded.

"Didn't he die in Vegas after... Oh, yeah. Great tragedy."

"If Chandler had to die young, and he did, he wouldn't have wanted to go any other way. The guy loved sex. I'm a little surprised at the circumstances, however. He wasn't the most creative guy in the sack," Ashley said.

"You're not a virgin," he said.

"I'm thirty-three," she answered him dryly. "How many thirty-three-year-old virgins do you know? But in answer to the unspoken question on your lips, I am not promiscuous. I have slept with only three guys in my thirty-three years, and two of them were going to marry me. The first was my college boyfriend. We did it twice, and then he broke up with me. I assume you've had a few adventures of your own, Ryan."

He laughed. "You are one candid lady, Ashley," he told her.

"You haven't answered my question," she said.

"Am I a virgin?" he teased her. "Nope."

Now Ashley laughed. "I think, to be fair, we should both have physicals if we decide to make this arrangement. Including tests for STDs. That okay with you?"

"Agreed," he said as the door to the conference room opened and their lunch was brought in.

The two waiters quickly set hot mats before them, covering them with linen place mats. Next came the silver, perfectly folded napkins, water, and wineglasses. Salads were set in front of them, and a small dressing boat was put on the table.

"Your entrées and the desserts are on the cart, Miss Kimbrough," one of the waiters said with a deferential bow. "I'll pour the wine, and then we'll be gone. Rick said you could serve yourselves."

"That's fine, Artie," Ashley said with a smile. "Thank you. The salad looks delicious, and you brought raspberry vinaigrette, my favorite." She poured a dollop on her salad.

While Artie poured them glasses of Pindar Winter White, the other waiter filled the water glasses. Then the two men hurried from the room.

"All the comforts of home," Ryan noted. "Your guys are pretty classy, considering you're country mice. Lunch in the boardroom."

"Usually it's yogurt, salad, or sandwiches," Ashley admitted as she ate the artfully arranged greens before her. "I generally eat at my desk. You?"

"Yeah, unless I have to take a client or a supplier to lunch. I try to keep those dates to a bare minimum. I don't eat breakfast except for coffee and juice. Lunch is a waste of time, and time is money."

"I eat three meals a day," Ashley said quietly. "I try to keep the carbs to the healthy kind. Good breakfast. Light lunch. Nice, but not too filling dinner."

"Do you cook?" he asked her.

"Actually I do, but not if I can avoid it. Mrs. B. cooks for me," Ashley told him. "If I had to cook after a long day at work I probably wouldn't eat, or eat all the wrong things. Having Mrs. B. to look after me is a great blessing."

"You have a cook?"

"I have a married couple, and a housemaid," Ashley told him. "When you came into town did you notice the large house on the hill overlooking the bay? That's my home, Kimbrough Hall. When you own a house like that you need help to keep everything running smoothly. The hall is on the National Registry of Historic Places in the state. I've lived there my whole life."

"Since you're your grandfather's only heir," he said, "I'm going to assume your parents are dead."

"They died in a boating accident when I was fourteen," Ashley told him. "They were totally in love to the exclusion of everyone else, including my brother and me. My father grew up at the hall, as my grandfather had. When he married, of course, my mother came to live there. They had two children, and then flitted off to enjoy themselves traveling the world. My brother and I were always getting marvelous gifts from their travels, and listening to them talk about their adventures on their rare visits home was really quite fascinating. Actually, my brother knew them better than I did. He was eight when they decided to go off on an extended holiday. I was just three."

"Who raised you then?" Ryan wanted to know. He was fascinated, and yet at the same time put off by the fact that she was so casual about a lifestyle that had left her virtually motherless. Would she, under the circumstances, have any maternal instincts herself?

"Well," Ashley said slowly, "Grams was around until I was eleven and Ben sixteen. After that it was usually Mrs. Byrnes who kept an eye on me."

"The cook?"

"Oh, no. The elder Mrs. Byrnes." Ashley laughed. "She was the housekeeper back when I was a kid. The Byrneses have been with the family for centuries. Grandfather always said they came with the house. My Mr. and Mrs. Byrnes are the elder Byrneses' son and daughter-in-law. But when they retire there'll be no more Byrneses at Kimbrough Hall. Their son is on Wall Street, and their daughter married a dentist. But Byrnes says he and his missus are good for at least fifteen more years." She chuckled. "I suspect they'll die in service, the way Byrnes's folks did. I just love them!"

Raised by servants. It just got worse, Ryan thought.

"Who brought you up?" Ashley asked him cheerfully, mopping the last of the salad dressing off her plate with a piece of roll.

"Our parents," he said.

"You've got siblings? I really miss my brother, Ben. He died in Desert Storm," she told him.

"I've got six sisters," he replied. "Bride is the oldest of us. She's fifty-three. Then comes Elisabetta, Kathleen, Magdalena, and Deirdre. There are four years between Dee and me. With five daughters my parents were reluctant to try again, but finally they did, and I was the result. They were so encouraged they did it one more time, but when my sister Francesca, Frankie, was born, they decided enough was enough."

"I can't help but notice your sisters' names. Irish and Italian," Ashley said.

"My mother's from Rome," he replied.

"That's why you don't look Irish despite your name!" Ashley exclaimed. "But you're very tall," she noted.

"My dad was tall," he told her. "That's the Irish part."

He had finished his salad, and he saw that Ashley was standing up and taking the covered plates off of the trolley. Removing the covers she set one plate before him and the other at her place. The plates contained four perfectly cooked raviolis with a light meat sauce sprinkled with freshly sliced mushrooms. Next to the pasta was a spoonful of thinly sliced pale green zucchini.

"Artie's Ristorante uses fresh local veggies. These must be the first zucchini of the season," Ashley said as she dug enthusiastically into the food on her plate.

As he ate he watched her eat. Other than his family he was used to women who picked at the food on their plates, but hardly ate a morsel. Ashley was obviously not one of those women. She was actually enjoying her food.

"I'll bet your mom makes great pasta," she said between bites.

"She does," he said with a smile, "but I have to admit Artie's pasta ain't bad at all. The sauce could use a bit more basil, but it's good."

When they had finished the pasta Ashley took their plates and returned them to the trolley. She came back with plates containing small meringue shells filled with fresh strawberries and drizzled with dark chocolate. "If you want coffee I can ask Judy," she said, "but frankly I'm enjoying the wine."

"Wine is good," he agreed.

"So," Ashley asked him as she ate her dessert, "do you have any bad habits? I'm not too good at tolerating fools. I'm a bit impatient. I tend to get sentimental over crazy things no one else would get sentimental over. I love animals. I've got two rescued greyhounds, Ghostly and Graybar. A very fat tortoiseshell tabby named Mr. Mittens. I feed the deer in the winter even though it appalls my neighbors. How about you?"

"I don't know," he said, considering. "My mother and little sister think I'm perfect. The five harpies who are my older sisters think I'm selfish because, now that they've all pissed through what Dad left them, I won't finance their extravagances. I've got other responsibilities, and they've all got husbands."

"Believe me, I understand," Ashley said. "People think if you're rich you can do anything. But you've got employees, and all the expenses that go with having employees. I've always paid my people what they're worth, matched funds for their retirement, paid their Social Security, and I even have a health care plan in place. I pay half and my employees pay half. Of course, even with the new stores opening I probably don't have as many employees as you do. But if people work hard they're entitled to earn a decent living and have all that goes with it. And many of your people are craftsmen and artisans, aren't they?"

"Exactly!" he said. Okay, so she was big and tall. She ate like a horse. She had been brought up by the help, and probably didn't have a maternal bone in her body, but she sure as hell understood business and how it should be run. She had ethics, and ethics were important to him. A marriage between them was going to be strictly business. If something else came of it, okay, fine. But at least if they married neither of them would lose everything they had worked so hard for over the past few years. They had to marry. "We've got a lot of people depending on us, Ashley, don't we?" he said seriously. "I'm told I'm not a bad guy, and I love animals too, although I don't have any. I'm not able to take care of them. Will it bother you that I travel a lot? I'm always looking for exotic woods, good hardware sources, that kind of stuff. Sometimes I'll go and oversee the packing of a client's antique for shipping to my shop for restoration."

"If we could live at Kimbrough Hall I wouldn't mind," Ashley told him. "The Byrneses are there, my creatures are there. I know how to be a good hostess, so if you wanted to entertain there we certainly could. My grandfather used to give the most marvelous parties when I was growing up."

"I could make Egret Pointe my legal residence," he said thoughtfully, "but I will want to keep my apartment in the city, because I'll have to stay in town three or four nights a week. This wouldn't be an easy commute."

"No, of course not," she agreed. "Now, we had better get the sex thing straightened out before we go any further."

"It's a marriage of convenience," he said. "If we get interested, fine. If we don't, no problem. But I want absolutely no gossip or scandal because you're sleeping with someone else. I assume you know how to be more than just discreet. And you'll have no problem with me that way, I assure you."

"Have you got a girlfriend?" she asked, curious, but then, even if he did he wasn't serious, or he most certainly wouldn't be considering a marriage of convenience.

"I don't have time for anything other than an occasional casual relationship," he told her. "I would have thought you'd figured that one out."

"I did, but I had to ask." Ashley swallowed hard. "And now here's another question I have to ask. Are you gay or bisexual? I don't want any surprises, Ryan."

"Good point," he said. "Nope. Straight as an arrow. Maybe we'll get to find out together someday, Ashley." He locked his gaze on her, and felt a small burst of satisfaction when she actually blushed.

"This is business, remember," she said primly.

"I know. The business of saving our asses. But we are going to have to sleep together in the same bed to prevent any rumors," he told her.

"My servants don't gossip," she said, irritated.

"All servants gossip, and these people have watched you grow up. They probably love you and want nothing but the best for you. You aren't going to tell them the truth of this proposed marriage, are you? What the hell do you think they would think of you under such circumstances, even if they said nothing? And I can see that you care for your Byrneses so you probably won't tell them what this is all about. That means we will have to share a bed, Ashley, on the nights I am out here. Am I wrong?" The brown eyes looked directly into her bright green ones.

"It's complicated," Ashley said. "But of course I'll tell the Ryrneses the truth. I have too much respect for them not to tell them. They understand my situation."

"My sisters could cause trouble," he said, "although my mom and Frankie are on our side."

"Why? Oh, yeah, you mean your older sisters." Ashley groaned.

He laughed. "Yep, the harpies, but actually it's my mother who suggested to Ray that he find me a nice wife. You see, she and Dad were an arranged marriage."

"Oh," Ashley replied. *Great! Just great!* He had a mother who had had an arranged marriage, and it was a happy marriage. And seven kids to boot. She would probably blame Ashley when she and Ryan divorced a few years down the line. Hell, Carson's mother blamed her because he was gay. Mothers and sons were a force of nature not to be reckoned with.

"Just *oh*?" Ryan said, curious.

"I don't know what else to say," Ashley admitted. "I thought arranged marriages went out a couple of hundred years ago, except maybe for third-world countries. How come an arranged marriage? I mean, you're a reasonably good-looking guy, so your parents have to be good-looking. It was the twentieth century. Couldn't they find each other another way? It seems so odd, but then, hell, this is odd, isn't it?"

"I liked it better when we were talking about sex," he teased.

"I don't remember us talking about sex," Ashley responded, feeling her cheeks grow warm again. It had been years since she had blushed, and now twice in the last few minutes he had managed to make her blush.

"The bed situation," he reminded her. "Have you got a king-size bed? I'm a big guy, and can only sleep in a king-size extra-long."

"I've got a double bed," she said. *And it's just big enough for me,* she thought.

"Gotta order a king, extra-long," he told her.

"We'll have to move into Grandfather's old rooms," Ashley said, thinking. "I'm like Goldilocks—my rooms are just right. For me. I hope you're not going to be more trouble than you're worth. Are you, Ryan?" Her eyes were twinkling.

He picked up the last strawberry from his meringue shell, popping it into his mouth. His tongue licked a drop of chocolate from the side of his lips. "Then we're doing this?" he asked her.

Seeing the tip of his tongue lapping at the chocolate had momentarily rendered her dizzy, but she still managed to speak. "I guess. You check out. You're not an ax murderer. You seem a reasonable man. Yeah, I guess we are doing it."

"*It?*" Ryan couldn't help leering at her. Bringing a blush to her pale cheeks was proving to be a lot of fun. He suspected from her consternation that it had been a long time since anyone had made her blush.

"Damn it, you're doing that deliberately!" she swore at him.

He burst out laughing. "Guilty as charged," he admitted. "I see you have a little bit of a temper too. I like my gals with spice," he drawled in his best Texas accent.

"And you seem to be a tease, *Mr.* Mulcahy," she shot back. "Okay. Yes. We will get married to preserve our fortunes and our livelihoods. It would seem that neither of us has any other choice, except to transfer our funds to numbered accounts in the Caymans, take on new identities, and run. And I've never run from anything in all my life!"

"Neither have I," he said, serious now. "How do we explain our marriage to everyone? It's going to seem really strange if we just do it without warning."

"I suppose we could date for a little while," Ashley suggested. "I could get to know your family. I have no real family left, but you could get to know my friends. But I don't want to have to plan another extravaganza, Ryan. When we set the date I want it to be simple. No fuss. No muss. Your mom. My friend Nina. That's it. I realize your family will probably want a big show, but I have ended up the Bad-luck Bride three times now. I'm pretty certain that the florist here in the village has put one kid through college on my three canceled weddings."

"But it has to be in church," he said. "Ma will insist on that."

"No problem. You're an R.C., I presume?"

"Baptized, confirmed, but I'm not much on church," he admitted.

"I'm an Anglican," she told him. "But I want your mother happy in this, because I can see she means a lot to you. St. Anne's is the Roman church. St. Luke's is the Anglican. We'll get married at St. Anne's. They've got a new priest, Father Donovan. He's a pretty cool guy. And my priest, Father Edwards, will co-officiate. That okay with you, Ryan?"

"You want to set the date now?" he asked her. "No one except the lawyers has to know we're going to be pretending to date."

"How about the last Saturday in August?" Ashley asked.

"That's good. I don't travel in August," he agreed.

"How are we going to say we met?" she asked him.

"No lie there," he said. "Our lawyers are cousins, and they introduced us."

She nodded. "Yes, it's the truth, isn't it?"

The door to the conference room opened, and the partners in the company of Ray Pietro d'Angelo came back in.

"Lunch was okay?" Joe asked.

"It was lovely," Ashley said. "Whoever chose the menu did a good job."

"Have you decided what you want to do?" Ray inquired of them.

Ashley looked at Ryan questioningly.

"You explain it," Ryan said.

"Ryan and I thought it might be better if a relationship between us seemed normal. We're going to have a whirlwind courtship," she said with a smile. "We will tell everyone that we were introduced by our lawyers, who are cousins—which is, of course, the truth, isn't it? And I think sticking to the truth is best. We will date for a few weeks, then surprise everyone by getting married. Ryan has agreed to make his legal residence here in Egret Pointe. We'll be married at St. Anne's, because it will please his mother."

"No," Ray said. "No church wedding."

"Why not?" Ryan wanted to know.

"Because this marriage isn't going to be a long-term thing. It's just to save your asses," Ray said. "One day you could find the love of your life, and you'll want to be married in the church. You can't if you've already been married in the church and then divorced. For this marriage we'll want a local judge. I want it to be legal in this state, especially because otherwise your sisters are going to raise hell when they see all that money Jerry Klein has promised them going bye-bye. They may even threaten legal action, although they won't have a leg to stand on. All your dad said was, married by forty. He didn't specify how or to whom or even how long. Now, how long is this union going to last for you two? I'd suggest a two-year minimum."

"That sounds fine to me," Ryan said. He looked to Ashley. "You?"

She nodded. "Yes, that seems right."

"Okay," Joe said. "We don't need you two now. We'll work out all the details. When we've got a working draft of the prenup we'll have you each look at a copy, make corrections, do a final draft, and you'll sign it. So when's the wedding?"

"August twenty-fifth," Ashley said. "And it will be extremely low-key."

"What?" Joe teased. "No twelve-piece orchestra? No thousands of dollars' worth of flowers? No catered feast? The hospital thrift shop is going to be very disappointed."

"None of the above," Ashley said. "If we can't do it in church then we'll do it up at the hall. You, Rick, Ray, and your wives. Nina. The Byrneses. Joe's mom and favorite sister. A nice sit-down dinner in the dining room afterward. The flowers will come from the gardens, and if you want to dance afterward we'll put a CD on. After all, it's a sudden wedding after a whirlwind courtship, gentlemen."

"Sounds good to me," Ray said. He turned to his client. "The limo will take you back into the city, Ryan. It was a good meeting, yes?"

Ryan nodded. "Thanks for solving the problem," he said.

"Would you have time to see Kimbrough Hall?" Ashley asked him.

"Why not? It's Friday, and I don't have to do the driving. Yes, I would very much like to see Kimbrough Hall. I never knew anyone who lived in a hall."

"We'll call it our first date then," Ashley said with a small smile. She turned to the partners. "Thanks, guys. And Joe, call Tiff. If you wait until you get home there will be no living with her." She turned to Ryan. "We'll tell the driver to follow me," she said. "That way you won't have to drop me back in town later." She led him from the boardroom and from the law offices of Johnson and Pietro d'Angelo.

Ryan went over to the limo and gave the driver his instructions. Ashley waved him over to her Solstice. He eyed the hot little car and climbed in on the passenger side. Ashley gunned the vehicle and they were off, heading back the way he had come, except when they came to a turn in the road she swung the car onto a narrow paved road. She moved so fast that he almost missed the stone pillars, and just barely caught a glimpse of two brass-and-bronze markers affixed to them. The trees thinned as they reached the top of the hill where the house sat. The view of the bay was spectacular.

The house was beautiful: brick with white trim, gracious and welcoming, with a portico of elegant white pillars in front. He could see the colorful gardens behind and around the house. Two greyhounds loped up to the car as it pulled to a stop. He felt as if he were in a 1940s movie. He hadn't thought houses like this existed anymore. All this land, and it was obviously hers. *I wouldn't want to lose it either,* he thought.

"Welcome to Kimbrough Hall," Ashley said as she stepped from the car, giving the dogs a pat. "I hope you'll like it here, Ryan. I realize it is very different from the city. Is your apartment big?"

"No," he said, getting out and letting the dogs sniff him. "I have a one-bedroom in a prewar. Three apartments to a floor. I've got the C apartment with a view of the backs of other buildings. I don't need a view, as I'm there only at night and first thing in the morning when I get up. This place...it's incredible. And you grew up here? Wow!"

Ashley smiled. She was pleased that he liked it. "I couldn't live anywhere else."

She led him inside as Byrnes opened the door as if he had been waiting for her.

"Good afternoon, Miss Ashley, sir," the butler said.

"Afternoon, Byrnes. This is Mr. Mulcahy. Would Mrs. B. bring us some iced tea out to the porch?"

"At once, Miss Ashley," was the polite reply.

She led Ryan through the house, and he couldn't stop turning his head as he spotted valuable antique after valuable antique. The house was pristine, and everything belonged. It looked like a perfectly dressed movie set. He was fascinated by it all. The porch on the side of the house was filled with wicker furniture, the chair cushions done in a green-on-white fabric. "Sit," Ashley invited him.

"How big is this place?" he asked her.

"This floor, kitchens, pantry, living room, dining room, library, the ballroom, although it hasn't been used in years, and a small office. Second floor is bedrooms, bathrooms, a nursery wing. There's a wing over the kitchens for Mr. and Mrs. B. Attics above everything else. They used to be servants' quarters in the glory days of the house, along with storage. Three-car garage, but we use only two bays—one for my car, the other for the Byrneses car. The housemaid who cleans lives in town, as does the gardener."

"Big house for just one girl," he noted.

"I know," Ashley said, "but it's home, Ryan, and maybe one day I'll find the right man to share it with, and have lots of kids."

"You want kids?"

"Oh, yes! It was such fun growing up with Ben, even if I was a lot younger than he was. He was a terrific big brother."

Ryan saw tears well up in her eyes, but said nothing.

The butler brought in a small silver tray with two glasses of iced tea, and set the tray down. "Will you require anything else, Miss Ashley? If not I'll want to go to the garden and pick some peas for dinner."

"No, this is lovely, Byrnes. Thank you," Ashley said, and the butler withdrew.

"You have a garden?" He was surprised. With the supermarkets offering such a variety of foods today, he was fascinated that there was some sort of garden here growing vegetables along with the beautiful flowers.

"Byrnes and Tony, our gardener, love doing a vegetable garden every year," Ashley told him. "Who am I to refuse fresh veggies?" She smiled. Then she surprised him. "Would you like to come out next weekend? I suppose we really ought to start being seen around Egret Pointe."

He thought a moment, and then answered, "Yes, I would. If I'm going to be living here I ought to get to know the village."

"Bring a bathing suit. I have a pool, and it's heated," Ashley said.

He was surprised, but why he was surprised he didn't know. She was obviously old money. Not the kind you heard about in the society columns—*real* old money. The old-fashioned kind that showed up only in wedding and death announcements. "I will indeed bring a suit. I love to swim," he said. Then he stood up. "I had better be going. I usually have Friday-night dinner at my mom's, and I don't want to be late. She'll want to know why, and I'm not certain I'm ready to tell her."

"Why not?" Ashley said. "After all, according to Ray it was her idea that you have an arranged marriage to save your inheritance. I think you would want to tell her right away so she would stop worrying," Ashley told him.

"You wouldn't mind? She might even end up calling you," he warned her.

"That would be lovely. Intimidating, but lovely," she said, and stood up. "I'll go with you to the door, and then I'm off back to the shop. It's only a little after three, and I've got a lot to do. June is always a busy month, with weddings and anniversaries."

The limo was waiting for him outside the house. They smiled and shook hands, and then, getting in, he settled back for the ride into the city. It had probably been the most interesting day of his life, Ryan Finbar Mulcahy thought.

Ashley watched the car disappear down the drive. The day had seemed like a dream, and yet it was reality. In a few short weeks she was going to marry a stranger. And this groom wasn't gay, or a con artist, or going to die in Vegas from too much sex. They had a similar problem, and united in matrimony they would solve that problem. And the wedding would take place. Suddenly she was afraid, but then she forced back her fears. He was handsome, well-spoken, and the only agenda he had was to hold on to his money. It was her agenda too, wasn't it?

Chapter Three

"You're late," Angelina Mulcahy said to her son as he came into the house.

"I've been in a little town called Egret Pointe meeting my bride-to-be," Ryan told his mother as he bent to kiss her smooth cheek.

"What?" Angelina Mulcahy looked astounded.

"Well, you did tell Ray to find me a wife, didn't you?" he teased her, sitting down in a living room chair and taking the aperitif from the small tray she held.

"Yes," she answered him slowly, "but I didn't think he could find a girl from the old country so quickly." She sat down opposite him.

"What old country? She's a nice American girl with the same problem I have. Her grandfather's will says she has to marry or lose everything. I saw some of the everything, Ma. Her house is called a *hall.* It's beautiful. It's going to be a wonderful place to entertain my clients," Ryan told his mother.

"I thought..." Angelina Mulcahy looked thoughtful. "I thought Ray would find you a nice young woman from Italy or Ireland. Where did he find this girl?"

"His cousin, another lawyer, is Ashley's attorney," Ryan answered.

"So this rich girl won't be rich if she doesn't get married?" She sipped her own drink slowly. "I don't know, Ryan. This isn't quite what I had in mind when I asked Ray to find you a wife. I thought a nice, unspoiled girl who would be a good wife and mother. But a spoiled rich girl who doesn't want to lose her inheritance ... I don't know."

"She's rich, Ma, but she isn't spoiled. She's got a degree in business, like I do. Her late grandfather invested in her business, and she's his only heir. She has to marry before she's thirty-five or she loses it all, including her shop, and she's just now expanding her little empire."

"She's nice?"

"Very nice," Ryan told his mother.

"Pretty?"

"As a matter of fact she is," he said with a smile. "But nothing like I would have thought I'd pick. She's got dark hair, very fair skin, and the greenest eyes I ever saw. And she's not a twig. She's got to stand at least five feet eight or nine inches."

"A big girl," Angelina Mulcahy mused. Well, that wasn't bad at all. She sounded like she was healthy. Angelina didn't approve of those women who starved themselves into wraiths and waiflike figures, but had the best boobs that money could buy. "Not fat?"

"No, just tall, and proportioned right," Ryan said. "And she likes her food, Ma. We had lunch together, and she scarfed down her ravioli like a champ. And bread too."

"Dessert?" Now Angelina was interested.

"Every crumb, Ma," he told her.

Angelina nodded. "So when do I get to meet her?" she wanted to know.

But before he could answer her the doorbell rang.

"This conversation is over if that's someone else for dinner," Ryan said.

"It's Frankie," Angelina said, getting up to go to the door and let her youngest daughter in, kissing her as she did so. Francesca Mulcahy O'Connor was thirty-seven years old, and the mother of a single child. She had lost her husband, an investment banker, during 9/11. "Ma," she said, returning her mother's greeting. "Hey, big brother." She took the aperitif her mother poured her. "So, what's new?"

"Ray Pietro d'Angelo found Ryan a wife," Angelina said, and then hurried to catch her daughter up.

"That is so cool," Frankie said approvingly. "So when's the wedding?"

"August twenty-fifth," he said quietly.

"You've set the date already?" Angelina was a little surprised.

"I don't have much time," Ryan said. "I'm forty in April, Ma. Remember?"

"Yes, I remember," Angelina said quietly. "I remember very well."

"So what kind of a shop does she own?" Frankie wanted to know.

"It's called Lacy Nothings," he said, and grinned when his sister squealed.

"Oh, my God! The *real* Lacy Nothings? The one I get my stuff from?"

"One and the same, although why a nice widow lady needs *stuff* like that, I don't know," he teased her.

"Shut up!" Frankie said. "Do you think once you're married she'd let me have merchandise wholesale?"

"What is Lacy Nothings?" their mother asked.

"It's a lingerie shop, Ma. Very high-end, very expensive lingerie," Ryan said.

"It's gorgeous, Ma," Frankie enthused. "Real quality. She's got a catalog, and my most recent one says she's opening two new shops. One is right near me!"

"You're marrying a girl who sells underwear?" Angelina said.

"She's marrying a guy who makes furniture," he countered.

"You aren't a craftsman," Angelina said. "You're a businessman, Ryan. Your father was the artisan, but not you. It's different." She was very proud of her son. She knew what he had done for his father, even if Fin never acknowledged it. Her late husband had had a very typical Irish attitude. Not once had he ever told Ryan he was proud of him.

"August twenty-fifth," Frankie said. "I can't wait to see the look on the girls' faces when I tell them you're getting married." She grinned almost maliciously.

"You are not to breathe a word of this," Ryan said quietly. "Either of you. The lawyers are handling the business end. Ashley and I will be seeing each other over the next few weeks, and it will be said to be a whirlwind courtship. You and Ma get to come to the wedding. The others will learn of it afterward. I don't want them trying to interfere. They are not going to get R&R."

"Dee is going to be furious." Frankie chortled. "She's already looking for a bigger house, although with her kids all grown I don't know why she needs one."

"Will we meet Ashley before the wedding?" Angelina Mulcahy asked her son.

"How about two weeks from tonight? Here. For dinner?" he suggested.

Angelina nodded.

"Can I come?" Frankie asked.

"Where's Michael? Isn't he home from school?" her brother said.

"Home from St. Peter's, and off to Mountain Lake Camp in ten days to be a junior counselor this summer," Frankie said. Her son, who was seventeen, had been given a full scholarship to his late father's old preparatory school after Mike had been killed at the Twin Towers. At first Frankie hadn't wanted to send her son away in seventh grade, but they had both grieved hard after Mike had been killed so tragically, and their grief fed off each other's grief. Frankie realized that the only way she and her son would be able to get on with their lives, and past that awful day, was for Michael to go to St. Peter's. And it had worked. Neither of them would ever forget that terrible day, but without each other they had no choice but to move on. Her son would be a senior at St. Peter's in the autumn. He was student body president, and Frankie knew his father would be very proud.

"I don't know why he can't stay home with his mother in the summer," Angelina said disapprovingly. "He was in England at Brixton School for his spring term. We've hardly seen him this year."

"Going to Brixton on the exchange program was a big honor, Ma, and he wanted to go," Frankie defended her son. "And he's been at Mountain Lake since before his dad died. He's always wanted to be a junior counselor. He gets his fee free this year, and a stipend of five hundred dollars for the summer. I like encouraging him to earn his own money. He's a very responsible boy."

"Maybe if your son were home you wouldn't work so hard," Angelina said.

"Nope. If he were home he'd be a latchkey kid, and I'd feel guilty," Frankie said.

Her brother laughed. "I think you and Ashley are going to get on very well together," he said with a grin. "She kept me waiting this morning because she had to take an overseas call from her lace supplier in Madeira."

"Having seen you now, sweetie," his sister teased, "I'll bet she doesn't ever keep you waiting again."

He laughed. He had been a little put off when she had been late, but her explanation had been perfectly logical and practical. And when she had looked directly at him with those gorgeous green eyes, he had to admit that he was intrigued. Why had he ever considered a blue-eyed blond the perfect ideal? Ashley's dark hair had been cut very fashionably short in a boyish bob, but he had to admit there had been nothing boyish about her body. It was, to use an old-fashioned expression his dad had been fond of, curvy. Her breasts had pushed out that red tee nicely, and her ass in those tight pants had been very tempting.

As he sat alone later that night in his own apartment, half watching *Letterman,* Ryan again considered his ideal, and decided that maybe he had a new ideal. He wondered what she would look like without that red tee and those tight pants. Did she wear her own merchandise? Having thumbed through his sister's catalog once, he had to admit Ashley sold some pretty provocative stuff. He remembered in particular a little thigh-high black silk robe with the model's boobs half-visible, and the smallest bikini bottom he had ever seen that matched it.

He considered how Ashley might look in such an outfit, and actually felt himself begin to get hard. *Damn!* How could you be attracted to a girl you had just met, who didn't at all meet your original expectations? He was horny, of course. It had been months since he had had any kind of a relationship with a woman. Business just kept him too busy. Maybe getting married wasn't such a bad idea. Except that she had told him they wouldn't have sex. But they could have sex if they wanted to, couldn't they? They would be married, and today a lot of people who weren't married had sex. Then he shook his head. He was an idiot. This marriage was going to be strictly business.

Yes, business, Ashley thought as she contemplated entering The Channel that evening. Her marriage was going to be a business arrangement, but God, he was the sexiest thing she had seen in ages. The height of a Celtic warrior combined with that beautiful Italian face had actually made her go weak in the knees. She couldn't wait to see what he looked like in a bathing suit. He probably had washboard abs. He looked like he had them. And he had been hung. Even in those elegant custom-tailored slacks she had been able to ascertain that he was a big guy, and he dressed to the left.

Ashley shivered. She was going to have to share a bed with him the nights he stayed at the hall. Share a bed, and no sex. Was such a thing even possible? Well, it would be, because she suspected she didn't appeal to him physically. Big men always seemed to like little women, just like little guys always liked having a big girl on their arm. Ashley laughed softly. So their marriage would be a business arrangement, and after a few years they would go their separate ways. But she always had The Channel.

She picked up her remote. She loved the new features The Channel offered now. Ashley didn't know who owned or managed The Channel, but it had to be a woman. Only a woman would have thought of having two fantasies available to each customer. It was like getting a two-pound box of Godivas. Contemplating the remote, she considered which fantasy for tonight. Her finger brushed over button A, but she wasn't in the mood to dominate Quinn tonight. Tonight she wanted to be dominated. Ashley pressed the on button first, watching as the wall opposite her bed opened to reveal her flat-screen television. Then she pressed the button marked B, and the one marked enter.

Almost at once she found herself at the booted feet of a tall warrior. Her hands were chained before her. Her long, dark hair was loose. Her *stola* was half ripped from her body, and her breasts were easily visible. Looking up at the blond warrior, she snarled, "Unchain me at once, barbarian! My husband will have your life for this!"

"You should have remained in your civilized south, Roman whore!" he snarled back. "Now you will serve me, as you made yon Celtic warrior serve you." He turned to Quinn. "You are free now either to return to your homeland or join with me. I am Rurik, lord of the Northmen, and I bid you welcome to my camp."

"I'll stay," Quinn said. "What do you mean to do with my mistress?"

"She's no longer your mistress," Rurik said. "She's my whore until I grow tired of her. After that she will service my men." His booted foot pushed at the woman at his feet. "What is her name?"

"She is the lady Cordelia, wife to Tribune Maximillian Alerio Patronius, who is kin to Caesar," Quinn said.

"And this tribune permits his wife to fuck a captive slave?" Rurik wanted to know. "He is most generous with his wife's favors."

"I was part of the tribune's booty after a battle in Gaul," Quinn explained. "He noted my, er, male attributes, and gave me to his wife to serve as a sex slave. Many highborn

Roman men give sex slaves to their wives. The lords know that if their women have sex slaves they will not stray and cause a scandal while they are away. They also know that no Roman matron would have a child not her lord's."

"He is either a practical man or a suspicious one, this Maximillian Alerio Patronius," Rurik noted with a laugh. Then he reached down his hand to wrap a hank of Ashley's hair about his fist. Roughly he yanked her up and kissed her mouth hard. "Is she good?" he asked Quinn when he had finished.

Quinn smiled a slow smile. "Aye," he said. "She has the tightest cunt I've ever fucked. Each time it's as if she were a virgin taking a cock for the first time."

Rurik nodded, and then he looked down into the green eyes blazing up at him. "Tell me, Roman whore, have you have entertained two cocks at once?"

Her eyes widened.

"No?" he murmured against her lips. "Well, my proud Roman beauty, you soon will. And you will learn to please your master in any way and at any time he demands."

"You will die for this, barbarian pig!" Ashley said furiously. "I will personally see you crucified in the most painful manner I can devise. I will whip you myself!"

"Aye, she enjoys whipping," Quinn remarked. "My back is permanently marked."

"So," Rurik said, "she likes punishment, does she? I think we should adjourn to my tent and give the bitch a taste of her own, eh, Quinn?"

"Let me go, you beast!" Ashley shouted, struggling as she was half carried, half dragged into the lord of the Northmen's tent and flung down upon a bed of furs.

Rurik then proceeded to tear her garments off with great precision. He unfastened the manacles about her wrists, laughing as he ducked a blow aimed at his head. Forcing her onto her stomach and holding her down by her slender neck, he proceeded to spank her as she shrieked her outrage and her bottom was burning and red. Then, pushing her into the position he desired of her, her torso and arms pressed forward, her buttocks elevated and high, he proceeded to enter her woman's channel.

Ashley screamed furiously as she divined his intent, but as she did, Quinn, kneeling before her, pushed his engorged cock into her open mouth, warning her, "If you bite I will see you punished in far worse fashion. Suck me sweetly, Roman whore."

She tried to moan as the thick peg of flesh filled her mouth. There was no other choice but to suck him. And as she did she became very aware of the enormous cock filling her cunt, stretching its walls as Rurik began to thrust into her with a skilled motion that left her breathless. When both men had emptied their load, Quinn down her throat and Rurik into her cunt, they fell away from her, temporarily satisfied. Ashley collapsed, gasping as she was pushed to the floor. She had needed the roughness tonight. Now, she knew, they would be pleased at having mastered her for the time being.

Rurik finally sat up and commanded her to come to him. Ashley hissed angrily at him, jumping when Quinn unexpectedly smacked her bottom hard. "Crawl," Rurik commanded her. "Crawl to me, my proud Roman whore. I have just begun to amuse myself with you. Quinn, my friend, you will find a bundle of birches in the far corner. It can bring a plump bottom such as the lady Cordelia possesses to a fine shine. Will you fetch it?" Reaching out, he yanked Ashley into his lap, her back to his chest, her buttocks seated upon his large cock. He began to lick the side of her neck, his hands reaching around her to cup her breasts in his palms. "You have fine tits, Roman whore," Rurik murmured in her ear with his hot breath. He squeezed the soft flesh as she squirmed in his lap. He could feel himself getting hard again against her buttocks.

Quinn had risen from the bed of furs and walked across the tent to fetch the bundle of birches, as asked. The bundle was tightly bound except at the ends, where the thin, flexible branches had been left loose. Returning to the bed, he rejoined Rurik and Ashley. "What do you have in mind?" he asked the lord of the Northmen as he displayed the birch before her eyes. "I hope you will let me use this on her. A bit of payback."

Rurik smiled. "Aye. I saw your back when you went to fetch the switches. She has not been gentle with you, my friend. Spread your legs, Roman whore!" he snapped at her, and when she refused to obey he pinched her nipples cruelly until she did. "Is she wet?" he asked Quinn.

"She needs a bit of priming," the Celtic warrior answered, and he began to finger Ashley's clitoris artfully, smiling into her green eyes when she began to whimper. Finally he pushed two fingers into her, moving them about teasingly until he was satisfied that her juices had begun to flow. "She's ready," he told Rurik.

The lord of the Northmen turned the woman in his arms about so that she was now facing him. Lifting her up, he lowered her onto his engorged penis. Then he drew her down into his arms and against his broad chest. "Whip her, and when she is well burnished, fuck her ass," he said.

"No! No!" Ashley cried, and she tried to struggle, but Rurik held her tightly as Quinn began to flog her buttocks with the birches. It was worse than anything she had ever imagined. The cruel little switches burned her flesh, and she tried to cry out, but she could not, for Rurik had taken her mouth in a fierce kiss, his tongue now doing frantic battle with her tongue.

"She has never allowed me to have her that way," Quinn said slowly.

"Then ream her well, my friend," Rurik said, tearing his mouth away from Ashley briefly. "You probably deserve it, though it is small payment for the scars on your back. There is a jar of cream here to aid you." Then he began to kiss his captive again.

For several minutes Quinn brought the birches down and across the hapless woman's backside. Then, satisfied with the deep pink color of the skin, he knelt directly behind her, and, reaching for the jar Rurik had indicated, he first greased his cock, and then generously lubricated her asshole. Then he slowly, slowly began to penetrate that most secret of places on a woman's body. The small opening resisted him at first, but then it began to give way beneath the persistent pressure of his penis. First the head entered, and then he carefully sheathed himself to the hilt.

Ashley almost fainted with his entry. She could feel Rurik's great weapon throbbing in her female channel, and now Quinn's cock was thrumming in her asshole. Rurik reached out and began to tease at her clit, and she moaned as he fingered her, teasing, stroking, pinching.

"Ah, my Roman whore likes being fucked and buggered at the same time, doesn't she? Perhaps I shall not give you to my men after all. You are providing me with a grand evening's amusement. I suspect you are going to be good for many an evening's entertainment."

"I hate you!" Ashley sobbed, and then to her shock they all came together in an orgasmic rush of lust fulfilled.

And afterward the two men cradled her and cuddled her, praising her for being such a good Roman whore, and when Ashley awoke she was in her own bed, as usual. Rurik and Quinn had been a bit rougher last night, but she had obviously needed them to be, because she felt absolutely wonderful. Yesterday had been a bit more unnerving than she had anticipated. Now she knew what all those heroines in the historical romance novels she loved so much felt like when bartered into arranged marriages. It was so strange to realize that in a few weeks she would have a husband. Her private number rang, and Ashley reached out to the table by her bedside to answer it.

"Good morning," a deep male voice said cheerfully.

"Who is this?" Ashley asked. "Are you sure you have the right number?"

"It's Ryan, Ashley. I got your number from your lawyer. Listen, I was thinking... I don't want to wait until next weekend to start getting to know you better. I know it's kind of short notice, but I'm halfway out to Egret Pointe now."

"Did you ever consider that I might have plans for the weekend?" she asked him, her heart hammering with excitement.

"Do you?" he asked candidly.

"No, but you might have asked first. Before you got halfway out," she scolded him gently. "You've never courted a woman before, have you? Are you driving while we're talking, Ryan?"

"No, I pulled over into a rest stop on the parkway," he said. "And, no, I've never courted a woman. I've done something wrong, haven't I?"

"Yes and no," she said. "I'll explain when you get here. I assume you mean to stay for the rest of the weekend? I'll need to tell Byrnes if you are."

"I did bring a bag," he admitted. "With a bathing suit," he added.

Ashley laughed. "We'll have a room ready for you when you get here," she said.

"Thanks," he answered her. "I should see you in an hour or so." The phone clicked off.

Ashley picked up her house phone and pressed the intercom.

"Good morning, Miss Ashley," Byrnes said. "Ready for your coffee?"

"Yes, please," Ashley replied. "And Byrnes, we're having an overnight visitor. Will you get the Washington bedroom ready for him, please?"

"Yes, Miss Ashley. I'll tell Mrs. Kramer, and she'll see to it at once," was the reply.

"Byrnes, I'll want to speak with you and the missus when I have my breakfast," Ashley said. "I'll be down in fifteen minutes."

"Very good, Miss Ashley," Byrnes answered.

Ashley climbed from the bed, stripping off her cotton sleep shirt as she headed for her bathroom. She showered quickly, washing her hair, and by the time she reentered her bedroom wrapped in a towel there was a small carafe of sweet, milky coffee on a table along with a china mug. Ashley filled the mug and drank half of it down. Then she got dressed. She had to go to work today. Nina was recovering from her dental surgery, and Brandy, the high school kid who usually worked in the shop on Saturdays, was getting ready for her prom. Saturday was usually a very busy day. Why hadn't she told Ryan to turn his car around and go home? Well, he would just have to amuse himself until she closed at four. Should she take him out to dinner?

Irritated at being caught unawares, Ashley yanked on pair of white silk briefs and then pulled up her pink silk slacks. Her bra and a cream silk shirt followed. Slipping her feet into a pair of custom-made burgundy leather loafers, she finished the rest of her coffee and hurried downstairs to the small breakfast room, seating herself at the round table with its single place setting. She picked up the glass of cranberry juice and sipped it. Almost immediately Byrnes was at her side with a hot plate of cheesy scrambled eggs, three sausage links, and a whole-wheat English muffin.

"Get a cuppa for you and the missus," Ashley said, "and come join me while I eat. I have something very important to tell you both." Picking up her fork, she dug into the eggs enthusiastically as she waited for them.

Byrnes retreated into the kitchens. "She wants us to sit with her while she eats. She says she's got something important to tell us," he told his wife.

Martha Byrnes poured two cups of coffee and handed one to her husband; then they reentered the little breakfast room off of the kitchen, sitting down at the small table with Ashley. They looked at her expectantly.

She had almost finished her eggs, and two of the sausages were gone from her plate. Now, as she spread some homemade marmalade on a half a muffin, she said frankly, "I'm getting married. But this time there will be no difficulties. The groom isn't gay. He won't go to Las Vegas before the wedding, and he isn't a con man. Joe Pietro d'Angelo has a lawyer cousin in the city who has a client with the same problem I do—an inheritance with a big string attached. He has to marry before he's forty or lose it all. We are a match made in heaven," Ashley said with a wry smile.

"Would he be the gentleman who came home with you yesterday, Miss Ashley?" Byrnes asked.

"Yep. One and the same. Ryan Finbar Mulcahy. He built up his dad's business in the city, made the guy rich, rich, rich, and then the old guy turns around and writes a will that says if Ryan isn't married by the time he's forty he loses it all. Nice, huh?"

"No worse than what your grandpa did to you, missy," Martha Byrnes said tartly. "Giving in to that hussy Lila Peabody! Well, it's a truth that there's no fool like an old fool. It wasn't enough for the shameless creature that your grandpa left her a goodly sum for services rendered, and I can only shudder to imagine what they could have been, and at his age too!" She huffed indignantly.

Ashley giggled. Never one to dissemble, Martha Byrnes had strong opinions.

"Mrs. Byrnes," her husband said warningly.

"Oh, it's all right," Ashley told him. "I agree with Martha. But you remember how Grandfather always thought a good woman needed a good man. After the first two unfortunate incidences with fiancés I honestly think he believed I wasn't trying hard enough. Putting that provision in the will soothed Lila, whose company he did enjoy, and it gave him comfort to know that I would marry to preserve what I had built."

"He's amenable to a prenuptial agreement?" Martha Byrnes wanted to know.

"Absolutely!" Ashley assured them. "Ryan and I will marry just to meet the terms of these two wills. In a few years we'll go our separate ways with our own possessions intact, and no one gets hurt in the process. I wanted you both to know because he'll be here shortly, and as soon as he arrives I have to go to the shop. He's a really nice guy. While he's hanging out here today waiting for me to get home, answer any questions he may have. Although he's keeping his apartment in town, he'll be making the hall his legal residence. We've got to start thinking about redoing Grandfather's old rooms for us."

"This isn't for public knowledge, I take it," Byrnes said quietly.

"No, it isn't. We've scheduled the wedding for August twenty-fifth. It's going to be very low-key. No more than ten or twelve people for dinner. We're doing it here, because he's Roman Catholic, and we don't want a church wedding to louse up his life after we're divorced. Actually I think it's better that way. No fuss. No muss. The flowers can come from the gardens."

"I'll tell Tony we're having a dinner party on that date, so he will be certain to have the right flowers on hand," Byrnes said. "You know how the flowers tend to go in August, so he'll need to nurse certain blooms along."

Ashley took the last bite of her English muffin, and then swallowed down the rest of her cranberry juice. She stood up from the table. "I'd better get ready to leave as soon as he gets here," she said, and walked from the breakfast room. "Well, if that don't beat all," Martha Byrnes said softly. "She's making an arranged marriage, Martin. It's a real shame she can't be allowed to fall in love like any other girl, but then, Miss Ashley isn't just any girl, is she?"

"No," he agreed, "she isn't."

"Well, if the lawyers have checked this young man out, then I suppose it's all right," Martha replied with a sigh. "Still, it makes me sad. I wonder what he's like."

"We'll know soon enough," her husband said. Then he stood up and straightened his tie. "I hear a car coming up the drive. That will be our guest, Martha. Run up to Mrs. Kramer and make certain the Washington bedroom is ready for him." Brynes hurried out to get the front door, peeping through the sidelights to see a vintage Jag pull up. Its driver climbed out, reaching behind him for a small overnight bag. Byrnes flung wide the front door. "Good morning, Mr. Mulcahy. I'll take your bag for you. You'll find Miss Ashley out on the porch. Can you find your way, sir?"

"Yes, thanks," Ryan said. Having a butler, or whatever Byrnes was, was going to take some getting used to, he decided as he made his way to the porch.

"Good morning, Ryan." Ashley came forward to greet him. "I can only stay with you a minute. My help at the shop is nonexistent today, and Saturday is always busy." And then to her surprise he reached out, drew her forward, and kissed her on both of her cheeks. "Oh, my," Ashley exclaimed as he set her back. "That was very…"

"Italian," he supplied the word for her with a smile. "I thought we had best get used to some form of kissing, since we're getting married."

"Yes," she agreed, thoughtful. "You'll have to kiss me on the lips at the wedding, won't you? People might talk otherwise. Well, kissing is a harmless enough sport."

"You've done a lot of it?" he asked.

"Again I remind you of my age," Ashley said.

"I like kissing," he allowed, his brown eyes twinkling.

"I've got to go," Ashley told him. The conversation was beginning to make her a little uncomfortable. Their relationship was a business one, and people in business didn't—or at least shouldn't—get intimate. "Byrnes will take care of you. I'll be home a little after four. He'll answer any questions you may have about the house." She managed to get past him. "Have a good day, Ryan." And she hurried off.

He made himself comfortable on the porch looking out at the blue bay sparkling in the bright June morning. He had made her nervous. Despite her misadventures she was obviously a very proper lady. Interesting. She was past thirty, a businesswoman, and had, in her own words, some small experience with men, but she was basically shy. Was it the situation in which they found themselves? Or was Ashley good at what she did, but clueless where relationships were concerned? He was one to talk, Ryan thought wryly. A discreet cough caused him to look up and find Byrnes standing there.

"Mrs. Byrnes thought that you had probably not had breakfast before you departed town this morning, sir. She's prepared you a small repast. If you will follow me to the breakfast room I'll bring it to you."

"Why, that's most kind," Ryan said, standing up and trailing after Byrnes. A breakfast room, no less, he thought as he entered the small room with its cheerful bright yellow-and-white striped walls. He allowed Byrnes to seat him, and then smiled as a plump woman appeared to put a plate before him. This, he concluded, was Mrs. Byrnes. "Thank you, ma'am," he said. "It looks most delicious."

"I gave you some of my fresh-baked blueberry muffins," she replied.

He looked up at her with a smile. "They smell wonderful, Mrs. Byrnes, but there was no need to go to such trouble for me. I would have been happy with a bowl of Apple Jacks," Ryan told her.

"Not in this house!" Martha Byrnes said emphatically. "In my kitchen we cook. Breakfast, sometimes lunch, and always dinner. Now, you eat up while it's hot."

He grinned at her and obeyed her directive. It was almost like having Angelina around, he thought. And then he realized that if the Byrneses were this caring of a stranger, then Ashley certainly hadn't suffered growing up. It was reassuring.

Ashley had sped into the village and parked her car behind Lacy Nothings. It was almost nine thirty. From the traffic on Main Street she could see it would be a busy day, and it was. From the moment she had opened the shop for business the little bell over the front door hadn't stopped ringing. By twelve thirty things had slowed down, and she was just drawing a sigh of relief when she heard the jangle of the bell again. Turning, she saw Ryan entering the shop with a small basket.

"Mrs. B. thought we might enjoy having a bit of lunch together," he said. "Where should we eat?"

"We can go back into my office, if you don't mind," Ashley replied. "I don't like to leave the shop even for lunch. A lot of people shop during that hour." She led the way into the tiny office, taking the basket from him to set it upon her desk. "Sit." She pointed to the chair behind her desk, seating herself in the chair opposite the desk. "It's easier for me to get out if the bell rings," she explained. Also my desk chair is bigger, and you're a pretty big guy."

All over, he thought wickedly as he folded himself into her chair. Now, what the hell made him think that? he wondered. Why was he getting sexual thoughts about Ashley? But he was. From underneath his dark eyelashes he was considering how she would look in a fuchsia lace bra and bikini bottom, like the one on the plastic dummy in her shop window. That rich purple-pink on her pale skin would be dynamite.

"Chicken salad," Ashley said, handing him a sandwich on a paper plate. "Mrs. B. already likes you. She doesn't do her chicken salad for just anyone."

He had gained a glimpse of her full breasts when she had bent over to hand him the sandwich. She appeared to be wearing a plain white silk bra, but nonetheless it was so sexy that he had wanted to lean forward and lick her skin. He closed his eyes briefly. He had just met this girl yesterday, and he was behaving like a damned pervert. Ryan Mulcahy couldn't remember a time when he had had such a strong reaction to a woman. Her fragrance had drifted up briefly from between her breasts. It was elusive, sensual, and clean smelling. He couldn't quite put his finger on it. "Nice perfume," he said casually. "What is it?"

"Do you like it? It's Vent Vert by Balmain. I've always loved it. It was my first real French *parfum*. My brother, Ben, bought it for me the summer we were in Europe. He was based in Germany, and got leave to meet Grandfather and me in Paris. It was the last time we were all together. He was killed the following year in Iraq during Desert Storm. I always think of him when I spritz it on," Ashley said sadly.

"Then why wear it?" he asked her practically.

"Because I like it," she told him. "And not wearing it won't bring Ben back."

"Mrs. B. makes a great chicken salad sandwich," Ryan said, changing the subject. He had seen the glint of tears in her eyes, and was touched by the love she still bore her late brother. He couldn't have cared less if his five older sisters were blown off the face of the earth. Now, Frankie was different, but the rest of them could be gone and he wouldn't have missed one of them.

"I've told the Byrneses that we're getting married, and why," Ashley said. "I know everyone was worried that they might think badly of us, even while understanding the dilemma that I—that we—face. They know there is no other choice for either of us. I'll need help redoing Grandfather's rooms for us, and I have to plan a wedding, don't I?"

"Frankie, my little sister, is a decorator. She works for Evelyn Claire," Ryan said. "She would probably help you if you asked. In fact, she'd die to help you. And she'd take her fee in your lingerie." He chuckled. "She's one of your big catalog customers."

Ashley laughed. "Hey, I'm amenable to a barter system," she said. "Give me her number and I'll call her."

"Done," he agreed. "I spoke to my mother."

"And?" She bit into her sandwich.

"She likes the fact that you aren't anorexic and enjoy your food," he answered. "She wants you to come to dinner in two weeks. Is that okay?"

Ashley nodded. "I'd like that."

They actually managed to finish their lunch without interruption, and when they had, Ryan gathered up the basket and they walked out together to the front of the shop.

"Look," he said when they had reached the door, "I know this is probably going to sound crazy, but I need to do this." He pulled her to him, and his mouth met her surprised mouth in a kiss. It wasn't a quick kiss. It was definitely an *I want to see where this goes* kiss. If it was going to go anywhere. And from the distinct tightening in his groin, it was going to go somewhere if they wanted. He had surprised her, but she didn't pull away, or even protest. Her breasts crushed against his chest, and he could feel her nipples hardening against him. The mouth beneath his was soft, sweet. Her lips parted beneath his, and their tongues touched. Slowly he broke off the embrace. "I'll see you later," he said, hoping she hadn't been put off by the fact that he had developed an enormous hard-on. Fortunately his car was at the curb in front of her shop.

"'Kay" Ashley managed to reply, and closed the door to her shop, grabbing at the counter to steady herself before she fell down. Boy, could he kiss! she thought. When their tongues had touched briefly she thought she was going to faint dead away. And he was obviously attracted to her, because she had given him one whale of a hard-on. He had practically limped to his car. But it wasn't love. They were both in lust.

Marriage of convenience. No sex. Well, she reconsidered, maybe not. Did either of them seriously believe they could sleep in the same bed and remain celibate for two years? She could go back on the pill. There didn't have to be any babies. But from the fire they were igniting in each other it was obvious that they were eventually going to have sex. Why not? Then Ashley shook her head. What was she thinking? This was to be a business arrangement, and here she was thinking with her cunt and not her brain. Still, Ryan Finbar Mulcahy was some kisser! And he was probably something else in bed.

He apologized after dinner, but Ashley would have none of it. "We're crazy to think we can do this with no sex," she told him. "You left me weak-kneed, and I gave you a hard-on. We're attracted to each other, much to my surprise. We only just met, Ryan, but there is definitely something there."

"It's lust," he said.

"I know," she agreed, "but what's wrong with a little lust between two consenting adults? We're getting married, after all. Unless there is someone else."

"There is no one," he said. "What if you got pregnant?"

"I'll go back on the pill," Ashley replied. "You may be a Catholic, but I suspect you don't object to the pill."

"You'd do that?" The brown eyes he turned on her were making her hot.

"Sure. I'll call Dr. Sam on Monday. I suspect you're like all the macho men—you don't like condoms. If we both get a clean bill of health, and you abide by my rules, then we can't rule sex out of the equation."

"Rules?" He raised an eyebrow.

"Look, all I ask is that if you're screwing me, you don't do other women. Okay? I certainly won't be doing other men." *Except, of course, my two boys on The Channel, but that's not really real so it doesn't matter,* Ashley thought. *And maybe I won't need them if you're as good as I think you're going to be.*

"Seems reasonable," he agreed.

"And I'd like to hold off until the wedding," Ashley said. "Or at least until we've both been given a clean bill of health."

"That's fair," he murmured, "but we could play a little, couldn't we?"

They were on the porch, and he was sitting on a wicker settee while she paced back and forth in the half-light. Reaching up, he pulled her into his lap.

"Hey!" Ashley said, surprised.

"I can't seem to help myself," he admitted. "All my life I had this picture in my head of the ideal woman for me. She would be petite. Blond. Helpless, and I would be her savior. You don't quite fit the bill, do you?"

"I guess I don't," Ashley agreed.

"But one look into those big green eyes of yours, and all I could think of was getting into your pants," he said. "I feel like a lecher, but damn it, you excite me!" His hand fumbled at the back of her shirt, seeking her bra snap.

"It's in the front," Ashley said, reaching to undo the bra herself. "Well, I don't know what I was expecting, but a guy six feet and a hundred inches tall, with a face like a model, wasn't on the agenda. You excite me too. And there's nothing wrong with good old-fashioned lust, Ryan Mulcahy. Just so long as we understand each other." She undid the top two buttons on her shirt.

His hand slid eagerly in to cup a breast in his palm. He sighed, feeling the soft weight in his hand. Opening her shirt fully, he pushed it off her shoulders and stared at her breasts. They were large, but not big. And they had nipples like blown roses. "God, these are beautiful," he said, and he began to kiss them.

Ashley sighed with pure pleasure. It had been several months since a man had made love to her. But oh, Lord, she knew it couldn't go much further. He was a passionate man, and she, for all her calm exterior, was a passionate woman. It would take very little to put them in a very compromising position. She could already feel his penis straining against the fabric of his slacks and her butt. But still, she closed her eyes and sighed again as his lips moved over her chest and up her throat to find her lips. He was pure heaven, and she was already wet for him. "Stop," she said, pulling gently away.

"Just a little more," he begged her, his hands fondling her breasts.

"No," she told him. "If we don't stop now I don't know what will happen."

"Yeah, you do," he countered, and fastened her bra back together before buttoning her shirt back up. "If we keep on like this I'm going to fuck the ears off of you, Ashley. You know that, don't you?" He nipped at her earlobe. "I cannot believe how hot I am for you."

She struggled to her feet, standing on shaky legs. "Me too," she told him.

"Tell me you want me to fuck you right now, Ashley," he said. "Tell me you want me to go deep and hard until you can't stop coming."

"No," she told him softly. "If I say it we're going to do it, and I'm not that kind of a woman, Ryan. And you really don't want me to be."

He nodded. "No, I don't," he agreed. "But I have never had such an instant attraction to a woman in my life. I don't understand it."

"When was the last time you were with a woman?" she asked him.

He thought, and then shook his head. "A long time, I guess," he said.

"So you're overdue for a good screwing," Ashley told him. "And we are going to get married in a few weeks, so you're ready to rumble. But I'm not. Do you excite me? God, yes! But I keep remembering the fraternity guy who did me twice in college and then bailed. And I remember the two men who were marrying me, but somehow never made it to the altar. So since we're making a marriage of convenience I think we'll just be old-fashioned and wait until our wedding night. Okay?"

"I'll wait quietly," he said, "but only if I can play with those again."

"I'll think about it," Ashley said with a grin. "Now I'm going up to bed. Good night, Ryan Mulcahy."

"Good night, Ashley Kimbrough," he replied.

Chapter Four

"Why, you're beautiful," Angelina Mulcahy said by way of greeting to Ashley. She took the younger woman's hands in hers and, leaning forward, kissed her on both cheeks. "Welcome to my home, *cara*. I hope we are, despite the unusual circumstances of this impending marriage, going to be friends."

"I don't think I've ever been greeted so sweetly, Mrs. Mulcahy. Thank you for having me," Ashley replied as her future mother-in-law slipped her arm through hers and led her into the living room of the gracious house.

"You must call me Lina, *cara*. All my friends do," Angelina Mulcahy said. She was pleased. Very pleased indeed. Ashley was tall and healthy-looking. She had a wide span between her hips, which was good for childbearing. Yes. Ray had done well, even if this girl was an independent American. And she had never particularly cared for the blondes that her only son said he preferred. This girl had beautiful coloring. She was like a Tintoretto Madonna. And she appeared to have manners, for all she had been raised by an old man and his servants. She sat Ashley on the settee. "Now, you will tell me all about yourself," Angelina said. "You had a brother?"

"Yes, Ben. He died in Desert Storm," Ashley answered.

Angelina crossed herself piously. "God rest him, and bless him for the service he rendered our country," she murmured.

The doorbell rang, and Ryan went to let his youngest sister in. "Hey, babe," he greeted her. "Ash is getting the third degree right now from Ma."

Frankie Mulcahy O'Connor stood for a minute in the entry between the living room and the hall. "God, she's beautiful, Ryan. You didn't say she was beautiful."

"First thing Ma said to her," he told his sister. "I think T was too busy getting past the she-isn't-a-blonde stage."

"You can be such a jerk sometimes," Frankie told him. Then, giving him a friendly shove, she walked into the living room. "Hi, Ma. Hi, Ashley. I'm Frankie, the good sister." She grinned mischievously.

"So I've heard," Ashley said with an answering grin. Then she hugged Frankie.

Angelina nodded her approval. A warm heart. This girl had a warm heart.

"Anyone want an aperitif?" Ryan asked. It tickled him the way his mother and his sister had taken immediately to Ashley. But then, he had taken to her too.

At the dinner table Angelina watched as Ashley devoured her cooking. She almost wanted to shout with joy, and when Ashley returned for a second helping of tiramisu she almost cried. "Do you cook?" she asked her guest.

"Not really. I've never had to," Ashley admitted. "Mrs. Byrnes does the cooking at Kimbrough Hall. I'm such a workaholic. But I would love your recipe for the chicken and artichokes. Mrs. B. is always looking for new dishes to make."

"I will write it out for you," Angelina said. "But then one day I will come and teach you how to make it. Work is good, but you should also know how to cook a few dishes. What if your Mrs. Byrnes became ill?"

"She'd do what we all do, Ma," Frankie said. "She'd order out."

"Not in Egret Pointe." Ashley laughed. "We have one pizzeria, and he just does pizza and heroes. But we do have some nice restaurants."

The evening continued in pleasant fashion. Ashley and Frankie began to talk about decorating the master suite in the house.

"I've got to run it by my boss," Frankie said apologetically. "She's a real Tartar about any of her decorators doing private work. She's scared one of them might walk off with her client list. I hope you don't mind."

"Evelyn Claire was a friend of my mother's," Ashley replied. "They were in school together. St. Hilary's. Tell her I'm Rosemary Leigh Kimbrough's daughter."

"A Catholic school?" Angelina put in.

"No. Anglican nuns," Ashley replied.

"Your children...?" Angelina said.

"I don't think Ryan and I have gotten that far yet, Lina," Ashley said candidly.

Later, as she and Ryan drove back to Egret Pointe, he apologized to her. "I haven't told Ma yet that the marriage is just a temporary one. She thinks it's going to be like her and my dad: two people marrying for practical reasons and making a go of it."

"Don't tell her," Ashley said. "It would upset her, and I don't want to do that."

"She liked you."

"I liked her, and I really like your sister Frankie. She and I are going to be good friends no matter what," Ashley told him. "You're staying the rest of the weekend, aren't you?" she asked as they pulled off the parkway. "I want to discuss several things with you. The wedding. Our bedroom. I want to do announcements to be sent out afterward. Personally, I like the old-fashioned black script on white or cream paper, but I'd like your opinion also. You've got a stake in this too. And I'll need a list of people you want to receive the announcement. I'd like to get the busywork out of the way so we can relax over the next few weeks, if that's okay with you."

"That's fine," he agreed. "We'll start in the morning." He pulled up in front of the hall.

The portico was lit, but Ashley had told Byrnes to go to bed because they would be late, and she didn't want her butler waiting up. They let themselves in and walked upstairs to their separate bedrooms. In the dim upstairs hall Ryan pulled her into his arms and began to kiss her. She slid her arms about his neck and ran her tongue across his lips. He followed suit.

"You've got the sexiest mouth," he told her. "Like that actress with the same name as my mother."

"Angelina Jolie," she said.

"Yeah, that's her." His hand began to fondle one of her breasts.

"Oh, don't," she said. "If we get started I don't know what will happen, Ryan."

"I miss the girls," he said softly in her ear. "You haven't let them come out to play since that night on the porch."

Ashley swallowed hard. His hands were big and gentle. She found she liked it very much when he touched her breasts. They were already growing firm, her nipples hardening, and she was absolutely getting wet between her thighs.

"I want to get naked with you," he whispered.

"No," she told him, but she didn't yet pull away from his hand.

"I took you to meet my mother and favorite sister. The prenups will be ready to be signed next week. I'm not gay, and I have no plans to go to Vegas or anywhere else in the near future." The hand fondling her breast slipped down, under her skirt, and up to caress the soft flesh of her thigh. "You're wet," he said. "You want this as much as I do."

Ashley whimpered. He wasn't telling her anything she didn't already know, but even if this was a marriage of convenience, she was going to do it right this time. Gathering every bit of her strength, she pulled away from him, her hand reaching for the doorknob. "On our wedding night, and not a minute before," she told him as she turned and stepped into her room, shutting the door behind her firmly, clicking the lock.

He was so hard he thought it would probably break off if he touched it. *Damn!* He really wanted her! Wanted to bury himself so deep he could touch her womb. What would she be like? he wondered. Would she cry out with her climax? Would she claw him? Or was she one of those silent types who just lay there? No. He didn't think she would be silent. Ryan rubbed his penis trying to ease the ache. That sexy mouth of hers could have tempered his discomfort. Would she do that for him? He sure wanted to go down on her. Wanted to peel back her labia, lick her clit, and then suck it until she was screaming with her climax. And she would scream. He entered his own bedroom.

In the morning it was as if the incident had never occurred. They sat at the table in the breakfast room and discussed the few guests who would come to the wedding.

Ashley had decided to have the local calligrapher do the invitations on pale cream paper. The gentleman had been sworn to secrecy.

They would do engraved announcements on cream as well, with elegant black script. The wording would be traditional, and there would be a separate card indicating their residence. The announcement cards were small.

Ashley Cordelia Kimbrough
and
Ryan Finbar Mulcahy
Announce Their Marriage on
Saturday, the Twenty-fifth of August
Two Thousand and Seven

The separate enclosure cards read: *At Home After September First,* with their address.

"My sisters are really going to be pissed," Ryan said with a broad grin. "And when they find out Frankie was there...well, Bride will split a gut. There goes her new big house, which she doesn't need. Betta ain't going to get her Ferrari, and Dee's spoiled brats are going to need loans to finish college. Considering their grades, I'm not sure they'll get them. My nephews like to party. As for Katy and Mags, their husbands are going to have to pay for those around-the-world cruises on the *QMII* they've planned."

"That is truly mean-spirited," Ashley said. "Your older sisters can't be that bad."

"Yeah, they can. Wait 'til you meet them," he said. "Those five bitches had already lined up a buyer for R&R, Ash."

"Well, then, let's hold a party at the end of September to celebrate our first month's anniversary," Ashley suggested mischievously. "Just family, okay?"

"You are a glutton for punishment." He laughed.

"I have to meet the wicked sisters sometime," she pointed out.

"True," he said, "and by that time you should have that well-fucked look that women get in the first month of marriage, and they'll know it's for real," he said softly, reaching out to take her hand in his. He nibbled at her knuckles.

Their eyes met, and Ashley felt her heart turn over suddenly. What was that all about? She had known him just a few weeks. She blushed, and he grinned.

"I like it when you blush," he said.

"And you seem to have a knack for making me blush," she told him. Then she drew her hand from his. "Let's decide on the menu for the wedding dinner."

"Are you a cock tease?" he asked her suddenly.

"No! I don't think so. Why would you ask a thing like that?" she demanded.

"I touch you and you retreat," he complained. "And yet if I can manage to kiss you, you're on fire almost at once."

"This started out as strictly business. But now sex is entering the equation," Ashley said slowly. "You obviously like sex, and I sure do, and yes, we're going to be married, but I don't want to jinx it this time, even if love is not part of the picture. I don't know how to explain it any better."

"This is the damnedest thing," he told her. "No, love is not part of this, and business is the reason we're getting together, but I can't believe how hot I am for you, Ash."

"You're flattering, but I meant it when I said not until our wedding night," she told him firmly. "You're a very healthy, lusty guy."

"You feel the same way about me as I do about you, and yet you are so cool about it as long as I don't touch you. But all I have to do is look at you and I want to pull your dress over your head," he growled at her. "How can you be so sanguine?"

"It's just a matter of self-discipline, Ryan," Ashley told him. *That and having The Channel*, she thought, and forced back the grin that was threatening to break out on her face. "I really want to do it this way, Ryan, please."

"I want to do it every way." He groaned.

"Then we should have one hell of a wedding night," Ashley said mischievously.

"I will make certain you don't walk for a week," he promised her menacingly.

"Ohhh, you are a very bad boy!" she teased him wickedly, and she waggled an admonishing finger at him.

"Are you a very bad girl?" he asked provocatively.

"I think I can be, with the right partner," Ashley said. Then she caught his hand up and began sucking on his middle finger. "Are you the right partner, Ryan?" Her tongue swirled about the finger slowly, and then she sucked hard on it. This was fun, she thought. She had never had this kind of a playful relationship with either of her two fiancés. It had been far more cut-and-dried. They had refrained from sex until she had an engagement ring on her finger, and then they had somehow fallen into bed. And both men had gotten far more out of it than she ever had, but she had assumed that was life. Now she was learning that it wasn't. She had never had a lustful attraction to any man until Ryan.

He closed his brown eyes briefly as he enjoyed the tug of her lips on his finger, and considered those lips fastening about his cock. *Damn!* He was hard again. He pulled his finger away from her. "If we're not going to fuck," he said, "then stop being such a bloody tease, Ash. You don't want Byrnes coming in and finding you on your knees in front of me with my dick in your mouth. The poor fellow would faint dead away."

Looking across the table at him, she considered. They could do a little sucking and licking. In fact, it would be very nice, and it would take the edge off of their appetites.

No! Was she out of what passed for her mind? The sexual attraction between them was much too hot. It wouldn't end with a little sucking and licking. That would be the beginning, and she damned well knew it. "You're right; I wouldn't," she admitted. "Okay, so we have done just about everything. Now, what do we wear? After the last three times I don't think I'm in the mood for another full-blown ninety-one-gun salute satin-and-lace wedding gown. I'd really like to keep it simpler, unless you want to see me in a 'Here Comes the Bride' outfit."

"Where are we doing the ceremony?" he asked.

"Garden if it's sunny, and if it isn't, the ballroom," Ashley answered him.

"What time?"

"Four thirty? Very traditional, and Wasp. Good luck to have the clock hands sweeping up, and not down," she said.

"I've got a pale gray pin-striped suit," Ryan told her.

"Who will we ask to be witnesses?" Ashley said. "I don't think we need to do the best man-maid of honor thing, do you?"

"I'll get Frankie to be my witness," Ryan replied. "You?"

"I'll ask Mrs. B. I'm asking Byrnes to give me away," she told him. "They're really my only family, so to speak."

"What's your favorite color?" he asked her.

"I guess any shade of pink or lavender," she answered. "Why?"

"It's a surprise," he told her, grinning. "Okay. We've got invitations, and the announcements, the dinner menu, where, when, and who will sign the registry, and clothes. Have we forgotten anything?"

"Wedding gown, or no?" she said. "You never said which you would prefer."

"I think you should be a bride," he told her. "But it doesn't have to be a Princess Di kind of gown. Something simple, but something that when you look back at the pictures of your first wedding you won't regret what you wore and cringe. They say the first time is always special."

"That's sweet, Ryan," Ashley said. "And thoughtful too."

"I'm a sensitive guy," he said teasingly, and then he rubbed his crotch suggestively, leering at her with a grin.

"You need a cold shower, buddy," she said.

"I'll settle for a swim," he responded.

"Good idea! Go change, and I'll meet you at the poolhouse. I want to take this menu to Mrs. B. first so she can begin considering the wedding dinner." Getting up, she hurried off toward the kitchens while he got up and went out to the pool house, where his bathing suits now permanently resided.

As he waited for her, swimming slow laps back and forth in the pool, he decided he was going to like this lifestyle. Ashley had told him that the pool was enclosed each winter, and heated so they could swim then. Yep, he was going to like it all. It was going to be getting unused to it in two years that would be hard. He climbed out of the pool and lay down on a chaise to get some sun.

She watched him from the pool house. Jesus, he was gorgeous! And that tight little European bathing suit he was wearing left absolutely nothing to the imagination. He had a fabulous butt, and he wasn't a guy who would ever need to stuff a sock in his shorts. From the size of his discreet wad he had to be as big as her two lovers on The Channel. Ashley pulled on the black one-piece suit, grabbed a towel, and stepped outside.

"How's the water?" she asked casually as she approached him.

"Good," he said, trying not to be too obvious as he assessed her. What a body she had! Those beautiful breasts of hers were very visible in that deceptively modest suit she was wearing. And her ass! *Mamma mia!* Round and tight. He fought himself not to reach out and grab it. She was not a petite girl, but there wasn't an ounce of flab on her, and she was in perfect proportion. Now he was really looking forward to seeing her naked. And he had another couple of weeks to go. He wasn't certain he was going to make it.

She knew he was looking her over despite the fan of dark eyelashes brushing his tanned cheek. She bent to carefully lay her towel on the empty chaise, giving him a nice long look at her tits. She slowly rubbed sunscreen on one leg, and then the other. On one arm, and then the other. Then she did her face and chest. "Do my back and shoulders, will you?" she asked innocently, handing him the tube. She sat on the edge of his chaise with her back to him.

He smoothed on the sunscreen with long, leisurely strokes of his palm, rubbing her flesh with a sensuous motion until it tingled. Her back was long and flawless. She had good skin. "I think I've got you covered," he finally said.

"Thanks," Ashley replied, standing, and then walking into the pool. "Nice," she said when she was waist deep.

He joined her, and they swam together for several minutes, back and forth, forth and back. She was a good swimmer, and so was he. "Ever swim naked in here?" he asked her with a mischievous grin.

"Sometimes," she allowed. "At night, when I know no one is about and can see me. And no, I am not going to swim naked now, and neither are you," Ashley told him firmly. "This is ridiculous, Ryan. We seem to have a case of raging hormones, and we just have to get past it. We aren't kids, damn it!"

"Then why do I feel like an eighteen-year-old around you?" he wanted to know.

"You're horny! You admitted yourself that you haven't had a woman in a while. And now that Dr. Sam has checked us both for STDs you'd better not! You are celibate until August twenty-fifth, and that's that!" Ashley told him. "If I can do it, you can do it. Don't be such a big baby, Ryan. I can't believe you can't stay out of trouble until then." She climbed out of the pool and stretched out on the chaise. She felt a twinge of guilt after that righteous little lecture she had just given him. Too bad he didn't have The Channel. She had really been getting her money's worth out of it lately, and it was actually the only way she had been able to resist his blandishments.

Quinn and Rurik were good lovers, but now that she had met Ryan Mulcahy she felt like a starving woman in front of a candy counter. She wanted to know what it would feel like to lie naked against his naked body. She wanted to feel his weight on her, his cock plundering her vagina, his mouth and his tongue on her, driving her wild with longing. Just thinking about it made her antsy, even though she had The Channel. If he felt the same way—and he obviously did—the waiting must be agony, but wait they would.

It wasn't easy, but Ryan's being in the city all week helped them both. And there was The Channel. Ashley was beginning to get a little bored with her two fantasies. Still, she didn't want to delete them. She had spent a lot of time perfecting them. Instead she decided to add a new element to the one with Quinn. It was time to introduce the lady Cordelia's husband, Tribune Maximillian Alerio Patronius, into the picture. She smiled. Yes, it was time the tribune came home from campaign. Stretching out on her bed, she pressed the button that slid the wall back to reveal her television, and then she pushed A.

The villa was bustling with activity as the slaves prepared for their master's homecoming from northern Gaul.

The lady of the house was stretched out as a slave massaged her body with a lily-scented cream. Quinn crept into the chamber and waited for her to recognize that he was there. Finally she cast a glance his way.

"My husband will be home shortly. You will confine yourself to your quarters until he has departed again. You know how he hates to see you and that lovely big cock of yours. Even though he gave you to me so I would behave while he is away, he does not wish to be reminded that you are foraging between my legs while he is gone. If he should catch so much as a glimpse of you, I will punish you severely, Quinn. I will send a slave girl to look after you. But you may not fuck her. Your cock is for me alone. Do you understand me?"

"Yes, mistress," Quinn answered her, his eyes lowered respectfully.

"Then get you gone," she told him, and turned back to the masseuse. "The ball of your thumb is too rough, Iris. Be certain to have it sanded when you massage me again."

"Yes, mistress," the slave woman answered, grateful not to have been hit.

There was the sound of trumpets amid the thunder of horses' hooves from outside the villa, announcing the arrival of someone of importance.

"The master is home!" she heard the slaves crying out.

Ashley smiled. Yes, this would add a *soupçon* of novelty to her fantasy. She arose from the massage table as her women scurried about her. Her long hair was scented with oil of lilies to match the fragrance arising from her naked body. A slave dropped a woven necklace of delicate white freesia about her neck, and handed her a second necklace. Then without a word the slaves ran from the chamber, and a moment later the twin doors into that chamber were opened, and her husband strode in. He had already been divested of his armor and garments. The tribune Maximillian Alerio Patronius looked exactly like Ryan Finbar Mulcahy, and he was as naked as she was. Ashley stepped forward and dropped the floral necklace over his head.

"Welcome home, my lord," she said in a husky voice. She hadn't thought he would look like Ryan, but then, she had been thinking about Ryan a great deal lately.

Reaching out, he swept her into his arms and kissed her deeply. "I have missed you, lady. The women in Gaul stink of animal fat and sweat."

"But you fucked them anyway." She laughed up at him. "Didn't you?"

"After I had them washed twice over, aye! Was your sex slave satisfactory?" he asked her. "Did he keep you entertained enough that you retained your chastity, and did not bring any scandal on my house, my insatiable Cordelia?"

"He is perfect, my lord. Not only does he fuck reasonably well, although nowhere near as well as you do, he has great stamina and is able to take a good whipping."

The tribune laughed. "I am happy to learn my gift was a success, lady."

"You are the perfect husband, Max," Ashley told him. "You are always thinking about me, and your gifts are delightful. I am the happiest woman in Rome. Now tell me," she said as she pressed up again him, "why are you home? I did not expect you for another few months."

"Caesar recalled me. He wished to replace me with one of his sycophants," the tribune replied. "Actually, if the gossip is correct Caesar is fucking the man's wife, and the fool tried to keep her too close. It was a simple matter to send the husband off to northern Gaul so Caesar might have easy access to his favored mistress. I can but hope the fellow doesn't find himself dead." He chuckled. "But now, my dear wife, it is time for you to welcome me home properly. On your knees like a good wife, Cordelia, and suck my cock. If you do it nicely I will fuck you. If you displease me, then I shall fuck one of your pretty slave girls. We have the afternoon, but then we are expected at the palace tonight for a banquet, which will certainly turn into a delightful orgy."

Ashley fell to her knees and lifted the long peg of flesh. She gazed at it carefully, as if deciding just what she was going to do. Then, holding it gently by its head, she licked it first up one side, and then back down the other. "Ummm," she murmured. "You taste of leather, Max." She took his penis into her mouth and began to suck on him. The long fingers of his big hand dug into her scalp, and he kneaded her head as she sucked at first with deep, strong pulls of her mouth. She stopped suddenly, and her tongue began to encircle the sensitive head of his organ. Then she nipped at it delicately with her teeth.

He growled. "Easy, my goddess," he warned her.

She began to suck him again. He grew thick and hard in her warm mouth, and he lengthened so that the tip of his penis was pushing just down her throat. She moaned, thinking how she loved the taste of him. Her hands slipped around him to fondle his tight buttocks. Her fingers dug into his flesh. She raised her eyes slightly to him, silently asking what he would have of her. Wordlessly he gave the command, and Ashley sucked harder and harder upon his cock until she felt him quiver, and then his sperm burst forth. She almost choked as she swallowed it down, so copious was the flow, but she continued to draw every last drop from him until he bade her cease.

"Jupiter and Mars, Cordelia, no one can suck me off like you can!" the tribune praised his wife. "Do you suck the slave?"

"My lord!" She was indignant. "That you could even ask me such a thing."

"You're a beautiful liar," he told her, laughing as he pulled her up into his arms. "You have an appetite for sex, which is why I bought the fellow for you. I'm glad he isn't boring you." He led her over to her large bed. "Now," he said as they lay down together, "you have been a very good girl, and should be rewarded appropriately. I have a taste for your juicy cunt, Cordelia. Open yourself to me," the tribune said, and he positioned her to suit his purposes. Then his head slid between her shapely legs.

He slowly licked the tender flesh of her plump thighs. His teeth grazed her delicate skin, nipping just enough to pinch. She squealed softly. His tongue ran up and down her slit several times. Then, pulling one of her nether lips apart, he licked at the inside of it, then probed beyond to find her clitoris. He slowly licked at the sensitive little organ, playing with it, teasing it with the velvet tip of his tongue. His mouth closed over it, and he sucked hard on it.

Ashley cried out as a small clitoral orgasm overcame her. "Ohh, Max!" she cried to him. "No one does that to me as well as you do." Her hand stroked his dark hair. "I know you need a moment to recover, but I beg you to put your fingers in me. I am burning with my desire, and it will but whet my appetites further," she told him.

He raised himself up and kissed her firmly. She could taste herself on his lips. Then he pushed two fingers into her vagina. Hard. "It isn't as good as I will be," he said. The fingers frigged her slowly at first, and then with increasing rapidity, but she found she could not come, and she whimpered with her frustration. He laughed. "I know, my goddess. Only a thick, long cock will do for you, and you shall have it." He swung quickly over her. *"Now!"* And with a single fierce thrust he filled her vagina.

Ashley screamed with delight, and wrapped her legs about her husband. "Fuck me, Max!" she begged him. "Fuck me hard, and make me come!"

He obliged her, and they finally collapsed as they came together. And when he had caught his breath he said, "No more for now, my goddess. Tonight when we return from the palace we will enjoy each other. But for now we must prepare to be the emperor's guests."

She called for their slaves, and she and Max were bathed and dressed. Max was attired in a purple silk toga lined in gold, to indicate his military victories. On his feet were slipped a pair of *calceus,* fine leather sandals painted gold and studded with amethysts. His dark hair had been cut once he had come from his bath. It was short, with several tiny stiff curls on his forehead and at the nape of his neck. His only jewelry was a gold signet ring he used for sealing correspondence.

The tribune's wife was garbed in a sheer violet silk tunic shot through with gold threads. Her body glowed through the fabric. It was sleeveless, and the draped neckline was low. She carried a matching shawl. Her hair was fashioned into a coil at the nape of her neck. Her leather sandals were decorated with gold leaf and pearls. The long, ornate earrings hanging from her ears were gold and pearls.

They were carried through the streets of the city in a large litter to join the other patrician guests in a banquet at the emperor's palace. Maximillian Alerio Patronius and his wife were shown to couches quite near the emperor. The ruler gazed down at them through a ruby set in gold, and acknowledged their presence with a wave of his hand. Around them servants brought food and refilled wine cups, music played, entertainers entertained. The noise was bearable.

"I have taken a new herb that is supposed to extend my stamina for sex," the emperor announced at one point. He pointed to the young wife of a senator. "I would fuck her," he said.

The senator pushed his blushing wife from their couch and sent her immediately to the emperor, who proceeded to use her publicly. When he had finished his penis was still hard, and he was yet unsatisfied. He pointed to the wife of another senator, and proceeded to lustily fuck her until the woman fainted with multiple orgasms.

"She was better than the first," the emperor said dryly, "but not good enough." He scanned the great banquet room again, and his eye fell upon the wife of Maximillian Alerio Patronius. The lady Cordelia smiled at him.

"Tribune," the emperor said, "is your wife pleasurable in your bed?"

"She is indeed, Caesar," Max replied.

"I would try her," the emperor said.

"Go to him, Cordelia," the tribune told his wife.

Ashley got up, and obediently went to the emperor.

"Remove your garment," the emperor commanded. He had not asked any of the others to do that.

Ashley unfastened her tunic and let it drop to her feet.

The vast banquet hall was so silent you could have heard a drop of wine fall.

"You must make me come," the emperor told her. "If you do not I will whip you." He lay back upon his couch in a half-seated position, and pulled up his toga to reveal his penis. It was a very long penis, but not particularly thick, and it was thrusting straight up. "You may mount me," he told her.

"Not until you have prepared me properly, my lord," Ashley told him, and then, going around the couch to his head, she straddled him, pressing her mons down on his face. "Lick, Caesar, and make me wet. When you do I will give you the finest ride you have ever had. And if I do not you may indeed whip me."

He yanked her nether lips apart and licked her furiously. He found her clit, and in very little time she was slick with her juices. Pushing her back he said, "Now mount me, you brazen bitch! And I will probably whip you afterward to punish you for your boldness. And then I will fuck your ass as well!"

She mounted him, slowly, slowly sliding down his slender hard penis until she had absorbed it all. She began to ride him, gently at first, and then more quickly. Reaching up, the emperor grabbed her breasts and squeezed hard. She moaned as he pinched her nipples and then leaned forward to bite them. But suddenly Caesar began to smile, and she felt him quivering within her vagina. She rode him harder, and he climaxed with a roar of pure satisfaction. The banquet chamber erupted with cheers and clapping as Ashley fell forward.

Immediately slaves leaped forward to pull her off the emperor. They held her upright, for she could not stand right away. The emperor was fed wine, and sweetmeats were pushed into his mouth. His genitals were gently bathed. Slowly he regained his strength and equilibrium, and when he had, he called for a leather tawse and commanded that his most recent partner be bound between two marble pillars. Then he stood up and began to lay the strap across her plump buttocks as a young slave girl knelt between his legs and sucked his cock back to a state of readiness. When it was ready, and Ashley's bottom was pink and warm, she was released, brought to her knees, then forced to stretch forward so that the emperor might mount her from behind.

She felt a thick oil being rubbed on and around her anus. She squealed as Caesar pushed slowly into her rear channel. He whispered all manner of lascivious things into her ear as he took her. Then, reaching forward, he found her clitoris and began to rub it. "Ohh, Caesar!" the tribune's wife cried. "Ohh, Caesar!" His fingers were having the desired result, and she was going to come. "Yes!" she screamed, knowing her obvious pleasure in his public performance would please him. "Yes! Yes! Yes!" And she climaxed, bucking wildly, as he came with a shout.

"I shall send your husband back to Gaul immediately," Caesar murmured as he helped her up. "You are the best fuck I have ever had, and I must have you again."

"I thank you, my lord emperor, for your praise, but Caesar can have any woman he desires. Poor Maximillian Alerio Patronius has only me. If you send my husband back to Gaul I would go with him," Ashley said.

The emperor nodded. He was not in the habit of being refused, but the woman had serviced him extremely well. She deserved to be rewarded, and sending her to Gaul with her husband would cost him nothing. "You will come to me one more time before I return your tribune to Gaul. And then you may go with him."

Gathering up her tunic, Ashley bowed. "As the emperor wishes." She backed away and returned to join her husband.

"You did well," Max said.

"He is returning you to Gaul," she told him.

"He wants you."

"I am going with you," she told him. "It is you I love, Max."

And then she heard the sharp ting of The Channel bell, and she awoke in her bed. *Wow!* Ashley thought. *That was some wild night. But I've been more than sexually satisfied. Ryan must think I'm a saint,* she thought. And she giggled. Where the hell did sex with Caesar come from? she wondered. *I didn't intend to add any more men to the picture.* Sometimes The Channel scared her. It was everything she wanted, but now and again something she had never considered seemed to pop up—like a Roman orgy and a sexually insatiable emperor. *Maybe I ought to practice a little abstinence for a while.* And what was she going to do with The Channel when she was married? Other married women had it. *Hell!* Probably all of its subscribers were women. And what if sex between she and Ryan didn't work out? *Yeah, right.* Like that was going to happen. But it was a temporary arrangement. Both of them had the right to be with people they loved.

Love. Everyone talked about love. But what exactly was love? Ben had thought he was in love for real just before he was shipped out. He had told her that he would probably ask Marianne to marry him when he got back. But he never came back. And Marianne had married someone else less than two years later. If you honestly loved someone, could you really do that? Could you love two men in a lifetime? Of course you could, she thought. She certainly had. Or had she really? What would have happened if she had married any one of the three? She probably would never have had sex with Carson if he had had the nerve to go through with their marriage. It would have ended in an annulment. And in disaster with Chandler, because there had to be more to love than just wild monkey sex. As for Derek, or whatever his real name was, he probably would have serviced her regularly as long as he got to spend her money. But that wasn't love.

This time she knew the wedding would come off. She was marrying to save her inheritance. Ryan was marrying to save his inheritance. They were crazily sexually attracted to each other. But love had nothing to do with it. It was all about money. And yet the lady Cordelia had told her tribune husband that she loved him. And he had looked just like Ryan Finbar Mulcahy. Subconsciously she had wanted him to look like Ryan. What else did she want subconsciously? It was starting to get very confusing, Ashley decided, and then she realized she had a headache. It was the kind she got maybe once or twice a year. Her temples began to pound and her stomach began to roll. She got up and stumbled to her bathroom, where she threw up. *Thank goodness,* Ashley thought. It always relieved the tension when she threw up, but she was not going to work today.

Ryan called her in midafternoon. "Are you all right? Nina said you were home sick today. What's the matter? Did you call Dr. Sam?" He sounded worried.

"I get a knockdown tension headache maybe twice a year," Ashley told him. "I think all the excitement and secrecy got to me. It's almost gone now."

"I've got to fly to London. I'll be in England for the next two weeks," he said.

"The wedding is in two weeks," she reminded him.

"I'll be back Thursday of that week, Ash. You and Frankie behave yourselves while I'm gone, okay? She says she's coming out to the house this week to start setting everything up in the master suite. Am I going to like it?"

Ashley smiled. "I think so," she said. "And if you don't we'll do it all over again," she told him.

He laughed. "Hey, babe, just because you and I are rich doesn't mean we should waste money. Just as long as Frankie hasn't done it up all Laura Ashley. I'm not much for flowers and butterflies."

"Oh, no!" Ashley gasped. "You don't like flowers and butterflies?"

He laughed again. "Nice try, but I'm not buying it, Ash."

She giggled. "It'll be very unisex," she assured him. "But remember, we're sharing, and it can't be all Ralph Lauren and leather, Ryan. What are you doing in England?"

"There are some house auctions I want to go to in London and out in some of the counties. Sometimes I buy; sometimes I just photograph details for the reproduction business. The newly rich want it authentic, even if they aren't quite certain what authentic is at first. They do learn," he said dryly. "And they expect value for their money. Our work isn't cheap, and we use the best materials. I think I may have found a new source for clock corners and drawer pulls up in York. They claim to have the original molds. I'll know when I see them. I can't just take anyone's word."

"When are you going?" Ashley wanted to know.

"Tonight," he said.

"Travel safe then," she said.

"Thanks. You take care now," he replied.

"I will. Thanks for calling."

"Yeah. Bye." And the phone clicked off.

Geez, Ashley thought. Could their good-byes have been any more impersonal? She lay back, but as she did she noticed that the pain had gone. But she knew she would have to relax for the rest of the day and evening. August was never the busiest month in the shop. But this week she had to go over the new catalog proofs. They would be waiting on her office computer for an okay. The printer would have to do a runoff this week if the catalog was going to be out on time. Then the pages needed to be bound and put in their envelopes for mailing at the end of September if they were going to get the Christmas orders out on time. She would have to do it tomorrow. Frankie was coming out on Wednesday.

She had seen Ryan's mother and youngest sister since that initial meeting several weeks ago. She had spoken at length with Frankie several times as they discussed what they were going to do in the master suite. Her sister-in-law-to-be arrived at nine thirty on a rainy morning, roaring up to the house in a sporty little red Miata. Byrnes was immediately outside with an umbrella to escort her into the house.

"Miss Ashley is waiting in the breakfast room," Byrnes said as he led her to it.

"Good morning," Ashley said, coming forward to greet her guest. They kissed. "How about some coffee or tea?" she asked.

"I don't suppose you have a cappuccino on you?" Frankie said.

"Byrnes, would you see to it, please?" Ashley said.

"You're kidding!" Frankie said as she sat down.

"We're very accommodating here at Kimbrough Hall." Ashley grinned.

"I'll say!" Her eye lit on a plate on the table.

"They were baked this morning," Ashley told her. "In your honor. Ryan told me how much you loved bialys."

"Can I live here?" Frankie said, smiling. "Please?"

Byrnes returned with a cappuccino and set it before the guest. Then he disappeared.

"Cappucino and a fresh-baked bialy," Frankie said. "I'm in heaven." She sipped, and then she took a nibble of her bialy. "Every bit as good as Rome!" she pronounced.

"You can tell Mrs. B. She'll be delighted," Ashley said.

"Ryan flew to England last night," Frankie said as she ate.

"I know. He called me to tell me." Ashley sipped her black tea. She always had black tea for breakfast the morning after a tension headache.

"Wow! He's getting thoughtful. Even Ma doesn't always know when he's going off," Frankie said. "I called his cell last night to yak, and he was at Kennedy waiting to board. I had to remind him to give her a jingle. So, tell me. No cold feet yet?"

"I can't afford cold feet," Ashley admitted. "Your brother seems like a nice guy, and at least he isn't after my money. We'll do fine."

"Have you signed the prenups yet?"

"Yes, last week," Ashley said.

"Ryan hasn't told Ma yet that this is only a business arrangement," Frankie said. "She thinks it's like when she and Da got matched up by the priest, and married. She just got the invitation Saturday, and wondered why you're not getting married in a church."

"Ryan has to explain that to her," Ashley said. "Lina is his mother, not mine. It isn't my place, Frankie."

"I know. But he isn't going to explain it to her. He doesn't want to understand that she thinks this is a till-death-do-you-part marriage," Frankie said. "An arranged marriage she understands, but not a marriage of convenience with an out clause."

"What am I supposed to do then?" Ashley asked, slightly irritated. This was just the kind of situation her brother would have fostered. Why were men such jerks about stuff like this? But they were. Honesty really was the best policy.

"Look, I'm staying a few days. Could you invite Ma out to lunch the last day I'm here? And I'll help you talk to her when she asks, because she will."

Ashley considered. Lina Mulcahy had welcomed her warmly. If Ryan wasn't going to explain the situation to his mother, she really owed it to her future mother-in-law to tell her that the marriage between heR&Ryan, while legal, wouldn't last, because they were marrying just to save their asses. "I could send Byrnes in for her on Saturday, and then she can ride back with you later that day."

"Would you?" Frankie sounded relieved.

"Of course. I'll have Mrs. B. do us a nice lunch, give Lina a tour of the house and the gardens. And we'll talk. I like your mother, Frankie. But I don't want her laboring under any illusions about this marriage."

"Do you think you could fall in love with my brother?" Frankie asked.

Ashley felt her cheeks growing warm. What was it about these Mulcahys that they could make her blush?

"Aha!" Frankie exclaimed. "Maybe you could."

"I don't know," Ashley admitted. "I've never been very good at picking men, but I do know your brother and I seem to have a sexual attraction toward each other."

"Ohh," Frankie said softly. "Have you done the deed then? I've heard rumors from some of his old girlfriends that he's very good in bed."

"No, we haven't slept together," Ashley said. "Not that he hasn't tried, but I'm not really into sleeping around. Oh, I did with two of my fiancés, and look how that ended up. I'm taking no chances this time. Do you know what they call me around here? The Bad-luck Bride. Well, I can't get jinxed this time. Besides, in the agreement we signed, sex between us is optional."

Frankie laughed. "You put that in the prenup?" she said.

"No, we have a small binding legal agreement in addition about what we can and can't do or have, where we live and entertain, et cetera," Ashley explained. "We needed to iron out the details of the little stuff, since this marriage is only so we don't lose our inheritances. It's all legal, and no one can say we aren't married. Neither of the wills involved said we had to marry for love or any other reason. They just said we had to be married."

"But you think Ryan is hot?" Frankie persisted.

"Yeah," Ashley admitted. "He's hot, but that isn't a reason to fall in love with him. However, I like him, and maybe that's a start. And it was nice of him to call me yesterday and tell me he was going away. He had called the shop, and Nina told him I was home, and why. He asked how I was feeling, and he really sounded as if it mattered. Of course, he was probably worried I might die before the wedding, and then he'd really be in a whole lot of trouble."

"No, not Ryan. He's not like that," Frankie defended her brother. "If he sounded concerned, then he was concerned. He really is one of the good guys, which is why Ma and I are so pissed off at the others. My five older sisters are like a damned pack of vultures, and Ryan doesn't deserve that. Dad was always tight with money. It was his upbringing. It was Ryan who was always getting Dad to help them out, and he's the one who made Dad give us each such a generous bequest in his will. So for them to have gone out and found a buyer for R&R stinks. Especially since the guy is Ryan's least favorite person in the whole world."

"I don't understand your sisters," Ashley admitted. "Ben and I would have done anything for each other."

Frankie shrugged. "What can I say? I don't understand it either, except it seems that the more my sisters have, the more they want." She drank the last bit of cappuccino from her cup. "Well, we had better get going. I've got a crew all lined up to do the painting and papering. They'll be here tomorrow."

"Where are you housing them?" Ashley asked, concerned.

"The motel just off the parkway," Frankie answered. "The new bed will be delivered Friday, and the rest of the stuff will be coming via FedEx this week. By the time Ma arrives on Saturday the rooms will be done. Hey, look, the sun is coming out. It's going to be a nice day after all. Can we go swimming? Ryan says your pool is wonderful."

"Of course," Ashley told her. "But let's get our work done first."

"Gee," Frankie noted with a grin, "you really are a perfect match for my brother. I hope you do fall in love and make this a real marriage."

Ashley smiled. *Maybe I do too,* she thought silently.

Chapter Five

Angelina Mulcahy stepped out of the Lincoln Town Car and looked about her. It was a beautiful hot August day, and a silvery haze hung over the bay below, which was dotted with several small sailboats. She turned to face the portico, and smiled as Frankie and Ashley came from the house to greet her. She kissed both women on their cheeks. "It's lovely," she said to Ashley. "What a beautiful house, cara."

"Wait'tilyou see the inside, Ma," Frankie said. "It's right up Ryan's alley, and the antiques are real. Been in the family for centuries, Ashley says."

"Francesca! Do not be so common," her mother chided her.

Ashley laughed. "Don't scold her, Lina. Like Ryan, she appreciates what my family has collected over the years. Come in."

The three women entered the house, and as it was only ten o'clock Ashley led them out on the porch for coffee, small cups of freshly made raspberry yogurt, and miniature Danish pastries that Mrs. B. had baked earlier. Seeing the gracious display Angelina raised an approving eyebrow, and Frankie winked conspiratorially at Ashley. After they had eaten, Ashley suggested a tour of the house.

"You'll want to see where Ryan will be making his home, of course," she said as she led her guests from the porch.

"Frankie has been all over the place this week, but as you will soon be my family, I wanted you to see the house before our wedding."

Although she was impressed by everything she saw, Angelina Mulcahy's handsome face remained a smooth, emotionless mirror barely reflecting her thoughts. The house was exquisite. The living room was large and gracious, with an elegant mantel above the fireplace. The formal dining room was something splendid, with its great Duncan Phyfe dining table and chairs with their beige-and-dark-green-striped satin seats. In the center of the table was a huge porcelain bowl filled with an arrangement of multicolored dahlias. The sideboard was balanced at either end with silver chargers, and a silver punch bowl and ladle was set in the center. There was a fireplace in the dining room as well.

Angelina admired the paneled library with its fireplace. "How many fireplaces do you have in this house?" she asked her hostess.

Ashley thought a moment. "Twelve, I believe. The bedrooms all have one, and the kitchen downstairs has one."

Living room, dining room, library, kitchen, Angelina thought silently. *That means there must be eight bedrooms. It's a house for a family. A nice big family.* She followed her hostess upstairs, where she was shown the new master suite, with its parlor, bedroom, two bathrooms, and two large walk-in closets. She was astounded by the size of it all, thinking of the small bedroom she and Finbar had slept in for much of their marriage.

"Well, whaddaya think, Ma?" Frankie said. "Have I done a good job?"

"It's amazing," Angelina replied, unable to keep the approval out of her voice.

They entered from the upstairs corridor into the parlor, which was painted pale green above its chair rail, and a dark cypress green below. The walls held several very good paintings—landscapes, and two obviously original ancestor portraits in muted gold frames. The carpeting was a pale cream color. A maple secretary stood in one corner, the wavy glass in its door attesting to its vast age. There was a couch upholstered in dark green duck cloth with several decorative pillows, and two comfortable club chairs that were upholstered in a large floral rose pattern, muted green on a cream background. There were small antique side tables, and several lovely lamps.

"Wait until you see the bedroom," Frankie enthused. "I got the bed from Ryan's place. It's a repro of a sixteenth-century English piece with an eight-foot linen fold-paneling headboard. Solid oak. Ashley's granddad lived in this room until he died several years ago. Strangely his bed was the only non-antique in here, and we sent it off to Habitat's store in the next town." She led the way into the bedroom. "Well?" she said, grinning.

"The bed is a bit overwhelming at first," Ashley said, "but the room can take it."

Angelina looked at the bed with its turned pillars at the foot and its dark green velvet bed hangings. The room was papered in a cream silk paper with delicate green ferns. There was a wonderful sixteenth-century chest-on-chest, and a seventeenth-century bureau with an exquisite mirror over it, among the other furnishings. "Just think," Angelina said softly, "you will create your children in that bed. Dynasties come from such beds."

"Look at the bathrooms, Ma," Frankie said, pulling her mother in another direction. "I've papered Ryan's in ducks on a taupe background. Real guy paper. And Ash's is pale pink lilies with green leaves on cream. Aren't they pretty?"

Angelina looked, and then moved on to see the other bedrooms, smiling when Ashley said, "You may pick whichever one you like best for your room when you visit, Lina. I hope you'll come often. They all have their own bathrooms. Byrnes will always be glad to pick you up and take you home again."

They returned downstairs and sat again on the porch as they waited for luncheon to be announced. A gentle breeze eased the heat of midday.

"Such a beautiful home," Angelina said. "And all those bedrooms for the children that you and Ryan, God willing, will have. Tell me, *cara*, why aren't you being married in church? You are of different faiths, I know, but certainly Ryan has explained that you must be married in the church, and the priest will have explained to you that the children must be baptized Catholic."

"Roman Catholic," Ashley corrected her. "Angelina, this is really something that Ryan should have told you, but like most men he is obviously not about to broach an unpleasant subject with his mother. This is not an arranged marriage we are contracting. It is a marriage of convenience. Both Ryan and I are faced with the possibility of losing our individual inheritances unless we are married by a certain age. That's the only reason we are getting married. We have both signed prenuptial agreements, and a separate agreement spelling out how we will conduct ourselves during our marriage.

"We are not getting married in church, or by a priest of either your denomination or mine, because the marriage will last only two years. If either of us should fall in love one day we want to be free to start fresh not just legally, but spiritually. I'm sorry that Ryan did not explain this to you. I don't know if he was embarrassed or afraid. I hope you will forgive him, and I hope you will forgive me," Ashley concluded.

"How will you be married then?" Angelina wanted to know. She had grown pale.

"Judge Palmer will marry us. It will be a civil ceremony—quite legal in this or any other state," Ashley explained. "Ryan's inheritance and mine will then be secured."

"That such a thing should be," Angelina said. "I can't come."

"Ma!" Frankie exclaimed. "Don't be so damned dramatic. What do you mean, you can't come? It's Ryan's wedding."

"It's a business arrangement," Angelina said, "and no true marriage. How can I approve such a thing, Francesca? Tell me how I can salve my conscience?"

"Enough with the religious fervor," Frankie said. "You know damned well that Dad wouldn't have had a twentieth of what he left if it hadn't been for Ryan. He could have gone to Wall Street and made a fortune, but instead he made Dad a multimillionaire. And Dad saw that you were lavishly provided for, and all his daughters given generous cash inheritances, but he couldn't die without dictating to Ryan from beyond the grave, could he? Ryan had to get married. Had to carry on the grand Mulcahy name or he would lose everything. Well, it stinks, Ma.

"You're the one who said to me that we couldn't let the others take R&R away from Ryan. You're the one who went to Ray Pietro d'Angelo and told him to find Ryan a wife. Well, he did, and now you aren't satisfied because it won't be a *real* marriage. What do you want, Ma? You want my sisters to sell Ryan's business—yes, damn it, Ryan's business—to

Jerry Klein? Sure, Jerry wants the R&R name and reputation, but he'll run it into the ground for a tax loss as quick as he can. That's what you want because Ryan and Ashley won't get married in the church and have a *real* marriage?"

"I want my son to have what your father and I had," Angelina said.

"And what the hell was that?" her daughter demanded.

"Frankie, please, your mom is upset, and I can understand." Ashley tried to mediate between the two.

"Your father and I were married in the church, the way people should be," Angelina said. "We had a real marriage with children, not a business arrangement. I wanted Ray to find a nice girl from the old country. Italy or Ireland."

"Wake up, Ma! There are no nice girls from the old country. It's one great big rock-and-roll, drugged-out, money-is-God world now. Ray found your son the perfect match. For God's sake, be satisfied and accept what's happening. You don't come to the wedding and my sisters are sure as hell going to attempt legal action to get their hands on Ryan's business by yelling fraud. You really want that, Ma?"

But before Angelina could answer her daughter, Ashley spoke up. "Lina, look, I wouldn't tell Ryan this for fear of scaring him, but I *really* like your son. I am very attracted to him, and I think that just maybe he might like me too. I've never really had a lot of luck picking my own men, but I didn't find Ryan all by myself, did I? No. Ray and Joe Pietro d'Angelo got us together. And so far, so good. We're approaching this marriage of convenience cautiously, and the honest truth is that each of us wants an out just in case it doesn't work for us on a personal level. But I think it might, and Frankie, if you say one word to your brother I will know it, and I swear I will kill you! Yes, we're putting the cart before the horse by getting married before we know each other. But didn't you and your husband do that too? Your priest put you together, and you didn't question it. You got married and made a go of it. Actually, I'm in a much better position than Ryan. I don't turn thirty-five for almost a year and a half. I have time. But Ryan is forty in seven months. He doesn't have time to look for the right girl. Even if you sent to Italy or Ireland for a bride you couldn't get her here in time, with all the immigration fuss and getting her papers. And wouldn't that give your other daughters more of an opening to go after Ryan legally? They would say he was marrying a girl like that just to protect his inheritance. True, his father's will didn't make any conditions for his marrying. It just said he had to be married by forty. They actually don't have a leg to stand on, Lina, but they would still try. But when he marries me they can't say anything, no matter what they may think, because they won't know this is a marriage of convenience."

Angelina Mulcahy was silent for a long few moments. And then she said, "You like him, *cara*?"

"Yes, I do," Ashley said, and she felt her cheeks growing warm. "He's smart, and he's funny, and he can make me blush."

"And he tried to get her into bed, Ma, but she told him not until they are married," Frankie put in with a mischievous grin.

Angelina nodded slowly. "He likes her," she said.

"More than I think he realizes, Ma," Frankie responded.

"You know, with Ryan the business is everything. And Ashley is probably the only woman in the world who can understand that, understand him. It really is a match made in heaven, even if it isn't celebrated in the church."

"Please come to the wedding, Lina," Ashley said.

"I'll come," Angelina Mulcahy said, "but only on one condition."

Ashley and Frankie looked to her anxiously.

"That when my *stupido* son realizes he loves you, you get married again by a priest in the church," she told her son's fiancée.

"Of course we will," Ashley said quickly. "I don't really remember my own mother, but I know she would have wanted the same thing of us, Lina. When Ryan decides we should make this a permanent arrangement then we will do this for ourselves, our children, and to make you happy."

"Luncheon is served," Byrnes said, stepping out onto the porch.

"Show Mrs. Mulcahy where she may freshen up, Byrnes," Ashley said. "Then join us back here for some food, Lina. It's a very light meal, but it's so lovely out here."

Byrnes led the older woman off.

Frankie turned to Ashley. "You handled Ma nicely, Ash."

"I meant what I said," Ashley told her. "If your brother decides he wants to make this marriage of convenience a permanent thing, then if it will make your mother happy I'll get the priest. In fact, I'll get two. I'll want my guy in on this also. And I want your mother's friendship, Frankie. I like her, and I like you."

By the time Angelina had returned to join them, Byrnes had set up a small table on the porch and covered it with an embroidered linen cloth. There were plates and glasses and silverware. And when he had seated the trio he offered them iced tea or lemonade, both of which had been freshly made.

"I'd do wine, but Frankie has to drive you back," Ashley said.

Each plate that Byrnes placed before the women held a small fresh fruit salad and a chicken salad sandwich on a little freshly baked soft roll. When they had finished the butler quickly cleared the plates, replacing each of them with another plate that held a slice of warm blueberry bread pudding with a mini scoop of homemade vanilla ice cream. Byrnes saw that the glasses were always filled during the course of the meal.

When they had finished Angelina Mulcahy said quietly as she laid her napkin aside, "You do not have to learn to cook, *cara*. Your Mrs. B. is a treasure."

Both Ashley and Frankie laughed aloud. And after another half hour her guests arose and prepared to leave. Byrnes had already stowed Frankie's luggage in the trunk of her Miata. Ashley thanked her soon-to-be sister-in-law for the beautiful decorating job she had done in the master suite. She kissed both Frankie and Angelina good-bye, and said she would look forward to seeing them at the wedding. Then she waved them off and reentered the house with a sigh.

Ashley felt bad that her future mother-in-law had misunderstood the situation. It had been different when Angelina and her sister had come from Italy after World War II. The world hadn't changed then. It was only just about to change. A marriage arranged by a priest was an acceptable thing, because girls were supposed to marry and have babies while their men went off to make a living to support those families. It had been a slower-paced life then. Not like now.

Ryan called her a few days later.

"I talked to Frankie. She told me what you did," he said.

"You should have explained it to Lina yourself," Ashley told him tartly.

"I know, I know," he admitted, "but I knew she was thinking it was just like her and Dad, and we both know it isn't going to be like that. Frankly I hoped to avoid the whole damned subject, and she'd never have to know. In two years, when we separated and she was sad, I'd remind her we weren't married in the church, which would mean I could start all over with the girl of my dreams, which would make her happy again."

"Well," Ashley said, "for now I'm the girl of your dreams, Ryan. You'd better get used to it, I guess. How's England? Did you get up to York yet?"

"I did, and damned if the guy doesn't have the original molds for the sixteenth – and seventeenth-century clock corners and other hardware. But he's retiring, so I bought them off of him. Now I've got to find someone who can do the casting with them back home. The sales haven't been that good so far, but I've got one outside of Worcester tomorrow that is rumored to have some excellent stuff, and another one in Herefordshire the next day before I head over to Gloucester, down to Devon, and then back to London."

"Sounds like you'll be busy until you fly back," Ashley said.

"Would it sound crazy if I said I missed you?" Ryan surprised her by saying suddenly. "And I miss Egret Pointe, much to my surprise."

"You sure it's me, or is it Mrs. B.'s cooking?" Ashley teased him.

He was silent a moment, as if considering her words, but then he said, "Nah, Ash, it's definitely you I miss. And, of course, the *girls*," he added.

She laughed. "You are so bad, but if the truth be known, the *girls* miss you too."

"I want to make love to you, Ashley," he said low.

"I know," she admitted.

"Are we going to make love?" he asked softly.

"Probably," she told him. "But not until after the wedding."

He chuckled. "I'm not going to disappear off the radar like the others," he said.

"Experience has taught me not to count on my bridegrooms," Ashley told him dryly. "Your sister has done us a gorgeous bedroom, by the way. The bed came from your shop, and it's incredible. It's got an eight-foot headboard."

"Bloody hell! The one with the linen fold paneling?" He didn't sound happy.

"Yes, why?"

"It was a special order for a client," he told her. Then he laughed. "But they're in Europe this summer, and I did say it wouldn't be ready until autumn. It will have to be late autumn. That headboard takes a long time to carve."

"I'm sorry," Ashley told him. "I didn't know."

"It's all right. Frankie does this to me once in a while. She comes into the workshops and plunders whatever takes her fancy," he explained.

"It's a hell of a bed," Ashley murmured. "We could have a lot of fun in it."

He laughed again. "I'm getting a hard-on just thinking about it," Ryan said. "Are you blushing, Ash? I get this distinct feeling you're blushing."

"Smart-ass!" she replied. "How do you do it? No one else can make me blush."

"No one?" he asked.

"Nope."

"Maybe this marriage of convenience is going to be something else," he suggested. "Maybe it'll end up being more."

Ashley was very silent, then she said, "Now, don't go getting all romantic on me, Ryan. We're just getting to know each other, after all."

"We're going to know each other better in a few days," he said.

"You've got sex on the brain," she told him. "And it's the middle of the night in England. You need some sleep. Go to bed."

"So you do care," he teased her.

"Maybe a little," she allowed. "Good night, Ryan Mulcahy."

"Good night, Ashley Kimbrough. See you soon," he said, and then he rang off.

Four days, she thought as she set the phone back down. Four days and she would be a married woman. Everything was ready and waiting. The judge. The guests. The dinner menu. The flowers. And a wedding dress. She smiled. It wasn't really a wedding dress per se. She had been browsing at a small, upscale mall twenty miles from Egret Pointe. There was an elegant, more traditional little dress shop there that she occasionally shopped in, and in the window had been the perfect dress for her wedding. It was cream-colored silk chiffon with a flirty calf-length skirt, cap sleeves, and a draped boat neckline. She went in, tried it on, and bought it.

"Special party, Ms. Kimbrough?" the saleswoman asked with a smile.

"No," she lied. "I haven't anywhere to wear it yet, but I hope I will. It's just so pretty I can't resist it, and it is in my size, after all."

"It actually looks better on you than on some of the smaller girls," the saleswoman said. "Funny how some dresses look better on one person than on another, especially when they all look the same on a hanger. Cash or charge?"

Ashley took the dress home and showed it to Mrs. B. "What do you think?" she said. "I thought this time something simpler might be better than something more bridal and formal."

"It's perfect, my dearie," Mrs. B. said with a smile. "And it is a bit bridal, if you don't mind my saying it. I think it's the length. You'll look beautiful in it."

And then Ashley realized that she was nervous. Especially when, on the day before the wedding, Nina gave her a bag as they were closing up. "What's this?" she said.

"You haven't picked anything for your wedding night," Nina said. "So I picked it for you. I know—I know everything you've said about marriage of convenience, but I've seen you with Ryan. You're attracted to each other, and if you don't end up in bed tomorrow night you will one night soon. So wear this."

Ashley opened the bag and peered inside. She immediately recognized the nightgown Nina had chosen. It was simple: a lavender silk number with spaghetti straps, that clung to the wearer like a second skin. It would reveal every asset she possessed, and then some. "You've got a wicked mind, Nina," she said, closing the bag.

"It's perfect for you," Nina replied with a grin. "Now, you are *not* to come in tomorrow, Ashley. Let me remind you, late August is as dead as a doornail in town. I might get a few browsers and maybe a sale or two, but I will not be busy. I'll spend my day updating the stock on the computer, close up at three, and be up at the hall all polished and brushed in time for the wedding."

"If I don't come in, what am I supposed to do until four thirty?" Ashley asked her.

"If I know you—and I think I do—you'll spend your time checking three times over to make certain everything is okay, and it will be. You'll pace, and finally nap before taking a shower and getting ready for the wedding. Is Ryan back yet?"

Ashley looked at her watch. "He should be landing at Kennedy right about now. Let me go and check." She went over to the PC in her office and went immediately to the British Airways site for arrivals. "Yes, they got in right on time. Five minutes ago."

"Go home then. He'll be calling, and trust me—he's going to need reassurance right about now. Bridal nerves aren't just confined to brides," Nina told her.

Ashley got into her Solstice and drove home. She had no sooner gotten through the door when her cell began ringing. She flipped it open. "Ashley here," she said.

"I'm home," his voice said. "Rather, I'm in a car service car on my way into town. When should I come out tomorrow?"

"Do you want to come with your mother and Frankie?" she asked him. "The limo is picking them up at two. Your mother is staying with your sister tonight."

"Yeah, that's fine. Tell the limo to pick me up last, okay? I'll carry my suit and change when we get there, if that's okay."

"Be shaved and shorn by then," Ashley said. "Depending on the traffic, you're just going to get here a half hour or less before the judge does his thing."

"No problem. You nervous?"

"A little," she admitted. "You?"

"Yeah, a little. I guess I never figured this would happen, and it probably wouldn't have except for my father's damned will," Ryan told her. "I might be a confirmed bachelor. I've never been sure."

"Don't you want kids someday?" she asked.

"Yeah, sure," he told her.

"Then you can't be a confirmed bachelor, Ryan. And with your mother you'd have to have a wife if you expected her to accept your children," Ashley said. "Lina is a very conservative and traditional woman."

"How'd you get her to change her mind about coming to the wedding when she learned it was a business arrangement first?" he asked.

"I told her that if by chance this marriage of convenience turned out to be more than just convenient, we'd call in the priest and do it the way she would want," Ashley said. "Didn't Frankie tell you that?"

She actually heard him gulp. Then he said, "No. Frankie just said you were wonderful with Ma, and eased her around her distress after you told her the truth. She said Ma really likes you, and let you sweet-talk her," Ryan answered.

Ashley laughed. "What I did was soothe your mother's conscience. She's a good woman, Ryan. I'm sorry we're disappointing her."

"Maybe we won't disappoint her in the end," he suggested softly. "Maybe before the two years are up we will call in the priest, Ash."

"Maybe we will," she allowed, her heart beating just a little faster at his words. Did he really like her enough already to be considering a real marriage? "Get some rest before tomorrow," Ashley said. "It's going to be a big day."

"I'm hoping for a big night," he said.

"You're waggling your eyebrows, aren't you?" she countered.

He laughed. "How can you tell?"

"You always waggle your eyebrows when you make suggestive remarks," she told him. "It makes me laugh, because it makes you look so naughty."

He grinned. "I'll see you tomorrow, Ash. Dream of me, okay?"

Dream of him? She almost laughed aloud. Her noble tribune husband on The Channel looked just like him. That was some dreaming, she thought. She was tempted to visit The Channel this evening, but she knew that if she did she would be tired tomorrow, and she wasn't about to spend a night on her fantasy when tomorrow she could have some reality. He wanted to sleep with her. No, he wanted to fuck her. And she was going to let him do it while she enjoyed every minute of it. Legally they would be married, so why not, if he wanted it? Their behavioral agreement gave them the choice. And there was no denying the sexual attraction between them. Maybe after they had done it a few times the thrill would pale for them. But even as she considered it, Ashley knew that wasn't going to happen. He was going to love doing her, and she was going to love letting him.

A weather front came through in the night, chasing the humidity out to sea and bringing rain that ended around ten in the morning. The day was suddenly perfect. *Well, why the hell not?* Ashley thought. She was a Kimbrough. This was her wedding day. And it was going to happen this time. No surprises. No embarrassment. It was going to happen! Byrnes had brought her coffee, and then she had gobbled a plate of scrambled eggs before hurrying out to the gardens to make certain everything would be just perfect.

Old Tony, her gardener, and young Tony, his grandson and sometime helper, had spent the summer coaxing a pair of Sterling Silver rosebushes up a trellis. They had pruned and fussed over the roses to make certain that today the trellis was covered in blooms. Some were fully opened, some half-opened but the effect was visually spectacular. Ten chairs covered in white cotton covers were set up before the trellis, five to each side. Urns filled with lavender and white flowers stood on either side of the trellis. Lavender was Ashley's favorite color.

"Will the flowers hold until four thirty?" Ashley asked old Tony.

He nodded. "The sun doesn't come around here this time of year until just after three thirty, missus. It's gonna look beautiful."

"Thank you," Ashley said. "Keep the dogs from it."

He nodded his acknowledgment.

Returning to the house, Ashley went to the dining room. It had already been set up. The table was covered with a white silk damask cloth embroidered with multicolored silk flowers along its border. "Where did this come from?" she asked Byrnes.

"It's been stored in the linen chest since your mother married your father," he answered her. "Hasn't been used since. We had to wash it and iron it to get the wrinkles out of it from all those years being folded up. I'd forgotten all about it, but you know how sentimental Mrs. B. is. She remembered, and thought it should be on the table today."

"The flower arrangement is spectacular," Ashley noted, approving the big cut-crystal bowl of purple, lavender, pink, and white dahlias, and greens.

"Did them myself," Byrnes said. "We're using the Royal Worcester and the Waterford tonight. Do you want the Gorham Fairfax or the Reed and Barton 1810?"

"Use the Fairfax. I like it better with the Royal Worcester," Ashley said. Then she left the dining room. There was absolutely nothing for her to do. The garden was ready. Byrnes had everything in hand in the house, and if she dared to venture into the kitchen she would hurt Mrs. B.'s feelings. She had canceled her regular Saturday massage, but she did have a noon appointment at Prime Cuts for a manicure and a pedicure. She glanced at the grandfather clock in the hall as it began to strike, and saw it was eleven forty-five. Ashley raced to her car.

At Prime Cuts she found herself surrounded by women she knew. Tiffany Pietro d'Angelo was there, along with Carla Johnson and Nora Buckley. They smiled at her conspiratorially. Emily Shanski, now Emily Devlin, delivered in late June of her first child, was in a wicker chaise getting a pedicure while the baby slept in a basket by her side.

"You look great for someone who just had a baby," Ashley said.

"You think so?" Emily said with a rueful smile. "I still feel like a bit of a cow about to calve." She chuckled. "When you get married one day—and you will, despite your previous misfortunes—look out for those extra romantic moments that sneak up on you. Writing a novel is far easier than being preggers, I can assure you."

"Yeah." Carla Johnson laughed. "Those sudden pleasures can really get you."

The other women all laughed knowingly. Each one of them was a subscriber to The Channel, but they were also happy, even the widowed Nora.

"Well," Ashley said, "I've never written a novel, but I suppose one day I might have a baby. When I do I'll let you know if the shop is harder." She smiled at them. Why was it that Nora Buckley seemed to grow more beautiful and younger-looking as each day went by? Ashley remembered a few years back, when Nora would never have ventured into her shop. She would just stand outside the windows looking sad and worn. But today she was one of Ashley's best customers, and the more suggestive a garment was, the better Nora liked it, though who she wore those lacy nothings for, Ashley didn't know. But then Nora, a widow, had always been a very private woman—except for that brief time when her husband was arrested and died in the lockup overnight.

A manicure table became available, and the pedicurist, having finished with Emily Devlin, moved over to do Ashley's feet as her hands were being tended to. By one thirty she was driving back up to Kimbrough Hall. She wanted a bath. Her nerves were becoming more jangled with each passing moment. A bath would soothe her, she decided as she poured oil of lilies into the hot water. Her cell rang, and she flipped it open. "Ashley here."

"We're on our way," Ryan's voice said. Then he lowered it. "What are you doing right now, Ash?"

"I'm in the bathtub," she said softly.

"Next time I'll be with you," he told her. "See you soon."

Ashley closed her eyes and imagined it. Yes, the tub could fit two easily. Her hand moved down between her legs, and she began playing with her clit. It didn't take long for her to come. Oh, yes! She needed to be fucked. She needed it badly, and so did he. Tonight could well turn out to be explosive. Ashley got out of her tub and stepped into the shower to rinse off. Then, drying herself off, she went to lie down for a brief while. Her clock was set for three forty-five, and she awoke immediately as it began to beep. She felt relaxed and refreshed now, but she lay quietly for a few minutes more. Then she went to get dressed. Her bridegroom and new family would be arriving, and then the few guests. Under the circumstances it wasn't necessary that she go down and greet them. Besides, they all knew one another. She slipped on her bra and panties. They were cream silk and lace, unlike her usual plain silk. Well, it was an occasion, she reasoned with herself. Her legs were smooth and tan, and she didn't bother with stockings. She was wearing pretty cream-colored leather sandals on her feet. She did her makeup, such as it was: a little bit of green eye shadow, some blush, a pink lipstick. Then she slipped into her dress, which buttoned in the back with two pearl buttons she was just able to reach herself. Looking at herself in the full-length mirror, she was pleased. The calf-length dress was lovely. Reaching for her hairbrush, she fluffed her short hair. Then she affixed her mother's antique pearl earrings in her ears. A knock sounded on her door and she called, "Come in."

Byrnes stepped through. He was dressed in a dark suit, white shirt, and a blue-and-white polka-dot silk tie. He was carrying a small bouquet, which he handed to her. "I believe we are ready, Miss Ashley," he said with a smile. "Oh, the wife said to make certain you wore your sapphire ring. You need something blue. Mr. Ryan's mother has left you the something old and borrowed." Reaching into his pocket, he drew out a small antique gold cross on a thin chain. "Mrs. Mulcahy said she hopes you'll wear it, and she'll tell you all about it later. Would you like me to fasten it about your neck?"

"Please," Ashley said, and watched as the little cross settled on her chest just above the neckline of her dress. "I guess we're ready then," she told Byrnes.

He escorted her downstairs and through the house out into the gardens. Tony had been right: The trellis was now awash in late-afternoon sunlight. She heard the bridal march as she slowly proceeded down the short aisle, preceded by Mrs. Byrnes in a lovely floral lavender silk dress. Mrs. B. was carrying a small bouquet of purple, lavender, and white dahlias. Ashley's nosegay was made up of small lavender roses, white freesia, and ivy. She wondered where the music was coming from, but then the music stopped magically as they reached the trellis where Ryan stood waiting with Ray Pietro d'Angelo and Judge Palmer. Byrnes proudly answered, "I do," when asked who gave the bride.

It was happening! Ashley thought. It was really happening this time! She was getting married. Married to a handsome, sexy guy she barely knew. But strangely, she wasn't worried. Fate sometimes actually did take a hand in your life, and it didn't have to be forever if they decided that they hated it. And then she thought that was a lousy attitude to have as you were being married. Maybe it would work out. Maybe there would be more between them than just sex. Maybe. Just maybe.

She hardly listened to what was being said, managing only to reply, "I do," at the appropriate place. She and Ryan had not had to go down to town hall to apply for their wedding license. Judge Palmer had made out the license himself to help them preserve their privacy. Ashley hadn't wanted anyone to know she was getting married before the fact. And if she and Ryan had gone to get that license, the *Egret Pointe Gazette* would have had it on the front page Thursday, when the paper came out. As Judge Palmer pronounced them man and wife under the laws of the state, Ashley realized she was no longer the bad-luck bride. She was a married woman.

"You may kiss your bride, Mr. Mulcahy," Judge Palmer said with a smile.

And he kissed her. Oh, yes, he kissed her—a long, demanding, hot kiss that sent the color flooding her cheeks. And when he released her and looked into her eyes, Ashley felt her legs go weak. She grabbed at his arm, and he smiled down at her.

"Wow!" Ashley said.

"How soon can we get rid of the guests?" he whispered to her.

"Ladies and gentlemen," said the judge, turning them about, "may I present to you Mr. and Mrs. Ryan Finbar Mulcahy."

There was much clapping and laughter as everyone pressed forward to congratulate them. Angelina hugged and kissed them both. Frankie was crying, along with Nina and Tiffany Pietro d'Angelo. Mr. and Mrs. Byrnes were standing proudly by, as pleased as if she were their own daughter. Ashley had insisted they hire servers so the Byrneses might be guests at the table today.

"So all's well that ends well," Ray Pietro d'Angelo said with a pleased grin. "Joe and I did good by you, huh? What do you think, Lina? Are you happy, *cara*?"

"For the moment," Angelina Mulcahy said with a meaningful nod to Ashley.

"Shall we all go up to the house now?" Byrnes suggested.

"Yes," Ashley agreed. "There are drinks and nibbles before dinner." She slipped her arm through her new husband's, and began to move toward the house.

"You're a beautiful bride," he told her quietly as they walked. "I thought you weren't going to wear a wedding dress?"

"It isn't a wedding dress. It's just a dress," Ashley told him.

"On you, it's a wedding dress. I want a picture of you in it," he told her.

"There'll be a photographer waiting up at the house," Ashley said. "I'm giving the local paper an exclusive. We'll be front-page news next Thursday." She laughed.

"You hired the paper's photographer?" he asked.

"No, the local photographer, but I'm giving him permission to sell the pictures to the paper. He just thinks he was hired for a social event. I told him it was a charity party. Is he in for a surprise." Ashley chuckled.

Ryan grinned. "You've got a wicked sense of humor, Ash," he said. "I like it."

She smiled up at him. She was married. He was her husband. He wanted to make love to her. He liked her sense of humor. Something akin to a tiny spark of hope bloomed inside her at that moment. Was it just possible that this *convenience* could turn into something else? She had never had any luck with men. Until now...?

They entered the house, leading their guests into the gracious living room. Almost at once there were servers with trays holding glasses of wine and canapés. Most of the guests had been in the house before. Ashley saw Frankie sneak off with Rose and Tiffany Pietro d'Angelo, Carla Johnson, and Nina. She knew full well that Frankie was taking the women up to see the master suite.

"You will forgive her, of course, *cara*," Angelina said quietly. She had seen them leave too. "Francesca is an enthusiastic woman."

"I like her," Ashley replied. "We're becoming friends. I thought I would hold a party in October sometime for the rest of your family. Will you tell your other daughters that Ryan and I have gotten married, Lina? The announcement cards are ready to go out on Monday, but I really think they should be told personally."

"I believe that chore is up to your husband," Lina said, her warm brown eyes twinkling mischievously. "Can you do one of those conference calls to all of them at once? It will give you an idea of how *passionate* my older daughters are. That is probably a good word to describe them. They aren't bad women, although Ryan and Frankie would have you believe it. They are simply middle-aged and bored with their lives. Some people, when they get that way, find useful things to do. My daughters, however, cause trouble for their own amusement. How they became so certain of their own righteousness I will never know. I did not raise them that way."

"I think it might be fun to call Ryan's sisters," Ashley agreed. "But is he brave enough to beard them all at once, I wonder?"

"Beard who?" Ryan had come up on his mother and bride. His arm slipped about Ashley, and he leaned down to kiss her cheek.

"We'll have to call your sisters tonight or tomorrow, and tell them you're married," Ashley said. "The announcements go out on Monday, and they can't learn of your marriage that way. It's cold and impersonal. It's bad enough we didn't invite them to the wedding, Ryan."

"I wanted us to have a happy wedding day," he said, "and with the harpies here it wouldn't have been. But you're right. We need to call them. We can do it tonight."

Byrnes had been watching for the women to return to the living room, and when they did he nodded imperceptibly to the head server, who then announced dinner. They all trooped into the formal dining room, oohing and ahhing at the table setting as they sat down. Immediately a clear vegetable broth was served and the wineglasses filled. It was followed by a salad of mixed lettuces—Boston, both green and red, endive, arugula, and peppery nasturtium flowers, dressed in a raspberry vinagrette. The main course was leg of lamb cooked with garlic and rosemary, fresh French cut green beans, slivers of yellow summer squash, and small white potatoes that had been roasted about the meat as it cooked. The wineglasses were filled again. When the meal had concluded the guests once more adjourned to the living room, where the wedding cake had been set up.

"The first one of you who starts singing 'The Bride Cuts the Cake' is going to get it," Ashley said grimly. "It's so corny."

"I'd like to get a shot of you two cutting the cake," the photographer said. When he had learned the charity party was actually Ashley's wedding he almost fainted. And then when she generously told him he could sell three pictures to the local newspaper, he was rendered almost speechless. He had taken a picture of both the bride and the groom together, with Judge Palmer, with Mr. and Mrs. Byrnes, with Angelina and Frankie, with their friends. He had taken a picture of Ashley seated demurely with her wedding bouquet, and then he had taken another of her seated and Ryan standing behind her, his hand on her shoulder, her hand on his hand. At one point she turned to look up at him and smiled. The photographer had photographed that too. Now he took pictures of the bridal couple cutting their wedding cake while the guests mischievously hummed the forbidden tune. Ashley fed her new husband a bite of cake. The photographer snapped. Ryan fed Ashley a bit of cake, and some of the frosting got on her nose. She laughed, and the photographer snapped. The cake was served with miniature scoops of lemon sorbet.

It was evening, and the party was coming to an end. A stretch limo had arrived to take Ray and Rose Pietro d'Angelo, Angelina, and Frankie back into the city. The local guests were departing in their own cars. The top layer of the wedding cake was wrapped, boxed, and put in the freezer to celebrate their first anniversary. The servers were busily cleaning up. Byrnes and his missus had disappeared, probably to their own quarters.

Ashley turned to look at her new husband. "I guess we had better call your older sisters now," she said.

"Yep," he agreed. "Business first. And then pleasure." Reaching out he pulled her into his arms and kissed her mouth gently. "I like the way you kiss, Mrs. Mulcahy."

"Ditto," she admitted as her cheeks warmed.

They went into the library, where there were two handsets for the telephone. Ryan pressed the appropriate buttons to set up the conference call, and then he dialed. "Bride, it's Ryan. This is going to be a conference call with all of you, so hang on," he told her, and before she could question him he moved on to the second number. "Betta, Ryan." And he gave her the same message.

"How can you be certain they're all at home?" Ashley asked.

"It's Saturday night," he said with a grin, and then he was speaking with his sister Kathleen, then Magdalena, and finally Deirdre. "Okay, girls, you all there?"

"Who's died?" Bride, the eldest, wanted to know.

"Is Mom all right?" Magdelena demanded.

"Nobody's died. Nobody's been in an accident. Nobody's been diagnosed with a wasting illness. Okay?" he said.

"So why a conference call with all of us?" Bride asked. "You know we have other things to do, Ryan, than listen to your foolishness."

Ashley raised an eyebrow. *Jeez, nice sister,* she thought.

"I have an important announcement to make, girls," Ryan said.

"You're drunk," Betta decided.

"Probably a little, because it's been an exciting day. I got married today, girls. Ma and Frankie were here with us.

Since the announcements go out on Monday I thought my big sisters would want to know before they arrived in the mail."

There was a long, very deep silence, and then Bride said, "Who is this person you married? Some little gold digger who thinks she's hit the jackpot by marrying you?"

"As a matter of fact, she's richer than I am. And it's old money, girls. Not new like ours. Old money. Beautiful home filled with antiques. Servants. Breeding and background. Her ancestors helped found the town."

"What's her name?" Kathleen demanded to know. "Just who is this rich girl?"

"Her name is Ashley Cordelia Kimbrough, and she's beautiful, with hair the color of good mahogany, and green eyes that I get lost in every time I look into them," he said.

"Oh, my God," Betta groaned. Her brother sounded as if he were in love.

"Is this a joke, Ryan? Because if it is, it's in very poor taste," Bride snapped.

"No joke, Bride. I'm married. I have a beautiful wife, and now if you don't mind I'm going to go off and spend a delightfully active wedding night with my bride. Actually, it was Ash who suggested I call you. She didn't want your feelings hurt."

"If she didn't want our feelings hurt she could have asked us to the wedding," Bride said acerbically.

"I didn't want you here," Ryan told his sisters bluntly. "You would have spoiled what has been an incredibly wonderful and happy day for us. I didn't want my wife having to look back on our wedding day with unhappiness because the five of you were sniping at her and bitching at me. You had better call Jerry Klein, girls, and tell him the deal is off.

Big brother has a beautiful new wife, and now he's going to go and fuck her."

Ashley almost burst out laughing at the collective gasp that arose from the women on the other end of the phone.

"Good night, girls," Ryan said. Then he hung up.

"Oh, Lord, and you say I've got a wicked sense of humor," Ashley said, laughing. "Those poor women are going to have a terrible weekend now."

He picked up the phone again and dialed. "Ma, I wanted you to know—Frankie too—that I've called the girls and told them. You'll probably have several messages on your machine when you get home tonight. Frankie too." He listened, and then laughed. "Thanks," he said, and then he hung up.

"What did she say?" Ashley asked him.

"She said I was to love you very gently on our first night together," he answered low, and his eyes were filled with his open longing.

Ashley felt her cheeks growing pink, and, laughing, he pulled her into his arms, nuzzling her soft dark hair. Her heart was hammering nervously. The tip of her tongue touched her lips briefly, and she put her palms flat against his chest, realizing as she did so that the house was suddenly very quiet, and that they were very much alone. And then his mouth took hers in a fierce kiss that rendered her weak-kneed.

Chapter Six

He looked down at her. "Are you all right?" he asked her. Ashley nodded slowly. "I think it's suddenly dawning on me that we're *really* married. It's not just a good idea anymore. It's been in my mind that this marriage is how you and I can save what we have worked for, and I did all the things I needed to do to make the day a perfect one for us and all our guests, but I never really considered the marriage part as anything else except a means to an end. Until now."

"Kind of scary, huh?" he said. "Listen, the sex thing... it is optional. You're tired, and the truth is that I'm still jet-lagged." His warm brown eyes looked into her green ones. "If you're not in the mood..."

"The truth is that I am kinda in the mood," Ashley admitted. "You were looking for a petite blonde, and I don't know what I was looking for, but I'm pretty sure it wasn't you. Yet here you are, and you are so damned sexy. Every time you kiss me I go weak in the knees. No one ever made me go weak in the knees. Not even hot to trot Chandler Wayne. I know women aren't supposed to say stuff like this, but, Ryan Finbar Mulcahy, I really want to jump your bones. But if you're not in the mood..."

Ryan grinned down at her. "Ashley, you are something else," he told her. "You say just what you're thinking, don't you? Well, so do I. I want to sink myself so deep in you. I want to make you come and come and come until you can't come anymore. I am more than definitely in the mood."

"I guess we had better go upstairs then," Ashley told him demurely, and she held out her hand to him. He took it, and they mounted the stairs together, then walked down the broad upstairs hallway to the bedroom suite they would share. "Nina made me take one of my sexy nightgowns home yesterday," Ashley said. "I'll go and change."

"No time," he told her, spinning her around to undo the two pearl buttons on her dress. He quickly peeled it off of her as Ashley stepped out of the puddle of fabric and kicked off her sandals. He unfastened the lace bra, and his hands slipped about her to cup her two full breasts. "Hello, girls," he murmured in her ear. "God, they are so beautiful. I don't ever think I've seen such a pair of gorgeous tits. They're real too, aren't they?"

"Uh-huh," Ashley managed to get out. His hands. Oh, his big hands cupping her breasts! She could hardly draw a breath, and when his two thumbs reached up to seductively rub her nipples she felt herself getting wet. She leaned back against him and sighed deeply. This was going to be good. Her gut told her it would be good.

He bent down to kiss the side of her neck, and his hands released her breasts so he might slip her little lace bikini bottom off. The Velcro closures at her hip bone gave way, and he tossed the scrap of fabric aside. One arm was now about her waist. His other hand moved down to her mons, and a finger slid along her slit. "You're wet," he said, sounding pleased. The big hand ruffled her pubic hair.

She managed to turn herself about in his embrace. "Take off your jacket," she said as she undid the narrow black belt at his waist and unzipped his gray trousers. Her hand slid in, moving though the opening in his silk boxers with unerring fingers, and closed about his penis. He was still half-soft, and he was huge, Ashley realized. She had created men with large penises in her Channel fantasies, but Ryan was to her unseen touch even bigger. She gave him a little squeeze, and he began to harden.

"I'm bigger than most guys," he told her.

"So I note," she said. "I want you naked, Ryan. I want to see for myself just how big." She released her grip on him to fondle his balls. His sac was large too. Well, she thought, her new husband was big all over, wasn't he? Why was she surprised that a man standing six feet, five inches tall had a supersized dick? Ashley took her hands from his genitals and began to unbutton his shirt. She almost moaned with delight at the broad, smooth, tanned chest. She slid her hands over it, kissing the warm flesh.

He had managed to get out of the rest of his clothing now, and stood back from her. "Well," he said, "do I pass muster, Ash?"

"Do I?" she asked him, staring at his penis. "How big is that?" she queried him.

"I measured once," he said. "Eleven inches. Just. Two in diameter."

"You *measured*?" She didn't know whether to laugh. She could not take her eyes from the thick column of flesh now bobbing before her. She wanted it in her so badly she was near to weeping. What was the matter with her?

"In college. Guys will do that, you know," he said, looking a little embarrassed.

"It's amazing," she told him.

"Look, I don't want to hurt you, so if I go too deep, tell me, okay?" he said.

"Uh-huh," she agreed. *Do it! Do it!* she was silently screaming. Then he was kissing her again, and his hand was squeezing her butt. They were still in the parlor of their suite, and he was backing over to the couch. Ashley kissed him hungrily as she felt him bend her back over the high rolled arm of the couch. Her back fit perfectly against it. Did Frankie know that when she had picked this couch?

"Put your legs up," he murmured, and she wrapped herself about him, almost whimpering as she felt the head of his penis beginning to penetrate her vagina.

"Oh, God!" she half sobbed. He was so big, so thick, so hot, and he was buried all the way inside of her. "Fuck me!" she begged him, but instead he leaned forward to fasten his mouth about one of her nipples, and he sucked hard on it. Ashley cried out softly as his lips and tongue teased her until she really thought she was going to die.

He bit down firmly but gently on the tender flesh. She cried out again. "Tell me what you want," he growled in her ear. "Explain it to me carefully, slowly, and if you're a good girl, I'll give it to you. Tell me what you want, Ashley."

"I want you to fuck me!" she gasped.

"Not good enough," he replied.

"I want that hot cock of yours inside of me, fucking me hard. I want you to make me come and come and come and come. Can't you feel how perfectly you fit me? My cunt was made for your big cock, Ryan! Do it! Do it, damn it!" Ashley cried.

He laughed low, and then he began, slowly, slowly at first, his penis moving with majestic strokes that pressed deeper and deeper. And then gradually he began to move on her faster and faster, until Ashley was sobbing and her climax began to roll over her with such force and intensity that she practically fainted. He had her bent back so far over the couch arm that the blood flowing to her head made her dizzy, but oh, God, it was wonderful! And then he stopped, giving her time to regain her breath. And her eyes widened with the knowledge that he was still very hard inside of her.

Gathering her up, their bodies still joined, he carried her into their bedroom and laid her on the edge of their big bed. He began to piston her once again, slowly, slowly, and then faster and faster. He laughed when her nails dug into his shoulders and shortly afterward raked down his long back. "Such a naughty kitty," he whispered in her ear. And then to her surprise he pulled out of her. "Roll over," he said. "I want to go deeper."

"I don't think I can move," Ashley said.

He laughed again, this time low and seductive. Then he helped her into the position he wanted her to take. Kneeling behind her, he grasped her hips in his hands and thrust smoothly back into the wet heat of her luscious body. "You are so tight," he groaned, delving farther into her channel.

Had she ever had a cock pushed so far into her body? The deep, hard thrusts were incredible. He hit her G-spot, and when she half cried, "Oh, yes, there!" he worked it until she was whimpering helplessly with the pure pleasure that he was giving her. She felt him begin to spasm, and as he ejaculated into her she climaxed so ferociously that Ashley thought she was going to die right then and there. "Oh, God, that was wonderful!" she managed to gasp as they fell apart. She rolled over onto her back, struggling for breath. "Tell me you can eventually do it again."

Ryan laughed weakly. "Eventually," he promised. "You were incredible, Ash. I mean really, really good. I don't think I've ever had better."

"Well," she told him, "that's nice, because I'm all you're likely to get for the next two years." Was he aware of what he had just said? she wondered. He was speaking to her as if she were just another one-night stand, and not his lawful wife. And then she realized that he had hurt her feelings. It surprised her to realize that he could do that, but then, it had just been sex for him, hadn't it? And if she were truthful with herself it had just been sex for her, but women didn't do things that way. For women sex was an emotional commitment. For men sex was just sex.

"What's the matter?" he asked her, realizing she was tense.

"I've never had sex just for the sake of it," Ashley told him. "I'm not sure that I like it." Well, that wasn't exactly true, was it? She had sex on The Channel just for the fun of it, didn't she? But that was different. "I mean, it was wonderful, but it meant nothing. Each time I've had sex before it was because I thought I was in love. We just had an absolutely fabulous wham-bam moment." She struggled to hold back the tears that were threatening to spill from her eyes. "So why do I want to cry?" The tears began to fall, and she was mortified when a soft sob escaped her.

Ryan pulled her into his arms and held her tightly. He didn't say anything at first, because she was right. He wasn't even sure what to say. This had all happened so damned fast, and all because Finbar Mulcahy was reaching from beyond the grave to try to run his life, just as Ashley's grandfather was doing to her. He hoped the two old boys were happy now. "Does it help that I really like you?" he finally said.

"You're just saying that to make me feel better." Ashley sniffed. She was snuggling into his arms, her breasts against his chest, and bare flesh on bare flesh felt so darned good. "I really like you too," she told him.

He smiled and kissed the top of her head. "Maybe it would be better if we tried to get some sleep now. I'm still jet-lagged, and you're obviously exhausted, Ash. Can I hold you for a while longer?"

"Uh-huh," she murmured. She could hear his heart beneath her ear. It beat strongly, with a reassuring *thump-thump*. "I guess I could use some sleep," she admitted. "I'm going to need all my strength if that's how well you perform when you're jet-lagged. You're likely to kill me when you're at full strength."

He laughed aloud. "Look who's talking," he countered. "You are an incredible partner, Ashley. I might find myself more than liking you if we continue to get on like this." He stroked her hair. "Now go to sleep, Ashley, baby."

Suddenly she was feeling better. And he had called her *baby*. She curled onto her side, and he pulled her against him, one hand enclosing one of her breasts. Ashley smiled.

When she awoke the following morning she heard him in his shower and contemplated joining him, but decided against it. It would certainly lead to another sexual encounter, and she wasn't certain she wanted one yet. She fell back to sleep.

"Wake up, sleepyhead," he called to her. "I've got coffee."

Ashley opened her eyes and rolled over onto her back. "The Byrneses have Sunday off," she said. "Where did you get coffee?"

"I made it," he told her, grinning and looking very pleased with himself. "And there was a covered plate of muffins out on a tray with butter and two cups."

"Mrs. B. must have put it out last night before she went to bed. How did you know where to find the coffee?" Ashley wanted to know.

"The coffeemaker was set up, and all I had to do was push the button," he said.

Ashley laughed. "Mrs. B. must like you, Ryan. She never sets out Sunday breakfast for me. I always have to go down and make my own."

She sat up, and then it dawned on her that she was naked beneath the covers. "Oh, Lord," she muttered. He grinned, and she blushed again. "Stop that!" she told him, but his grin just expanded. "Close your eyes," she said.

"Why?"

"Just close them, Ryan." And when he had she jumped from the bed and ran into her dressing room to slip on the nightgown she had brought home from Lacy Nothings on Friday night. Then, mustering her dignity, she came out of the dressing room.

His eyes widened as she strolled across the floor to the bed and climbed back in. "*Mamma mia!*" he said expressively. What had ever made him think petite blondes were his ideal? Ashley's tall curves set off in the clingy lavender silk were gorgeous! Perfect! Utterly and totally seductive. He felt a tightening in his groin just watching her walk.

"I take it you like the nightgown," she said dryly as she reached for one of the small muffins on the bed tray and began to butter it.

He nodded and splashed some half-and-half in his coffee. "I woke up about six," he began, "and I've been doing some hard thinking, Ash." He took a sip of his coffee. "When you cried last night because you weren't comfortable with sex just for the sake of sex, I suddenly realized that maybe we should try to make something more of this marriage than just the fact that we've saved ourselves the difficulty and irritation of having to start all over again. I know we did this for one reason, but maybe we should try to really make a go of it, and not just consider that in two years we can walk away with everything that belongs to each of us, and nobody gets hurt. Because I think after two years together, with the kind of sexual chemistry that we seem to have, we would both get hurt." He sighed. "Am I making any sense, baby?"

Her heart was hammering fiercely in her chest. "Are you proposing that instead of a marriage of convenience we have an arranged marriage, like your folks did? A real marriage, not just a pretend one with mind-blowing sex?"

"Yes," he told her, "yes, I am. But can we keep the mind-blowing sex?"

"Why?" she asked him, suspicious. She had learned long ago that if something looked too good to be true then it probably was.

"Well," he said, "I've never found a woman interesting enough to hold my attention long enough to court. I'm one of those guys who really loves his work. The restoration of beautiful furniture has fascinated me ever since I was a kid. And then when I started the reproduction end of it, I was blown away by the fact that we could, using many of the same hand techniques used hundreds of years ago, and finishing with the myriad new materials, stains, and finishes available to us today, create new pieces every bit as good as the old pieces. It's an amazing procedure, and I've been wrapped up in it. My dad was a wonderful craftsman. As Ma says, he was the artist and I'm the brains. It's true, but I can still love and appreciate the creative process involved. And I spend a great deal of time figuring out new ways to make what we do even better. There just hasn't been any real time for women. I've had girlfriends for a few weeks at a time. The hardier ones have lasted a few months, but given up after that. And until last night, when my convenient new wife cried because she wasn't comfortable with sex just for the sake of it, I didn't care."

"But you do now?" Ashley sounded skeptical.

"Yes, I do," he answered her.

Ashley had to admit to herself that he did sound earnest about what he was saying, and she licked some butter from her fingers. "Well," she allowed, "I haven't exactly been a success in the finding-a-mate department myself. I'm a terrific merchandiser, but I'm lousy at picking the right man. I'm probably not as passionate about my business as you are about yours, yet I do love what I do, and I really like expanding Lacy Nothings and doing my catalog. But I've always wanted to get married, and have kids too. Maybe subconsciously that desire is the reason I kept taking up with the wrong guys. I wasn't applying Principles of Business One to Picking a Husband One," Ashley said with a small smile.

He chuckled. "So maybe fate took a hand in putting us together," he suggested.

"You believe in stuff like fate?" she said, surprised.

"Hey, I'm half-Irish," he reminded her. "Look, don't you think it's a terrific coincidence that our lawyers are first cousins, and that they each had a client who *had* to get married or lose their inheritance? And you and I do have a few things in common."

"Like what?" Ashley wanted to know.

"Well, we both come from families with a strong work ethic. We both majored in business at college. We both started our own businesses and have made them successful. We're careful with our money. You like my mother and Frankie. I love 'em. You want kids. So do I. All boys, though. Well, maybe one girl. And we are incredibly wonderful together in the sack, aren't we, baby?"

He shouldn't have been making sense. But he was. They did have a lot in common, and it was a lot more than just being sexually compatible. Her first fiancé, Carson Kingsley, had been a lot of fun—funny, quick, sweet, and with incredible taste. But there had been no sex involved, and it confused her until she learned why. Her second fiancé, Chandler Wayne, had wanted nothing but sex. He was fun and he was energetic, but he also drank too much in the off season, and could get nasty when crossed. And then there had been fiancé number three. Tall, blond, and handsome. A thirty-five-year-old preppy with a great wardrobe, a wonderful backhand, and perfect manners, who knew just what to say. *Always.* Sex with Derek had been nice. Yes, in retrospect, *nice* was the right word.

But what the hell had she had in common with any of those guys? It shocked her to realize suddenly that she had had nothing at all in common with any of them. But she certainly shared much with Ryan Finbar Mulcahy. And yes, they were wickedly, wonderfully compatible sexually. "Do you think this fate of yours helped Joe and Ray to get it right for us?" she wondered aloud.

"Could be," he said. "Look, we've got the prenups protecting both of us financially. And if we really want it the out is there. But instead of concentrating on that out, why don't we concentrate on making this marriage work?"

"I could do that," Ashley answered him slowly, "but there is one condition."

"And that is?"

"No babies until we're absolutely sure that we can be happy together, and that you want me and a family more than you want to spend time in your office. Okay?" Her green eyes engaged his brown ones.

"I'm used to spending most of my time there," he said. "It could be hard at first, but I can try, Ash. I will try. And you've got to help me, because sometimes I don't see the plain truth staring me in the face."

"You're asking me to nag you," Ashley said, but a small smile played at the corners of her lush mouth.

He grinned. "Yes, I am." Then he grew serious. "I'm a bit of duh sometimes, but I'm not a complete jerk. I'm discovering you're a very special girl, Ashley. You're beautiful, sexy, smart, kind, thoughtful, and sensitive. I know I'd be a fool not to try to hold on to you. I planned to go into town on Monday, but I'll call in then and tell them I won't be back until the Tuesday after Labor Day. There's nothing at R&R that can't wait."

"That's ten days!" She gasped.

"Well, we really should have a honeymoon, shouldn't we?" he answered her.

"But I didn't plan anything!" she wailed. "We should honeymoon on some exotic island, or fly to Europe and stay at a grand hotel."

"I thought it might be nice if we stayed home, let Mr. and Mrs. Byrnes take care of us, and you show me all around Egret Pointe and its environs. Can Nina handle Lacy Nothings for the next ten days?"

"I suppose so," Ashley said. "The catalog is under control for now, and this is usually our quiet season, and I'm here in case of a real emergency."

"Then call Nina today so she's prepared tomorrow morning when she goes in to work," he suggested.

"Okay," Ashley agreed. "She'll be okay. Brandy can come in five days a week instead of just three. She's saving for college, and this is her senior year. She'll welcome the extra cash. She's been checking at the IGA the days she doesn't work with us, but I pay her more, so she'll change her days there." She finished the coffee remaining in her china mug. "That was good. Thank you."

He stood up and took away the bed tray. "I think we ought to seal our new agreement with something."

"A little sex, perhaps?" she teased.

"A lot of sex," he growled, diving back into the bed.

Ashley squealed and squirmed out of his grasp. "I need a shower," she said. "You had one earlier. And the next one we'll take together, okay?"

"That's fair, but hurry up, baby. I'm getting hot just thinking about you naked again," Ryan said, his brown eyes caressing her long body.

And then she slid the spaghetti straps off her shoulders and, turning, walked slowly and seductively into her bathroom, her hips swaying as she went. Halfway there the nightgown slid down her frame, and without losing a step Ashley stepped out of it, treating him to the delicious sight of her graceful back and delightfully firm buttocks. He gave a long, appreciative wolf whistle, and she turned slightly to grin at him as she closed her bathroom door.

Ashley let the warm water from the twelve spigots in her glass and marble shower pour over her. She picked up the cake of Florentine olive oil soap and rubbed it over her sea sponge until it was foamy. Then she washed herself thoroughly and rinsed. But she wasn't of a mind to get too quickly out of the privacy of her bathroom. Something wonderful had just happened. Something totally unexpected. Certainly she had never anticipated that Ryan would suggest they try to actually make a go of what had begun as a marriage of convenience. Perhaps she had hoped a little bit that something good might come of their marriage, eventually. Yet they had known each other only two and a half months. But the day after the wedding? He had no reason she could think of to make the suggestion. Unless, of course, he thought he might be able to actually care for her. That he believed she could learn to care for him. Now she really did know how the heroines in romance novels felt when put into marriages not of their own choosing.

Ashley turned off the shower and, stepping out, wrapped herself in a large bath sheet. She took a towel and rubbed her arms and legs dry. Then, going to the sink, she brushed her teeth and swished a bit of mouthwash around her mouth. Picking up her hairbrush, she ran it through her hair, fluffing it up. *Beautiful.* He had said she was beautiful. She looked hard at herself in the mirror. Pretty. She would admit to pretty. Wrapped in the bath sheet, she exited the bathroom and reentered their bedroom.

Ryan was sprawled naked on the bed. He held out his hand to her. Ashley dropped the bath sheet and, coming across the room, took his hand, letting him pull her down onto the bed with him.

"You've got a body like the Venus de Milo," he said softly, reaching up to caress one of her breasts. "Last night it was hard and hot, Ash. Now let me do it to you slow and sweet." He didn't wait for her to answer, but pressed her down onto the mattress and began to kiss her. His mouth was firm and warm. His tongue ran along her lush mouth, encouraging it to open, sliding in when it did to play with her tongue.

Ashley let herself relax completely, putting herself into his care without any reservations. She had learned last night that he was a skilled lover, and he had given her no reason to distrust him. The kiss melted into another, and another, and another, until her head was swimming. The sensation of her breasts against his bare flesh was exciting. And then his mouth began to move from her lips, going beneath her chin, sliding easily down her throat. He kissed her shoulders. His tongue traced a line between her breasts. He kissed those pale mounds of flesh, sucking briefly on each nipple. She didn't see his smile when she sighed with appreciation.

His mouth moved down and across her long torso. The flesh beneath his lips was soft, and faintly perfumed with an elusive scent that set his pulses racing with the odd sensation that the fragrance was familiar, but he couldn't place it. He kissed her down one long leg, reaching her foot, nibbling on her toes, pushing his tongue between them suggestively. Ashley sighed again, and made small noises of pleasure.

He moved up her other leg, this time using his tongue on her skin. Her legs fell open, and he teasingly nipped at the soft, tender flesh of her inside thigh. Her pussy was a full thicket of mahogany-colored curls, and he wove his fingers through it. He could see she was already growing slightly moist. He slipped two fingers between the lips of her labia and, finding her clit, played with it, smiling again as it swelled beneath his ministrations. Then, carefully, he pushed those two fingers into her vagina, and she whimpered and began to encourage him by moving her hips. His fingers pushed as deep as they could, moving gently, but with increasing rapidity. He felt her tense and bedew his hand with her juices. "Tell me what you want," he whispered in her ear.

She was silent for several long moments, and then she said, "Lick me, Ryan! Please! And then fuck me! I want you inside of me."

"Whatever my baby wants, she will get," he answered. His head lowered, and, opening her with his fingers, he could see her swollen clit and the pearly juices of her arousal. The tip of his tongue touched her clit, and she shivered. He licked slowly around it, and her hips moved restlessly. He bent closer and, taking her clit in his mouth, sucked hard on it several times.

Ashley actually screamed softly. He was driving her wild, and it was wonderful!

Ryan was hard with his lust. He was ready to take her now. Giving her clit a little bite, he pulled himself up, mounted her, and pushed into her vagina slowly, slowly, until he completely filled her. Then he began to fuck her with measured, deep, deliberate strokes of his engorged cock.

Ashley felt him. He was almost desperate with his need for her. She wrapped her legs about his torso so he could go deeper. He was so big, and he seemed to stretch the walls of her vagina, but he didn't hurt her. Eleven long, hard, hot inches plumbed her tight depths. She squeezed her vaginal muscles around his eager cock. "Oh, yes, Ryan!" she encouraged him. "Yes!" Her head was beginning to spin. Fireworks burst behind her closed eyes as she climaxed with a cry of undiluted pleasure, and at the sound she felt him drenching her with his juices. It was a good thing she was on the pill, Ashley thought. It was going to be easy to make babies one day with Ryan Finbar Mulcahy.

"Oh, baby! Oh, baby!" Ryan groaned as he spasmed and spasmed with his ejaculation. Then he collapsed atop her for several long moments before finally rolling off of Ashley. Propping himself up on an elbow, he looked down into her face. "You," he told her, "are absolutely wonderful!"

"So are you," she returned. "I'd have us take a bow, but I don't think either of us can stand up quite yet. Where did you learn to make love like that? Or do I not want to know? No," she decided, "I don't want to know."

He chuckled, but he didn't answer her right away, and though she was curious, Ashley let it go. "One day," he said finally. "But not today, baby. Okay?"

"Okay," she agreed, and, pulling his head down to her, she gave him a quick kiss.

"That was nice," he noted.

"I like the idea of really trying to make this a real marriage," Ashley said. "I think your mother would be pleased, but could we hold off on telling her right away? I don't want to disappoint her if we can't do it. Let's at least wait until we've spent our honeymoon together to see if we can honestly stand being together long enough to do this right."

He nodded. "Agreed. But I've got a good feeling about us, Ashley."

She called Nina later that day and then she and Ryan went to ground, not bothering to answer the telephone during the next week, letting Byrnes take messages. Finally after one desperate message from Frankie, Ashley relented and called Ryan's sister.

"Where have you been?" Frankie wanted to know.

"Ryan and I are honeymooning. Isn't that usual for newly married couples?" she teased her new sister-in-law.

"He took time from work?" Frankie said, sounded amazed. "My God! He must like you!" She paused when Ashley said nothing. Then she shrieked. "He does like you! Is the sex fabulous? Does he live up to his reputation? Tell me now! I can't talk at home with my kid there, and he doesn't go back to St. Peter's for three more weeks!"

Ashley laughed. "Yes, he likes me, and I like him. And yes, the sex is fabulous, but that's all I'm going to say. What's the matter? Is Lina all right?"

"It's my sisters," Frankie said. "They all got their marriage announcements, and I swear that they are going crazy. They descended on Ma today and demanded to know just what was going on. Incidentally, they didn't call me to join them. She told them if they got the announcements then they knew what was going on. You got married. She and I were there. You're lovely. He's lucky. But she could tell it wasn't enough for them. She reminded them that Ryan called them last Saturday night to tell them himself, but they said he was blind drunk, and they hadn't talked to the bride. Ma hasn't answered any of their calls this week. She didn't want to be bothered. Ryan didn't answer any of their calls. Ma called me after they left because she's not certain what they'll do."

"I think maybe you should talk to Ryan about this," Ashley said. "It's your family, after all. I don't know them yet, but I thought I'd have everyone up over the Columbus Day weekend. Save the date, will you? Here's Ryan."

"What's up, sis?" he asked Frankie, and then he listened. Finally he said, "Okay, you tell Ma not to worry. I'll be back in town after Labor Day, and in the meantime I'll call Bride. She can calm the rest of them down. After all, I did speak with them after the wedding. What did they think? That I was joking?"

"They said you were drunk, and they did think you were joking," Frankie answered him. She giggled. "Those formal engraved announcements have really done them in, Ryan. I think they're suddenly beginning to realize that you actually did do it."

"Tell Ma I'll take care of everything, and I'll call her later," Ryan said grimly. "Thanks for the heads-up, kid." He hung up the phone. Then he pulled out his cell. "I'm going to call Bride now," he told Ashley, "She has caller ID, and I don't want her getting the house number. She's a real pit bull when it comes to ferreting out information." He turned back to the cell and pressed a single number. The phone rang, and then he heard his oldest sister's voice as she answered. "Bride," Ryan said, "what the hell is the matter with you and the others, hassling Ma like that?"

There was silence, and then Bride said, "You *really* got married?"

"Yeah, I really got married. And I'm on my honeymoon right now, and I'm having to deal with you and the others, Bride. I'm not happy."

"How could you do this to us, Ryan?" his eldest sibling asked him.

"Not ask you to the wedding? Now, why would I do that, Bride? You and the others would have made it all about yourselves and spoiled what was an incredible day for Ashley and me. Incidentally, we're inviting you all for the Columbus Day weekend, so tell the others and save the date. And be on your best behavior, because if any of you cause trouble, you won't be invited again. Ma and Frankie are crazy about her, Bride, and Ashley already loves them." He was ignoring the real meaning behind his sister's question. Ryan knew damned well she was talking about money, and not hurt feelings.

"You know exactly what I mean, Ryan," Bride said, unwilling to let it go. "We're going to hire a lawyer. You can't do this to us!" Her tone was venomous.

He laughed at her. "But I did, sweetie. And incidentally, none of you has a leg to stand on, Bride. Dad's will only said I had to marry before my fortieth birthday, which isn't until next April. That was it. I'm married, legally and lawfully under the laws of this state. I didn't even have to have a church wedding, just get married—and I did." Bride hung up on her brother, and Ryan closed his cell, sticking it back in his pocket.

"I take it she wasn't happy," Ashley said softly. "I'm sorry, Ryan."

"They're only interested in the money," he told her. "Don't feel bad, baby. Frankie and I were always the outsiders where the five harpies were concerned. Bride was thirteen when I was born, and fifteen when Frankie came along. Dee, who's the youngest of them, was four. And I was a boy, and suddenly the family had its prince." He grinned. "They have never been happy with me." He chuckled.

"I'm sorry," she said.

"Don't be." He caught her hand up and kissed it. "Frankie and I were partners in crime. Ma and Dad spoiled us. And the harpies didn't count for us."

And then they heard a strident voice. "Don't bother announcing me, Byrnes. I know my way to the porch."

"Jesus Jenny!" Ashley swore softly as a plump blonde in a pink-green-and-white summer dress came into view. "It's all right, Byrnes. Let her in, please."

"Ashley! What did you do?" the woman cried, and, seeing Ryan, her blue eyes grew wide with both surprise and admiration.

"Hello, Lila. It's been a while," Ashley said. "The paper is out, I take it. Ryan, this is Lila Peabody, Grandfather's friend. Lila, this is my husband, Ryan Mulcahy."

"Why, Mr. Mulcahy," Lila Peabody cooed, suddenly all sugar and spice, "aren't you just the handsomest thing! Ashley, dear, you really are very, very naughty keeping such a secret from all of us, but then, of course, after your last three attempts at marriage I can certainly understand. She did tell you that she'd been engaged and planned three weddings before she married you, didn't she?" Lila purred.

"One was gay, one died, and the survivor is wanted in two states and three countries. Yes, she told me," Ryan answered. "Ashley and I don't have any secrets from each other, do we, darling?"

"Not a one," Ashley replied, struggling not to laugh. "Lila, dearest, would you like to see the proofs of our wedding photos? We got them a few days ago, but we've been so busy with ..." She giggled. "Well, I expect you know what we've been busy doing."

"Why, yes, I would like to see them," Lila Peabody said. "There were only three pictures in the paper, and they were rather grainy."

Ashley slid the proofs from their envelope and spread them on the porch table.

"You were married in the garden," Lila noted. "How long have you known each other, dear?"

"A little over two months," Ashley said.

"It was love at first sight," Ryan added.

"Oh, my," Lila commented. "The judge married you. He rarely does that, you know. No church wedding?"

"We're deciding which church," Ryan said. "I'm a Roman Catholic."

"Oh, dear!" Lila made a little moue with her cupid's-bow mouth. "I don't think dearest Edward would have approved of that at all, Ashley."

"Then he shouldn't have put that clause in his will, Lila. Or he should have at least stipulated more clearly the kind of man he wanted me to marry. I figured Ryan was sexy and rich and he didn't need my money, which certainly made him a good bet."

"And besides, we can't keep our hands off each other," Ryan put in with a wicked grin at Lila Peabody. "Neither of us wanted to start a scandal." He chuckled.

"Oh, my!" Lila exclaimed, flustered.

"That's my mother-in-law"—Ashley pointed to one of the pictures—"and Ryan's sister." She shook a warning finger at him, but she was close to laughter.

"My goodness, what a handsome woman, and your sister is certainly pretty. She isn't married?" Lila wanted to know. "And your father? Is there a picture of him here?"

"Both my sister and my mother are widows," Ryan responded.

"Oh, the poor dears!" Lila exclaimed. "I certainly know the sorrow and loneliness of being a widow." She sighed dramatically, her hand going to her heart.

"Yes, Lila has really struggled valiantly to overcome her pain," Ashley remarked sweetly.

Lila reached out with a plump and very beringed hand to pat Ashley on her slender hand. "You always understood me, dear," she said. "Edward was forever remarking on your kind heart and infallible instincts where humanity was concerned. And dear Edward was never wrong. No engagement ring, dear?" But her sharp eye noted the superior quality of Ashley's diamond wedding band.

"It was a whirlwind courtship," Ashley said.

"Actually, I'm having a ring made for Ash in Italy by a jeweler friend," Ryan said. "My business requires that I travel now and again."

Now Ashley drew Lila away from the pictures, saying, "Lila, dear, I hope you won't think us terribly rude, but we're on our honeymoon this week. Ryan has to go back into town on Tuesday. It was so sweet of you to stop by." She began leading their guest from the porch through the living room and out into the foyer of the house.

"Then you'll be moving to the city, dear?" Lila said.

"My dear Lila—I may call you Lila, mayn't I?" Ryan murmured as he took her hand and put it through his arm. "We would never trade Egret Pointe and this beautiful home for a city apartment. I may go in a day or two a week, but I can easily run my business from here."

He smiled down at her, pleased when a glazed look overcame her.

Lila Peabody sighed. "You have just gone and married the most charming man, Ashley, dear," she said. "I hope you will bring him to tea one afternoon this autumn."

Before Ashley could answer, Ryan did. "I would be delighted to take tea with such a lovely lady, Lila," he told her. "Just give me a little time to settle in, my dear."

Byrnes was opening the door, and Ashley stood spellbound, watching as her husband saw the now awed Lila Peabody to her car and stood in the drive before the house, waving her off.

Byrnes was chuckling softly. "I think you've married a dangerous man, Miss Ashley," he told her with a smile.

"I suspect you are right," Ashley agreed. "I've never seen that wretched woman managed so well, and she didn't utter a word about SSEXL."

"Yes, she did," Ryan said, coming back into the house. "When I kissed her hand and tucked her in her Ford Taurus, she told me coyly that SSEXL's loss was certainly Egret Pointe's gain." He laughed. "Now if only the five harpies could be handled as well."

They spent the remainder of the week and the long weekend alone, eating, drinking, and making wild, passionate love. When Tuesday came Ashley found she was unhappy to be letting him go.

"When will you be home?" she asked him as she stood by his car.

"Thursday night," he promised. "Don't make any plans for the weekend. I want you all to myself. Now that I've had a little taste of married life I find I like it."

"Don't go all possessive on me, Ryan," she teased him. "What you really like about marriage is fucking the ears off of me between naps."

"Yes, I do," he agreed amiably, and raced his engine several times. "You are a very receptive partner, and I expect by Thursday night you will be well rested, and ready to pleasure me once again, woman."

"Yeah, sure!" She laughed. "You're going to miss me, big guy, and every time you think about us you'll get hot. Drive carefully, husband."

He grinned, blew her a kiss, and drove off down the driveway.

Ashley got into her Solstice and drove down into the village to her shop. It was almost ten when she arrived. Nina had already opened up, but the mornings were traditionally slow. Most women in Egret Pointe would be hurrying to get last-minute school supplies and clothing for their children, because school started tomorrow. "Hey," she greeted Nina as she came in the back door of the shop.

"How was your time off?" Nina asked her.

"Strangely wonderful," Ashley said. "It seems that we're very compatible."

"I'm glad you're here," Nina said. "Odd little man came in first thing this morning. He wanted to know if I was you. I told him no, and asked if I could help him. He said no, and left. But I've seen him across the street, and I think he's taking pictures of the shop with his camera phone."

"Where?" Ashley asked.

"There." Nina pointed.

Ashley picked up the shop phone and dialed. "Bobby, it's Ashley at Lacy Nothings. Funny little guy came into the shop before I got here and started asking Nina all kinds of questions. He's across the street, in front of the pharmacy, taking pictures of the shop right now. Can you send someone around to check him out? Thanks, Bobby."

"Wow, you play rough!" Nina said.

"Ryan's five older sisters are very unhappy," Ashley told her. "I suspect this has something to do with them. Oh, look. There's the cop car."

They watched as the local patrolman got out of his car and faced the man down. The cop took the guy by the arm and marched him across the street into the shop. "This the guy, Nina?"

"That's him," Nina said.

"He's a licensed PI from the city," the cop said, looking at Ashley.

"Would you like to tell me why you were looking for me, and why you are photographing my assistant and my shop?" Ashley said.

"I'm on a case," the man said. "It's confidential."

"Well," Ashley replied, "you tell whichever of my husband's sisters who hired you that if they attempt to invade my privacy again I will take legal action against all of them. Now, I am going to call Ryan and tell him of this incident. I'm certain that shortly after I do you will receive a call to cease and desist your harassment. Got it?"

"Got it," the man said.

"Shall I escort him out of town, Ashley?" the cop asked.

"If you would, Bill, I would appreciate it. And tell Bobby I said thanks."

"You got some pull here, lady," the private detective said.

"My family helped found the town," Ashley told him. "Now, that's something you can tell your employer. You won't be going back empty-handed."

The man gave a short laugh as the cop escorted him from Lacy Nothings.

"What was that all about?" Nina said. "Why would his sisters set a private detective on you? What did you do?"

"I married their brother. They were expecting to come into his wealth in a few more months, and I've spoiled it for them. They told Ryan they were getting a lawyer. It won't do them any good, but they're unhappy."

"Geez," Nina exclaimed. "What a bunch of bitches. The mother likes you, and so does the sister called Frankie. What's the matter with the rest of them?"

"Ryan and Frankie call the older ones the five harpies," Ashley said with a chuckle. "I'd better call him now. Hold down the fort while I go back to my office." She already had her cell out, and it was programmed to reach his cell.

"This is Ryan," his voice said. "Talk fast. I'm on the parkway."

"Your sisters set a private investigator on me," Ashley said. "I've had the cops escort him out of town. Call them when you get into your office. I'll talk to you later."

"Shit!" he said as she hung up.

Ashley laughed out loud. What was that old saying about being able to pick your friends, but not your relations? She was glad Ryan's mother and youngest sister liked her. She liked them. But the older five, she suspected, would never be her friends. They would always consider that by marrying Ryan she had cost them his money. It had been an incredible ten days with her new husband, but this incident this morning had been irritating and downright annoying.

She managed to put it out of her mind for the rest of the day, but once she was home again it nagged at her to the point where she couldn't sleep. There was no television in the bedroom she shared with Ryan. Getting up, she went down to her old bedroom and climbed into bed. Taking up the remote, she pressed the button that slid open the panel covering the television screen. She clicked the set on, went to channel sixty-nine, and after a moment or two of silent debate she pressed A and enter. And she was back in her villa in Rome, and the sex slave, Quinn, was kneeling before her, offering her the strap she would shortly use on his bottom. But she didn't want the handsome slave. She wanted her tribune, Maximillian Alerio Patronius. And she wanted him now!

Chapter Seven

"Where is your master?" the lady Cordelia asked Quinn. "You are not supposed to show yourself if he is in the house."

"He was called to the palace, mistress," Quinn replied. "I have missed you."

"Bold creature!" she scolded him, looking down at the big hands holding the leather tawse. "How do you know where he has gone? The tribune cannot bear the sight of you, so why would he inform you of his whereabouts?" She did not take the tawse up.

"One of the other slaves tells me where the master is at all times so I will not offend him even by accident," Quinn answered her. "If I have displeased you, mistress, then you must punish me." He looked up at her hopefully.

"No," she said. "I am not in the mood to punish you now. How long has my husband been gone?"

"Less than half an hour, and it takes that long to get through the midday streets to the palace, mistress," he said slyly. "He will undoubtedly be kept waiting by Caesar for some time. Perhaps the rest of the day. And then he must make his way home again. You may not see the master until midnight, mistress, or even tomorrow." Reaching out, he slipped his hand beneath the hem of her tunic and up her leg.

Ashley looked down at him thoughtfully. If what he said was true, then it would be some time until she saw the tribune. Fingers caressed the soft flesh of her inner thigh. They slid through her nether lips, seeking her clit. "You are a bad slave, Quinn," she told him as he began to tease at the sensitive little nub. "Ummm, yes, that is nice."

"I but live to serve you, mistress," Quinn answered her.

She pulled her tunic up over her head and off, tossing it aside. "Lick me, you bad creature," she ordered him.

He parted the lips of her labia with his two thumbs, holding them wide. Then his tongue began to draw over her flesh, first up one side, and then down, repeating the action on the other side of her nether lips. The tip of his tongue delved about her clit, probing, teasing at it, until it began to swell with her arousal. The sounds coming from her told him he was succeeding in pleasuring her. Leaning as close as he might get to her, her scent filling his nostrils and exciting him, he took her clit into his mouth and sucked hard upon it. She screamed softly, squirming. He sucked harder, two of his long fingers now pushing into her vagina. Two strokes, and she climaxed.

Without asking her permission he pulled her down to the floor with his big hands. Spreading her wide, he mounted the woman beneath him and thrust his engorged penis into the hot swamp of her fevered sex. Her nails raked his long back, and she scolded him for his boldness, all the while exhorting him to fuck her hard and deep. "I live to serve you, mistress," he repeated, his long, thick rod flashing back and forth with increasing rapidity while she thrashed beneath him in a frenzy of lust. And then she came. Her juices flowed copiously as he spasmed within her.

"Get off of me, you great beast!" she finally said. "Now I will whip you for your presumption, Quinn!" She pushed at him.

"If I were still the warrior I was born," he told her daringly, "I would fuck you again and again, mistress, until you begged for my mercy."

"Would you?" she purred at him as he rolled away from her. Then, getting to her feet, she picked up the leather that had earlier rested in his hands. "Get on your hands and knees now, Quinn!" she ordered him. And when he had obeyed her she laid five strokes upon his broad back, now well marked by her sharp nails. "Now leave me," she told him when she had finished. "You are beginning to bore me, I fear."

He scrambled to his feet, a puzzled look upon his handsome face, and left her. The lady Cordelia called to her slave women and went to her bath, where she was scraped free of the dirt and sweat upon her body, bathed, rinsed, and then left for a short while in a perfumed bathing pool. When she finally emerged she was thoroughly dried, and then massaged with fragrant creams until she was completely relaxed again.

The sex slave had taken the edge off of her lust, but she wanted her husband, the tribune, between her legs, not Quinn. If Caesar did indeed return him to Gaul she would go with him. And she was going to sell Quinn. General Flavonius's wife had admired him from the first time she had seen him at a party several of the women held for their amusement while their husbands were away. Indeed, many of the women had coveted Quinn. She would hold an auction and let him go to the highest bidder. She spent the rest of the day napping, eagerly awaiting her husband's arrival home. And when he finally arrived she melted into his arms.

"I have missed you the day long, Max," she told him.

"I am to be sent back to Gaul," he said, his lips brushing hers.

"I will go with you," the lady Cordelia said.

"It is not Rome," he replied.

"We will make it our own little Rome," she responded.

"My villa is not large, and it has not the amenities of this one," he warned her.

"We will enlarge it and add what we need, Max. I don't want to be without you any longer. And I am going to sell Quinn. Many of my friends have admired him. I should realize a nice profit from the sale, and I will use it to make our new home perfect."

"I think you will regret your decision, Cordelia, but I am not unhappy to have you come. It is lonely in northern Gaul, and cold," he warned her.

"And your whores smell," she teased him. "Now you will not have to avail yourself of those savage females, Max, for you will have me to fuck whenever you want to, my darling!"

"I am of a mind to fuck you now, wife, for your speech excites me," he told her, pulling her into his arms, one hand kneading her breast. "Yes, I very much want to fuck you right now!" he said, yanking his garment off.

She felt his cock—thick, hard, long—against her belly, and she was so eager for him. And then Ashley heard the *ping* of The Channel's warning bell. "Damn!" she swore as she felt her fantasy sliding away, and she awoke in her bed alone. Wednesday. It was Wednesday, and she had two long days and another long night ahead of her before Ryan got home. She rolled over, and slipped back into sleep for a few more hours.

He hadn't gotten back to her yesterday after she had called him about his sisters, but she expected he would eventually. The five harpies were his problem. Yesterday's little incident had made it certain in her mind that she wasn't going to like them at all. She and her brother had never been like that with each other. They had gladly shared everything they had between them. If one had a success, the other cheered that success. Oh, yes, she and Ben had had their disagreements, but neither of them would have ever deliberately tried to hurt the other. She didn't understand how his sisters could be that way. It wasn't as if their father hadn't remembered them when he died. Two hundred and fifty thousand dollars each was a damned nice inheritance. And it had been Ryan who had seen that they got that money. Money he had made for their father.

Lacy Nothings was being inundated with new merchandise when Ashley got down to the shop. Jerry, their UPS man, was lugging it all in from his truck and piling it on the counters and floor.

He grinned as he handed her the clipboard to sign. "Looks like Christmas is coming," he said. "Do you think that teddy I ordered for my girlfriend is in one of those boxes? It sure looked sexy in the catalog, Ms. Kimbrough. And thanks for getting it in her size. Not many shops carry sexy stuff above a twelve."

"I'll go through the shipment today and see," Ashley promised him, signing, and then handing him back his clipboard. "It should be in this shipment or the next. We'll have it in time for her birthday next month, I promise. And it's Mrs. Mulcahy now. I got married August twenty-fifth."

"I thought I heard some gossip around the village about that," Jerry admitted. He had been the UPS man in Egret Pointe for almost fifteen years now. He knew everyone and just about everything that happened in the town.

"What's the gossip on Emily Devlin?" Nina asked boldly.

"I just delivered some baby things over there on Friday," Jerry said. "Essie says she won't get a nanny cause she likes being a mom. She's hurrying to finish her latest book," Jerry informed them. "You can tell she's real Egret Pointe, like you are, Mrs. Mulcahy. She's got that good work ethic. Well, gotta go. Truck is pretty full today."

"That man knows everything that's to know," Nina said with a chuckle.

Before Ashley might answer, her cell rang, and, pulling it from the pocket of her slacks, she flipped it open. "This is Ashley," she said.

"Hey, wife," she heard Ryan's voice. "I got your message yesterday. Sorry I couldn't get back to you. I had to take care of the problem personally, Ash. You aren't upset, are you? I really apologize for the harpies."

Ashley moved from the shop floor into her office as he was talking. Now she sat down at her desk. "Yes, I was upset," she said. "But I got over it. What the hell is the matter with those women, Ryan? A private investigator? What do they think you married, anyway? I don't know whether to laugh or get mad."

"Well, first off, they're sure the marriage isn't legal. And they're sure you're nothing more than a gold digger out for my money, and I'm too dumb to realize it," he said. "Flattering, huh? But what do I know? I only took a nice little restoration shop and morphed it into a multimillion-dollar business."

"How did they find me?" Ashley wanted to know.

"Kathleen is married to a cop. Well, actually he isn't a beat cop anymore. He's up there in the police hierarchy. He used some contacts of his to track you down, at my sister's urging. Kevin is actually a decent guy. Not too bright, but decent."

"That is a serious violation of my privacy and my rights," Ashley said angrily.

"Look, I spent all day yesterday visiting each of my sisters personally. And I went downtown to One Police Plaza and spoke with Kevin. I had him call Judge Palmer, and we got him to fax a copy of our marriage license to Kevin. I told my brother-in-law that I would be visiting all my sisters with the copy, and he was to talk with the other brothers-in-law, and tell them that if their wives tried any more nonsense, our next step would be legal."

"And?" Ashley said.

"Kevin took care of the guys, and I took care of my sisters. They aren't happy about the fact that I'm married, but they're stuck with it," Ryan said. "Ash, I apologize. I never thought they would go crazy-crazy. I didn't realize how out of touch with reality the thought of getting their hands on all that money would make them." He sounded very embarrassed, and for a moment she felt sorry for him.

"Right now I'm not certain I want to meet them," she told him candidly.

"I don't blame you," he responded.

"But I'll do the October thing for your mom's sake. Not a whole weekend, like I was planning, though, Ryan. If your sisters were counting on grabbing your money that much, then they aren't going to have calmed down in a month. They might never calm down over this, and while that's their problem, I don't want to have to put up with it. I'm good to a point," Ashley told him.

"I understand," he said.

"We'll invite them for the day, and make it easy for them by hiring a stretch limo to bring them out and take them home," Ashley said.

"Let's do it Saturday, so we have the rest of that long weekend just for us," he suggested. "Now, don't let this go to your head, but I missed you last night." His voice was warmer than it had been previously.

She smiled. "Yeah, me too," Ashley admitted. "Do you have to stay away until Thursday night?"

"Yeah, I have to, baby. I lost a whole day yesterday running uptown, downtown, and into suburbia dealing with the harpies. And then I had to stop and tell Frankie what went down, and go see Ma, and tell her everything was all right. I didn't get to my office until late afternoon. That's why I didn't call you. I worked until almost one this morning, and then I just crashed where I was. I haven't even gone back to my apartment yet to change my clothing. I'll do that later, as I have clients coming in from Europe. I just wanted to make sure you were all right."

"I'm fine, Ryan. I'm tough, and I don't collapse too easily," Ashley told him. "Anything special you'd like for dinner tomorrow night? And incidentally, what time do you think you'll be home?"

"Steak," he said with male predictability. "I'll try to get there by eight."

"I'll see you then," she said.

"Say hello to the girls for me," he teased her, and then he asked mischievously, "Are you blushing, Ash?"

"Bite me!" she shot back, and she heard his laughter as she flipped her cell shut. She *was* blushing. She didn't need a mirror to feel the warmth flooding her cheeks. And her nipples were tingling with the thought of his mouth on them. *Damn!* What was the matter with her? She had always enjoyed good sex, but now her mind was consumed with it, despite her evening on The Channel. The fantasy wasn't enough. She wanted reality. She wanted her sexy husband, a man she hadn't even known three months ago. Tonight she would try the B fantasy. Maybe being dominated by Rurik would ease her.

"Oh, no!" she heard Nina's voice exclaim.

Ashley got up and went back out into the shop. "What's the matter?"

"Elegance sent the wrong size for Jerry's girlfriend's gift. They sent a six instead of a sixteen," Nina said irritably. "And you know how long it always takes to get an order from them, Ashley. Her birthday is early in October."

"You know what to do," Ashley said. "Call. Get tough, but remind them we have two new shops opening this autumn, and I can't do business with a firm that's unreliable," she said. "Listen, can you handle the shop alone for a while?"

"Are you all right?" Nina asked, her voice concerned.

"I just need to take a ride," Ashley told her.

"You miss him, huh?" Nina cocked an eyebrow.

Ashley sighed. "Yeah. Who would have thunk it?"

"Are you falling in love with him? Wouldn't that be nice," Nina remarked.

"I don't know. Maybe. If he loved me back, but he's as wrapped up in his business as I am in mine," Ashley said.

"You're not so wrapped up now," Nina noted.

"But he is," Ashley said.

Nina watched the younger woman as she left the shop and climbed into her Solstice. The car's top was down today. It pulled out of the back parking lot with a small roar. Nina knew exactly where Ashley would go. She'd drive up to the Egret Pointe Overlook, park, and sit looking at the bay until she had sorted out whatever it was she needed to sort out in her head. Nina picked up the phone and dialed Elegance.

The sky above her was crystal blue as Ashley drove out of the village and up the coast road. The sun was bright, the air clean. She could feel autumn coming, and it was her favorite season of the year. She pulled into the overlook and parked, her bumper just an inch from the stone wall. There was one nice-sized sailboat crossing the bay below, but with Labor Day over and done there wouldn't be too many boats out on the weekday water until next summer. The weekends would be busy for a while, but then it would be empty but for migrating whales and the seals.

Nina's question had really touched a nerve. Was she falling in love with Ryan? And if she was, how was she going to keep it from him? Because of course she would have to keep it from him. They had married for practical reasons. Yet their marriage might last. He said he wanted it to last. And the sex was beyond great. It was true that they had a great deal in common with each other. And the sex was incredible, she thought again. But there was no cause for her to go falling in love with her husband and messing things up. She wasn't going to push him to the wall, like his older sisters did. She was going to be a good friend, wife, and lover. And if it ended maybe they could remain friends.

So why was she thinking about babies? She had always assumed she would have kids when she got married. But this wasn't that kind of marriage. Yet she had been thinking about babies ever since that first night. A plump, roly-poly infant with dark curls and big brown eyes. A boy. He wanted a boy. She could almost hear a baby giggle. "What the hell is the matter with me?" Ashley asked herself out loud. Above her a gull squawked noisily. It had to be her biological clock, she decided. She was going to be thirty-four in December, and that clock was ticking louder with each passing day. She needed chocolate. Chocolate always calmed her when she found herself filled with irrational thoughts like this. With a deep sigh she turned the car's engine on and, backing out of the overlook, headed to the village. It was a workday, not a holiday.

"Have a nice think?" Nina asked as she reentered the shop.

"Did you reach Elegance?" Ashley inquired in return, ignoring Nina's question.

"They were not pleasant about it," Nina said. "At first they accused me of poor handwriting on the order, until I reminded them that this order was phoned in, so if the handwriting was had it was their own, not mine. Then they said they were already in the throes of making and shipping stuff for Christmas, and they didn't have time to make a single item. So I reminded them that Lacy Nothings has been a client for five years, and that we will have two new shops open by Thanksgiving. If they expect to see their merchandise in those shops they will get that teddy in a size sixteen to us ASAP."

"And they agreed," Ashley said.

"They said they will try," Nina replied, and then stepped back to wait for the explosion that was certain to follow.

"Call them back. Tell them if that teddy isn't here by Friday that Lacy Nothings will be canceling our current orders and returning the merchandise currently in our possession. And before they make any decision to irritate me further, they might want to check to see how much business we do with them annually. Now I need to redo the front windows," Ashley said. "I think we should do a back-to-school theme."

"With underwear?" Nina giggled.

"Why not?" Ashley said with a grin. "I'll go the mall, and get some school supplies at Wal-Mart." And she was out the door again.

By late afternoon the two front windows of the shop were done, and both women had to admit it was a successful venture. Some of their most modest yet outrageously sexy garments were displayed among black-and-white composition books, bright yellow Number Two pencils, rulers, colorful folders, crayons, protractors, and big pink erasers. Each window had an antique circa-1940s school bag and tin lunch box, next to which was a bright red polished apple. In one window was an old-fashioned blackboard pointer. In the other was an antique paddle once used by teachers to punish recalcitrant students.

"Too suggestive?" Ashley asked her assistant.

"No, it's daring," Nina said. "And I'll bet we get asked if they're for sale more times than not. Where did you get the paddle?"

"I borrowed it from the Egret Pointe Museum's Little Red Schoolhouse," Ashley said with a laugh. "It pays to be the last descendant of a town founder."

Nina laughed. "Hey, I'm all for nepotism," she said. "Well, if you don't need me to lock up, I'm off. I want to eat early tonight. I've programmed a new fantasy for myself having to do with a guy who looks like Cesar Romero."

"Dirty girl!" Ashley chuckled. "Have fun!" She waved Nina off. She remained in her office for another two hours, catching up with the paperwork. Then, locking up, she headed for her car. She didn't bother going to the bank. She kept the shop's proceeds with her when she went home. When she had first opened someone had broken in during the night, but as her register was empty they had gotten nothing. She had put in a security system, reinforced the doors, and never been robbed again. Even Egret Pointe, perfect as it was, had its modicum of crime.

Wednesday was one of the Byrneses' days off, but Mrs. B. had left Ashley a small chicken pot pie that only needed heating up. She poured herself a glass of iced tea and carried her meal out into the kitchen garden to eat at a small round table that was set up there in the warm weather. She ate slowly, shooing away the wasps that always seemed to appear at an outdoor meal in late summer. She had had a call today from the contractor working on the two new stores. They would be ready for viewing next week. She would have to spend a few days in the city interviewing prospective employees for that shop, and then she would have to go into suburbia to interview for the mall store. It was going to be a busy few months. She wanted both stores open by mid-October. She would have to make a reservation at a hotel—and then it dawned on her that her husband had an apartment. Why couldn't she stay there?

Finished with her supper, Ashley returned to the kitchen and put her plate and glass into the dishwasher. Spying a covered plate of Mrs. B.'s rich, gooey brownies, she took it with her upstairs. The house was quiet. Stripping off her clothing, Ashley stepped into her shower for a leisurely wash. She had just gotten out and wrapped a towel around herself when her bedside phone rang. Picking it up, she heard Ryan's voice.

"What are you wearing?" he asked provocatively.

"A towel. I just got out of the shower. Why?" she asked.

"Unwrap it and get naked," he replied.

"Hold on," Ashley said, laughing. "I'm putting you on speaker. Okay. The towel is gone, Ryan. Now what?"

"I want you to begin to fondle the girls, baby. Close your eyes and cup them in your palms. Now begin to tease those sexy nipples of yours. Do you know how badly I want to suck on those pretties? I want you to think about me doing that, Ashley. Think about my hot mouth closing over your nipples one at a time, drawing on them, my tongue lapping at them, nibbling them, until you want to scream. Pull the nipples out, baby, and pinch them. Doesn't that feel good?"

Jesus Jenny, he was starting to excite her with his words! "Ummm," she murmured. "I'd rather it were you, Ryan," she told him.

"I want you to lie down on the bed now," he said. "You know what I'm doing? I'm unzipping my pants and pulling my cock out. I'm already getting hard just thinking about those delicious tits of yours. Press them together, Ashley, and think about my cock sliding back and forth between them."

Ashley lay back on her bed and contemplated his words. She was surprised to find herself getting hot. "Your big boy likes playing with the girls, doesn't he?" she purred at her husband. "Ohh, he's getting so hard, and he's being very naughty. He's kissing my nipples." She had never had phone sex before, and she decided it was fun.

"I want you to slowly let your hands move down your body, Ash," he said softly. "I want you to close your eyes and think they're my hands. I love touching you, baby. You have such incredibly soft skin, and it always smells so damned good. I'm touching you, and my mouth is following my hands. I'm kissing your belly, and now I'm sliding between your thighs and kissing them."

"Ohh, yes!" Ashley said. This was exciting, and it was fun.

"I want you to play with yourself, baby. I want you to find your clit and play with it the way I do. Pretend my tongue is doing you. Are you getting wet?"

"Yes!" she told him. She was indeed getting wet.

"I've got my cock in my hand now. I'm thinking about your lips closing over it and sucking me. Yeah! Yeah! That's good, baby. Do you want to come? I'm close, but I'd much rather be at home pushing myself deep inside of you. Think about it, Ashley. I'm hard, and I'm moving faster, and faster, and faster. You want it so badly you're aching to come. When I get home tomorrow night I'm going to fuck you that way." He could hear her breathing, excited and quick. "Tell me you want me to fuck you, Ash!"

"Oh, God, yes!" Her fingers worked her clit hard, and then she sobbed, "Oh, I'm coming, Ryan! I'm coming!"

"Me too." He groaned. "But it's just not enough. I need the real thing!"

"I know." She gasped. And then as her heart slowed a bit, she said, "Maybe we could figure a way for you to work from home? At least until we're a little less hot for sex with each other."

He laughed weakly. "It's definitely a thought, baby."

"I thought you had clients in from Europe? Didn't you take them to dinner?"

"Drinks. They had theater tickets," he said. "So here I am all alone in the apartment, thinking about my hot wife."

"You think I'm hot?" She was surprised.

"I think you're very hot," he replied. "Don't tell me no one ever said you were hot, Ashley?" He was surprised.

"Nope. I've been called beautiful, pretty, smart, clever, sexy. But never hot," she told him. "I'm glad you think I'm hot. I like being hot for you."

"Ashley?"

"Yes, Ryan."

"I do think this might work for real," he said low. "And it isn't just the sex."

"We haven't known each other that long, Ryan," she told him. But she was smiling. "I don't want you to be disappointed. I don't want to be disappointed."

"But we're married, baby," he said.

"A marriage of convenience," she reminded him.

"But it doesn't have to be," he said again.

"No, it doesn't," Ashley responded. "But let's give it a little more time, okay?" Oh, this felt so right, she thought. And he felt it too. Or was it just relief at having preserved their assets, and the easy sex? Guys didn't always think straight when their dicks were involved. "I liked the phone sex," she said softly.

"I liked it too, but I think the real thing is better," he answered her.

"Much, much better," she agreed. "You have the most talented cock. All eleven inches of it." Then she giggled. "I can't believe you measured it. Or are you just joking?"

"Got a soft tape measure?" he asked.

"In my sewing box," she said.

"Get it out and we'll measure it tomorrow night, baby," he said.

"Ryan!" she squealed.

"No, no! You've impugned my dick. I need my honor restored, and the only way we can do that is for you to measure it. And after you have then I'm going to stick it as deep inside you as I can and fuck the ears off of you, Ashley Mulcahy. So just think about that before you go to sleep tonight. That is, if you can sleep. Thinking about you all naked and sweet-smelling right now, I don't think I can sleep."

"I'm going to sleep like a baby," she teased him. "Good night, darling."

"Good night, baby," he responded, and the line went quiet. She had called him *darling*. He smiled.

Ashley stuck the phone back in its charger. Getting up, she went into her dressing room and took a sleep shirt from a hanger, putting it on. Suddenly she didn't feel like The

Channel. She didn't need it. Instead of going down the hall to her old bedroom she climbed into their big bed, and actually did fall asleep clutching the pillow Ryan used, smelling the faint scent of his aftershave. She didn't need the fantasy of rough sex tonight. She had a sexy husband to keep her happy.

The following day seemed to drag. To her amusement Jerry's teddy arrived FedEx overnight express. It was a size sixteen, and the right color. But she had caught up with all her paperwork, and the shop was busy all morning and then slow all afternoon. But people kept stopping and looking in the windows, the men thoughtful, the women giggling and poking one another.

"We ought to start thinking about the Halloween windows," Nina said.

"We'll do a variation on the usual," Ashley told her. "I found some really fabulous carnival masks, the kind you might see in New Orleans or Rio or in Cannes. I want you to look through all the new stock and pick out the sexiest black outfits we've got. The naughtier the better. I'll be watching the farm stands for the perfect pumpkins. I'm going into town next week for a few days. The contractor says the new shops are ready. Do you mind holding down the fort while I'm gone?"

"What about staffing for the new places?" Nina wondered.

"I'll be doing that. Any suggestions?"

"I've got a friend in the city who was just retired from the garment biz. She'd been with this company for thirty years, but the boss, an old fart himself, got talked into hiring a younger woman by his son. It's a mistake, but Suzette is really too young to retire. She's only mid-fifties. She would make a great manager for the city store," Nina said. "If you're interested I'll call her, and you can meet next week."

"Yes, please call her," Ashley said. "She sounds ideal, if she would be interested. Tell her I'll pay health insurance and contribute to a retirement savings for her, as well as her salary. She and I can negotiate that."

Nina nodded.

"Ryan's coming home tonight, so I'll leave you to close the shop," Ashley said.

"Sounds like you'll be glad to see him." Nina chuckled.

"Yeah, I will. Say, how did Cesar Romero go?" she asked the older woman.

"Didn't live up to his promise, I'm afraid," Nina said dryly as she waved her boss off with a grin. "It was like I knew him, but I didn't know him. It got uncomfortable."

"Be more daring," Ashley suggested, waving back. She was surprised to find Ryan home when she got there. Entering the house, she smelled roast beef cooking. Running upstairs to their bedroom suite she found him just coming out of his shower. "You came early!" she said happily.

"Mrs. B. says dinner won't be served until seven. Get out of your clothes, baby, and go fetch that measuring tape," he said. "You're home early too, and we have time for a nice leisurely fuck. I almost had an accident getting off the parkway thinking about you," Ryan told her.

Ashley giggled. "And just what were you thinking?" she asked him teasingly.

"Putting you on your back," he said predictably as he began to unbutton her shirt. He pushed it off her shoulders and, reaching out, unhooked her bra. Her breasts spilled out. "Hello, girls," he purred, tweaking each nipple. Then his hands clasped about her waist, and he lifted her up onto a small footstool. Unzipping her slacks, he pulled them down. Leaning forward, he began to lap at her nipples with his tongue as she kicked off her leather loafers and the pants at her feet. His hand reached out to cup her through her briefs, while his other hand held a breast so he might suckle on it.

She pressed herself against his palm, rubbing her pussy against him. "You're making me hot," she said softly.

In response he lifted her out of the pants around her ankles. "Go get the tape," he told her.

Ashley complied, taking the tape from her little wicker sewing basket and returning to stand before him. "It doesn't look like eleven inches right now," she said.

"That's because you haven't done your wifely duty," he told her. "I want you to suck me to a stand, baby. Then we'll measure."

Ashley slipped to her knees, and, taking his cock in her hand, she brought him to her open mouth. Her tongue slowly licked around the tip of him while her other hand slid beneath him to cup his balls in her hand, rolling them about her palm. She smiled at his intake of breath. Then she took him into her mouth and sucked hard. "Ummmm," Ashley murmured. She felt his big hand kneading her head as she sucked him sweetly. He was easily aroused, and shortly his cock was stretching her cheeks. She released him. "Time to face the truth. Are you in truth eleven inches long or have you begun to shrink with age?" she teased him wickedly as she picked up her tape, unrolling it from root to tip.

"Well?" he said, holding back his laughter.

"Wow! Eleven and a quarter inches, Ryan."

"Now measure around," he said.

"Ryan!" *Damn!* She felt her cheeks growing red, but she drew the tape about his cock, eyes widening as she saw the measurement.

"Well?" he growled.

"Two inches even," she squeaked, dropping the tape as his hands began to fondle her buttocks.

"And you are going to take every single inch of it, woman," he told her, and, pulling her close, he met her mouth with his in a scorching kiss. Their tongues intertwined in a leisurely dance. "Tell me you want it now," he murmured in her ear.

"Oh, yes," Ashley breathed. This was the perfect end to the last several days.

"You want me to put it in you, baby, don't you?" he teased her.

"Yes! Put that big cock of yours into my hot, wet pussy and fuck me senseless," she said, sliding her arms about his neck. "I want it, Ryan! I want it now!" She rubbed herself against him. Their naked bodies were heated. "Do it to me! Please!"

He didn't bother going to their bed. He sat down in the wing chair by the fireplace, pulling her with him. Ashley straddled him, and then slowly, slowly she impaled herself on his long, thick rod, sighing as she took it all inside her eager cunt. His hands reached up to grab her breasts, pinching the nipples, his eyes closed, his face blissful as the walls of her vagina enclosed him.

Oh, God, he felt good inside of her. Ashley sighed with pleasure as his length and width plumbed her heated depths. He actually throbbed within her. She rode him gently, at first moving from a walk to a jogging trot to a graceful canter, and finally into a frenzied gallop. His cock touched her G-spot, rubbing it, and she screamed softly with delight. "Oh, Ryan," she half sobbed, "this is so damned good! I'm going to come! I can't help it!" She felt the soft quivers as her climax began to rise up and roll over her.

He groaned, and his cock stiffened, then shuddered as his juices exploded, filling her, running down her thighs and into his pubic hair. "God, Ash! You are incredible!" He pulled her down and kissed her passionately, his fingers threading through her short dark hair.

She lay atop him for several minutes, breathing raggedly, feeling as limp as a rag doll. She had never had sex like this with anyone. Even the always-horny Chandler Wayne. But sex wasn't love. Wasn't a lifetime commitment. But it was becoming more for her than just that, Ashley realized. She was falling in love with him. It wasn't too soon. People fell in love at first sight, didn't they? But how did he feel? She was pretty good at reading people, but while she knew he liked her, she couldn't tell if it was more.

He held her close, feeling her heart beating in time with his. This was so right. Ashley. Kimbrough Hall. Coming home to her. If it got any more perfect he was going to think that he had died and gone to heaven. Just one thing was missing: He wanted kids. Did she want children too? Could he stay married to her if she didn't? Hell, wasn't that why the old man had put that damned clause in his will? He wanted Mulcahy grandchildren to carry on the name. And suddenly Ryan realized that so did he. So the apple didn't fall far from the tree after all, he thought wryly. He kissed the top of her head. "Maybe we ought to think about getting up?" he said.

"I know," she said, and straightened up. "But we have time. We'll have to shower before we get dressed and go down."

"Yeah," he grinned, waggling his eyebrows at her. "Let's shower."

Ashley laughed. "Oh, no," she said. "You'll go to your bathroom and I'll go to mine, darling. That way we'll get down to dinner on time, and Mrs. B.'s roast won't get overdone. Grandfather always said you don't want to shock the help or be late to the table, even if they are your friends. We'll probably eat out on the porch. It's still warm enough." She slipped off of his lap and headed for her bathroom.

He watched her go, appreciating her prettily rounded buttocks. She had a really nice butt, he thought to himself. Most of the women he had slept with looked great in their clothing, but not as good out of it. They had small breasts and virtually no butts. Ashley looked great both in and out of her clothing. He hauled himself out of the chair and headed for his own bathroom. Wild sex in an antique wing chair, he thought with a grin. Now there was something new for him.

Ashley wore a colorful cotton kaftan down to dinner. Taking his lead from her, Ryan had put on a pair of jeans and a dress shirt with the sleeves rolled up to the elbow. They were both barefooted.

"You don't mind if we're casual at dinner, do you?" she asked him. "Grandfather always wanted us to be formal, but after a long day at the shop I'm happy to be clean and comfortable." She dug into her salad.

"We can be formal when we entertain," he replied. "I like this."

"I have to be in town next week. The contractor is finished, or says he's finished, with both the shop there and at the mall. Could I stay at your apartment?"

"The bed is big enough for both of us," he said, smiling. "The place is small, though. I've never needed a big place, and I don't entertain there. Can I come with you when you see your contractor? I may not be the artisan my dad was, but I know good work."

Her first reaction was to be offended. Did he think she was some ditsy little idiot who didn't know if the contractor was stiffing her? But then, she thought, the truth was that she had never dealt with anyone outside of Egret Pointe until now. Oh, the contractor had come highly recommended, but still, it couldn't hurt to have an expert eye checking everything out. "I would appreciate it," she told him. "I know my own merchandise, but a new shop is a whole other thing. And it's got to be right. I want those stores open by the first week in November. Getting established in a new location for the Christmas trade is very important to my bottom line. But can you spare the time?"

"I can always spare the time for you," he said quietly. He had seen her hesitation, and it hadn't been difficult to imagine what she had been thinking when he made his offer. He was impressed that she had been able to swallow her pride and accept his help. It said a lot about Ashley's character, and the more he saw and learned, the more he realized that he honestly did like her. His mother had always said you should like the person you married as well as love them, because when the passion cooled you would have a best friend as well as a lover. He smiled, thinking his mother was a wise lady.

"Why are you smiling?" she asked him.

"I was thinking about something Ma always said. And I've just discovered that she's right." Then he told her.

"And that made you smile because...?"

Byrnes cleared the salad plates from the table.

"Because I realize that what began for us a few months ago as one thing is, at least for me, morphing into something entirely different," Ryan said softly. And his brown eyes engaged her green ones.

Ashley felt a warm wave of pleasure sweep over her. "For me too," she admitted, ignoring the blush spreading over her cheeks. It had become a fact of life: Ryan Finbar Mulcahy could make her blush.

"I don't want to pressure you into something you don't feel," he continued.

"I didn't say anything because I didn't want to push you either," Ashley replied.

"Then if I said I loved you it wouldn't send you screaming into the night?" His handsome, sexy face was suddenly boyish and hopeful.

"No." Her voice was practically a whisper. "And if I said I loved you, would you feel as if I had trapped you into a corner?" Her beautiful face held an anxious look.

"No, I wouldn't. I'd like to be in a corner with you," he told her. "Putting you right up against the wall, and—" He stopped as Byrnes set a plate before him.

The butler's face was totally impassive, and Ryan might have believed he was both deaf and dumb except that his ears were turning quite a bright red. But without a word the dignified Mr. Byrnes turned and made his way from the porch with his usual grace and decorum.

A fit of giggles overcame Ashley, and Ryan couldn't help chuckling himself.

"Oh, I'll never forgive us for embarrassing him like that," Ashley said.

"Sorry. I forgot myself for a moment," Ryan apologized to her.

"Oh, don't chastise yourself too much," Ashley said. "Once he was out of our sight I'll bet he ran all the way to the kitchen to tell Mrs. B. that we've fallen in love." She stopped, and then continued, "We have fallen in love, haven't we, Ryan? Or did I misunderstand you and make a dope of myself?"

Reaching across the table he took her hand and, raising it to his lips, kissed it. "You didn't misunderstand at all; nor did I. Yeah, I've fallen in love with you, baby. And I've never loved another woman before. Lusted after them, yeah. But never loved."

"And I love you too," Ashley said, tears in her eyes. "But I can't claim to have not said that before, because I have. But now I realize I didn't really know what the devil I was talking about. I didn't feel anything for Carson or Chandler or Derek that I feel for you, Ryan. I never thought about babies with them."

"You're thinking about babies with me?" His mouth turned up in a smile.

"Yeah, I am. A little boy with dark curls and big brown eyes like his daddy," she replied. "Crazy, huh?"

"How many babies?" he asked her.

"How many do you want?" she responded, smiling back at him.

"Three too many?" he said.

"Three's a good number," she agreed.

"Ashley?"

"Yes, Ryan?"

"I *really* do love you!"

"And I *really* love you," Ashley answered him. "Now eat your dinner, Ryan. Mrs. B. won't be very happy with us if we let this perfect roast of hers go to waste. And we won't be getting good corn like this much longer now that autumn's coming."

After dinner they made love again, and this time with such tenderness that Ashley cried when she came to climax. She was loved. She loved. Their crazy marriage of convenience had by some miracle turned into a love match. They were even talking about a family. She began to think that they would have to start thinking about a religious ceremony to formalize the love they admitted to having for each other. Lina would be so pleased, but first things first. She had two new shops to staff and open.

Ashley drove into town on Tuesday with her husband. They stopped at his apartment first. He introduced her to his doorman, explaining that his wife would be using the apartment now and again. The doorman, he knew, would spread the word to the superintendent and the other help in the building. Ashley already had a key, as they had had one made the previous day in Egret Pointe.

Her appointment for the city store was at eleven in the morning. Their car parked in his building's garage, they hailed a cab and headed back downtown. The contractor was a big, jovial fellow. Ashley had met him only once before. They had conducted most of their business on the telephone once she had hired him. He let them into the store, and Ashley's first reaction was delight. The fresh gray paint with its elegant white trim looked perfect. The pale silver-gray carpeting was plush. The display cases were ebony and glass. The lighting fixtures were discreet but for the elegant gold sconces on the walls. She checked the stockroom, the manager's office, the bathroom, the small lunchroom she had insisted upon for her employees. "What do you think?" she asked Ryan.

"It's good, but has the electric been upgraded to handle the computers, the register, and the security system?" he asked the contractor.

"I got the papers from the city inspector right here, Mr. Mulcahy," came the response. "The security system ain't hooked up yet, but the guy is coming next week."

"We're opening the first week in November," Ashley said.

"It'll be ready before then, I promise," the contractor replied.

"And the window painter for the shop's name and logo?" she wanted to know.

"Tomorrow. I wanted the best guy, and he's hard to get," the contractor explained. "You know about those things, Mr. Mulcahy."

"You know me?" Ryan said.

"My father knew your father," the contractor answered. "It's a small world when you're a woodworker."

Ryan nodded. "When can we see the mall store?"

"Tomorrow be all right, Miss Kim...Mrs. Mulcahy?" The contractor wisely addressed the question to Ashley. After all, she was paying him, not the husband.

"How about Thursday afternoon instead?" Ashley suggested. "Then we can just head out of town from there. Three o'clock?"

"That's fine with me, Miss Kim...Mrs. Mulcahy." He laughed. "I'll get it right eventually," the contractor promised.

"You had better," she said with a smile. "If these two shops do well I'll probably be opening a few more in the area."

"Yes, ma'am!" he responded with a broad grin.

Ryan left her afterward, and Ashley hurried to a luncheon meeting she had scheduled with Nina's friend Suzette. The two women met at Felicity's Tea Shoppe on Madison. Nina had reminded Ashley that the two women had met briefly when Suzette had visited Nina the previous year, and sure enough they recognized each other. They were seated, and as they ate lunch Ashley explained to Suzette what she wanted. Suzette assured her that she could handle the shop, asked some salient questions that impressed Ashley, and then the two women negotiated a salary. Ashley was rather relieved at what Suzette wanted. It was less than she had been prepared to pay, but as Nina told her later, Suzette's boss had had an investment retirement fund for his employees, and under the law Suzette had taken hers with her. She was comfortably fixed, and with Ashley picking up her medical insurance and adding to that fund, she could accept less of a salary.

"Do you want me to do the hiring for the shop?" Suzette asked. She was an elegant, well-spoken woman in her late fifties with stylishly cut short salt-and-pepper hair. Her makeup, Ashley noted, was flawless and natural-looking, her jewelry good. Suzette was just what Ashley was looking for. Nina was going to get a bonus for it.

"It would be a help if you did," Ashley replied.

"How many girls do you want?"

"Start with two. If you need more let me know. You might have to hire someone to temp for the holiday rush. I'm putting you in charge of the employees to start. Once you've learned the stock and what sells on the Upper East Side, then I'll probably ask you to do some ordering."

Suzette nodded. "I come from dresses and suits, but I learn fast," she said.

"Would you mind coming out to Egret Pointe soon? I'd like you to work with Nina and get an idea of the merchandise," Ashley said. "We're opening the first week in November. Hire your girls to begin the last week in October for paid training."

"No problem," Nina said.

Ashley spent the following day visiting the showrooms of some of her largest suppliers. She also found a new small showroom with some rather interesting and one-of-a-kind garments. She placed an order. On Thursday she and Ryan headed up to the suburban mall to meet the contractor and inspect the mall store. It was identical to the shop in town and in Egret Pointe. There were two women from a local employment agency waiting for her when they arrived. She interviewed them before the contractor got there, and hired one, a Mrs. Babcock, who had solid retail experience. She explained, as she had to Suzette, what her duties would be, and that she would be responsible for the hiring.

"You will have to come up to Egret Pointe shortly, along with the manager of the city store. I'll see you're both put up, and pay your expenses, of course."

"Certainly," said Mrs. Babcock, a slightly younger version of Suzette. "My husband is home every night, and the kids are in high school and presumably civilized. They can all manage without me for a few days."

Ashley was feeling very good as they returned home. Everything seemed to be going along perfectly. She was in love, and loved in return. Now all she had to do was face down her horrific in-laws. But with Ryan by her side she decided she could triumph over just about anything. And one day very soon her birth control pills were going to be dumped down the commode. Now that she had birthed three shops, she was ready to have that baby. And they were going to make such beautiful babies too.

Chapter Eight

The leaves had begun to turn, and Main Street in Egret Pointe was decorated once more to fit the season. The trees lining the street were surrounded with tall dried and colored cornstalks tied with wide bright-orange ribbons. Large, fat pumpkins in every possible shade a pumpkin could be grown, along with piles of green, yellow, white, and orange gourds, encircled the trees amid baskets of red and yellow apples. A large banner advertising the local Harvest Festival was slung across Main Street.

"We get to go on Sunday," Ashley told her husband. "We've got the harpies on Saturday. I'm going to ask your mom and Frankie to stay over."

"I thought we were going to have the rest of the weekend to ourselves," he complained. "Besides, Frankie won't be coming. It's parents' weekend up at St. Peter's, and she never misses one. And this is her last, as my nephew graduates in June."

"Can't I ask your mom?" Ashley said. "I like her, Ryan. I have only the barest memory of my own mother, because she died when I was fourteen. Oh, I've got a picture of her, but very few memories. And I missed having a mother. Your mother is cool. Look how she went to Ray to find a wife for you. And look how nice she's been to me, even if I wasn't quite the daughter-in-law she was expecting. Besides, do you want her having to ride home with the harpies and their husbands?"

"You're too softhearted, woman," he said, pulling her into his arms and giving her a kiss. "All right. Ask Ma if she'd like to stay. And call Frankie. She's been worried you'd be upset she couldn't come, but she didn't want to disappoint her kid."

The next day Ashley called her sister-in-law Frankie. "It's okay," she said to her. "I'll just deal with the harpies myself. I was going to ask you and your mom to stay over just to piss them off."

Frankie laughed. "Ma told me you called her this morning. She thinks you're sweet asking her to stay, and of course she's going to do it, because she had such a good time last time. I'm sorry to leave you with the harpies—well, not really, if you get my meaning—but my kid comes first, Ash. You'll understand when you have your own."

"So you'll come for Christmas with him and your mother, okay?" Ashley asked.

"Yes, we'll come," Frankie replied. She paused, then finally said, "You sound different. Really happy. I guess everything's all right with you and my brother."

"If that's your clever way of asking what's going on, I don't mind telling you. It seems that against all odds we have fallen in love," Ashley told her sister-in-law. "We're even talking babies, although I'm not quite ready to give up my birth control pills. I need to get these two new shops open and running smoothly."

"Oh, my God!" Frankie gasped. "I am so glad, Ash! For you and for my brother. He really is a good guy, and I want him to be happy. Does Ma know?"

"We're going to let her figure it out for herself." Ashley chuckled.

"Ashley, don't stop loving Ryan after you've met the harpies. *Please!*" Frankie said. "They'll start off semi-charming, but the mood will degenerate as the day goes on. It's the way they are. They've got the sibling-rivalry thing down pat, I'm afraid."

"I have to admit that I'll be glad to get it over and done with," Ashley admitted.

"I've got to go," Frankie said. "I've got a client coming in any minute. Good luck on Saturday, sweetie."

On Saturday morning they arose, ate a leisurely breakfast together, and then dressed to receive their guests. Ashley was wearing light wool slacks in a red-yellow-and-black Royal Stewart plaid, along with an off-white cotton cable-knit sweater with a round neckline. She had comfortable black leather boots on her feet. Ryan was wearing pale gray slacks and a taupe-colored Italian knit sweater in silk and cotton. He had expensive leather loafers on his feet. They were the picture of wealthy country casual.

At a little after eleven Ashley's cell rang. "This is Ashley," she said, picking up.

"It's Bill, Mrs. Mulcahy. We're five minutes out," a voice said.

"Thank you, Bill. After you drop my guests off, Byrnes will show you around to the kitchens, where you can get lunch and later dinner before you return to town."

"Thanks, ma'am." The phone clicked off.

"Who was that?" Ryan asked.

"The driver," Ashley told him. "We are now about four minutes from touchdown, darling. Gird your loins."

"I'd rather still be up in bed grinding them against yours," he said. "You are too delicious today, baby. And I'm going to be thinking all day about tonight after we wave them off. And don't look at me that way, Ash, all soft and melty-eyed. You want to really start a brouhaha, you'll let me greet the five harpies with a hard-on for my beautiful wife." He sighed dramatically, making a shaking motion with his hand. *"Mamma mia!"*

Ashley laughed. "You can't be that horny after last night," she said.

"I can't get enough of you," he replied.

"Stifle, big man!" she warned him. "Uh-oh. I hear the limo coming up the drive. Let's head to the door, and remember, smiles, everyone."

Now it was his turn to laugh. *"Fantasy Island* my foot," he said.

She flashed him a grin.

They stood on the portico of the house, arms about each other as the extra-large black limousine drew up before them in the drive. Bill, the chauffeur, was out of the vehicle immediately to open the door. First out was Angelina Mulcahy. Both Ryan and Ashley greeted her warmly, Ashley giving her a big hug.

"Be brave, *cara*," Lina murmured softly as one by one Ryan's older sisters were carefully handed out of the car. Their husbands had gotten out on the far side, and now stood bunched together, not quite certain what to do.

"Welcome to Kimbrough Hall, everyone," Ashley said, smiling. "I'm so glad the weather is perfect for you."

"It's a long ride from the city. I am Bride," a tall, dark-haired woman said. She smiled, but Ashley noticed that the smile didn't reach her eyes.

"But I hope it was at least comfortable for you," Ashley answered.

"Oh, yes, very nice, but certainly expensive. We could have driven our own cars. I'm Elisabetta." She was smaller than Bride, and her hair was quite red.

"Kathleen," said a third woman, holding out her hand to Ashley. She was platinum blond, and her handshake was feeble and limp.

"Magdalena," said the fourth woman. She was plump, and looked the most like her mother. Her gray hair made her look older than the others, although she was younger.

"I'm Deirdre," the last of the sisters said. Like Bride her hair was dark.

None of the sisters made any move to kiss Ashley.

"Good morning, ladies," Ryan said cheerfully. "Nice to see you all together."

"Yeah," one of the men said with a grin. "If you wanted to take them out, this would sure as hell be the time and place, Ryan."

"It's a good thought, Kevin, but I know how much you guys would miss them," Ryan joked with his brothers-in-law as, laughing, the men came forward, and Ryan introduced them to Ashley. On the whole the men seemed friendlier than Ryan's sisters.

"Come into the house," Ashley invited them, then settled them in the living room. She turned to her butler. "Byrnes, if anyone would like coffee, will you please bring it?"

"At once, Mrs. Mulcahy," Byrnes replied with a slight bow.

"You have servants?" Bride asked as she settled herself in a large wing chair that allowed her a full view of the room and everyone in it.

"They came with the house," Ashley joked, and the men laughed. "Yes, I have servants. They helped raise me after my parents died. Thanks to Mr. and Mrs. Byrnes the house runs like clockwork. I couldn't do without them."

"My daughters are striving to remain polite, Ashley, but they are dying to learn how you and Ryan met," Lina said. "I hope you'll tell them *everything, cara.*"

Ashley threw her mother-in-law a look of thanks. There were going to be no secrets now, and she was glad. "We were introduced by our attorneys in my lawyer's offices several months ago. Because Ryan and I were faced with a similar problem, we decided to make a marriage of convenience. Actually, it was Lina and Frankie who spoke first with Ray Pietro d'Angelo, and asked him to find Ryan a wife. Ray mentioned this rather odd request to his cousin, Joe Pietro d'Angelo, who is my lawyer."

"And just what problem did you have that was similar to our brother's?" Bride demanded to know. Her face was stony.

"Your father wanted to make certain Ryan married, because he knew that just being consumed by his business wasn't a good idea. A man ends up alone that way. And my grandfather thought a woman needed to be married to be happy and safe. And both of these old gentlemen added clauses to their wills. Ryan had to marry before he was forty. And I had to be married before I was thirty-five. If I didn't marry before that birthday, my father's old girlfriend's cockamamie organization, the Society Seeking Extraterrestrial Life, or SSEXL, would get everything: my house, my investments, and my monies. For your brother the penalty was as bad. To lose the business he had built up would be terrible for Ryan. I'm sure that now that you've all had time to think about it you appreciate that."

The five sisters all glared at Ashley, and then Bride said, "Your marriage can't be real. I think you should know we've hired a lawyer, and we're going to be suing you, Ryan. You only married to spite us, damn it!"

"Bride, do you hear yourself?" Ryan asked her.

"Fin's will only said your brother had to marry, Bride," Lina said quietly. "It didn't say to who, or even what kind of a marriage. It just said he had to marry."

"But it's a fraud!" Bride said angrily. "It's nothing more than a business arrangement. It isn't a *real* marriage! They weren't even married in the church by a priest, so it can't be a marriage at all."

"Our lawyer says we may have a case," Kathleen chimed in.

"We were married under the laws of the state, and that makes it legal no matter your religious beliefs," Ashley said quietly. "We signed prenups, and even have a written agreement as to what our marriage is and how it should work."

"There's a sex-is-optional clause," Ryan said wickedly. "And, of course, we exercised it immediately. I can't seem to keep my hands off of her." He leered at his five sisters, who were briefly silent.

"Don't be vulgar!" Bride finally snapped. "So you have sex. Everyone has sex today. That doesn't make it a real marriage in our eyes."

"Sister dearest, I don't give a damn what you think. Or the rest of you, for that matter. Ashley and I are married. We have sex daily when I'm here. We—"

"When you're here? Just what does that mean, Ryan?" Deirdre asked.

"I'm in town two nights a week," Ryan said. "But my legal residence is now here in Egret Pointe. And yes, I still have the apartment. I'm trying to figure out a way to telecommute to the studio and only have to go in now and again. Give it up, girls. You are not going to sell R&R. And you haven't a hope in hell of getting a court or a judge to say our marriage isn't legal. Besides, we love each other."

"You love each other?" Bride said shrilly.

"Yes," Ashley said. "Isn't it wonderful? All the years Ryan and I looked for love, and only thanks to those silly wills were we fortunate enough to meet, marry, and then fall in love. It's a miracle, a fairy tale, a dream come true."

"Ridiculous!" Magdelena, silent up to now, said. "No one falls in love that quickly. Love at first sight is a myth. The pair of you are just doing this to cheat us."

"Please," Ashley said. "You are guests in my home, and for us to get into a quarrel like this is terrible. I invited you so I might meet you and get to know you and your husbands. I've planned a lovely day. I want to show you Egret Pointe. My ancestors were among the group who founded it. My brother and I were the last Kimbroughs. Ryan and I have really fallen in love. We're happy, and I want you all to be happy too."

"That's real nice of you," Kevin McGuire, Kathleen's husband, said. "I agree with Ashley. Ryan is married. The money wasn't ours to begin with, so let's cut the crap and be a family, like we should."

"Kevin!" his wife exclaimed.

"Yeah, I agree with Kev," Robert Napoli, Deirdre's husband, spoke up.

"We all do," Frank Butler, Magdalena's husband, said, and the other men nodded.

"All very well and good for you men to say. It wasn't your father's money," Bride responded sourly.

"It wasn't your father's money either," Bride's husband, Pete Franklin, said. "Your old man was a great craftsman, Bride, but his business couldn't have taken in more than a hundred thou a year until Ryan took over. Ryan made the money, and Ryan saw that Fin remembered each of you generously. The guys and I have had enough of the five of you whining and bitching about it. We let you do what you wanted with the money you inherited, and you all pissed most of it away. Too bad. Boo-hoo. This ends today. Get past it, girls." He turned to Ashley and said, "Welcome to the family, sweetie. Ryan sure got himself a pretty girl. And a smart one too."

Ashley stepped forward and gave Pete a hug. "Thanks," she said. "But how would you know if I'm smart or not?"

"I'm an accountant," Pete replied. "You got one store, you're opening two more. You sell what women want. You're smart."

Ashley laughed. "Yes," she said, "I am." Then she turned to her other guests. "I thought I'd show you the house and grounds. Then we'll have an early lunch. This weekend is our annual Harvest Festival, and I thought you might enjoy going later. But if not we'll just sit and talk. Ryan and I plan to go tomorrow either way."

"How lovely, *cara*," Lina responded. "Yes, I for one would love to go to this festival. Do they have handicrafts?"

"Oh, yes," Ashley told her. "The festival proceeds all go to our local hospital. There are homemade treats, knitted goods, birdhouses, and our local author signs her latest book. Her publisher donates the books so everything can go to Egret Pointe General Hospital."

"Who's the author?" Bride asked, curious in spite of herself.

"Emilie Shann is her pen name. She's really Emily Devlin. She'll probably be there, although she does have a new baby. She's old Egret Pointe too, and way back we're probably related. I'm sure a Kimbrough married a Dunham somewhere along the way." Ashley laughed.

"Emilie Shann lives here?" Elisabetta's eyes were excited. "I love her books! And especially since she's gotten sexier. Do you know her?"

"Yes," Ashley said. "We went to school together."

"We've got to go to this festival," Elisabetta said. "She is my favorite author. Do you think she'll sign a book for me?"

"For a price, sure," Ashley said. She was secretly tickled that her sister-in-law was one of Emily's fans. "And remember, it's all for charity. But now, how about Ryan and I show you the house? Frankie did our bedroom suite, and it's lovely."

"Even the floral chairs," Ryan said, and his brothers-in-law chuckled.

The Mulcahy sisters were, in spite of themselves, fascinated by Kimbrough Hall. The wide boards in the floors amazed them, and Ashley was quick to tell them that the boards came from trees found growing in the area when the house was built in 1724, a year after the town was founded. "My ancestor, Edmund Kimbrough, wanted to replicate the manor house in England where he had grown up."

"There's a house like this in England?" Magdalena asked.

"Yes, in Devon. It's also Kimbrough Hall. That branch of the family is still going strong."

"How did your family make the money to build a house like this?" Elisabetta inquired. She taught history in a local city private school.

"Rum, molasses, and slaves to begin with," Ashley replied. "Pretty much like all the successful early families. Then in the 1840s we got into the China trade. And some of the family's fleet were whalers. And then the Kimbroughs got involved in helping to build railroads, started a few banks, and eventually got a seat on the New York Stock Exchange. Grandfather sold that before he died. The Egret Pointe National Bank is mine, or rather the Kimbroughs'. I'm on the board, of course, although I have little to do with running it." She smiled at them. "My late mother's family came here from Ireland in the middle of the nineteenth century, before the Civil War. They were all shopkeepers, so I guess I come by it naturally. Nobody left on that side. They weren't much on reproduction, I'm sorry to say."

Ryan's five older sisters looked slightly shell-shocked by this recitation. Their husbands were openly impressed, and perhaps just a little bit awed. This was certainly going to erase any doubts the harpies had about Ashley's motives for marrying him, Ryan thought as he caught his mother's eye and winked.

"Well, come on now," Ashley said brightly as they moved from the formal dining room to the breakfast room and the library. "There's the rest of the house to show you." She led them upstairs, flinging open the door to the first bedroom. "The rumor is that President Washington himself stayed here once when he was either coming or going from New York, the capital in the early days. It was this bedroom."

Everyone looked around the room. The furnishings were definitely eighteenth century. Even the draperies at the windows and the bed hangings looked authentic.

"Not many people know that New York was the first capital," Elisabetta remarked. "Are the hangings real?"

Ashley shook her head. "Very good reproductions. The originals were in the room until about twenty years ago, though. But they just became too hard to clean."

The other bedrooms were admired, and then they came to the bedroom suite shared by Ryan and Ashley. The sisters pushed into the parlor, taking everything in.

"Nice couch," Robert Napoli said with a grin. "Looks real comfortable."

"Shut up, Bob!" his wife said.

Both Ryan and Ashley laughed.

"It is comfortable," Ryan allowed.

The sisters next looked at the master bedroom, and someone gasped at the size of the bed.

"We needed it extra-large because your brother is such a big fellow," Ashley said.

"I saw dormers on the roof," Kathleen remarked.

"There's a third floor. In the old days when the house had a full staff of servants they lived there. Now it's pretty much empty. Just attics and storage," Ashley told her. "Well, this is it, ladies and gentlemen. I expect that luncheon is ready by now, and Mrs. B. really doesn't like to be kept waiting."

She led them briskly downstairs again to the dining room, which was set with embroidered linen place mats. There were place cards at each setting. Ryan sat at the head of the table, Ashley at the foot, and Lina had been put on her son's right. Byrnes, along with a girl brought in for the day, served. There was clear soup to start with, and Waldorf salads were set to the left at each place. A large roast turkey was set on the sideboard, and Byrnes carved, laying bits on each plate, which the maid then distributed among the diners. The side dishes were then passed about. There were mashed turnips, French-cut green beans, and sweet potatoes whipped with butter, maple syrup, and cinnamon.

"I wasn't certain what you would all enjoy, but I know everyone likes turkey," Ashley murmured. "Bride, do try some of those tiny corn muffins. Mrs. B. is famous for them. And the cranberry that's in the sauce comes from a local bog. They grow wild."

"The veggies are all from the estate garden," Ryan told their guests. "And the turkey is local. When was the last time any of you ate so fresh?"

"I suppose living in the country has some advantages," Bride allowed.

Ashley couldn't help but notice how quiet the table was as her husband's relatives ate, and ate, and ate. There were audible sighs of bliss when the dessert was served on individual plates. It was chocolate mousse with fresh raspberries. Finally every morsel had been consumed, and they began to rise from the table.

"Let's go to the festival now," Ashley said brightly. "Bill can follow Ryan and me. Byrnes, tell the driver we need him, and why."

"Yes, Mrs. Mulcahy," Byrnes said, and he hurried off.

"Well, you know what the prince of Wales always said," Ashley remarked. "Never miss an opportunity. If anyone wants the bathroom I think the time is now. There's a powder room, second door on the left in the hall, and one with every bedroom upstairs." She grinned as her guests scattered.

"Well," Ryan said when they were alone, "I don't know if I could say you've won the harpies over, but you've kept them from fighting. It's amazing."

"The day isn't over yet," Ashley warned. "I could kiss your brother-in-law Pete, however. He really put everything in perspective with that little speech of his. I never saw anyone so outraged as Bride when he was speaking."

"The in-laws are all good guys," Ryan told her. "Pete generally lets Bride have her head, but when he's had enough he says so, and she generally listens. They've all had enough. None of them ever counted on getting R&R. For them it was a long shot. They're all smart guys, and they knew I wasn't going to let it go over that damned clause in Dad's will. But if it weren't for that clause," he said, pulling her into his arms and kissing her heartily, "I would have never had you,

Ash. My sexy, smart, beautiful wife. When are we going to start making those babies?"

"Soon, I promise," Ashley said. "Oh, let go, Ryan! You're starting to get a hard-on. What if the others see?" She pulled away from him.

Their guests returned. The limo was waiting outside, and with Ashley and Ryan in her Solstice leading them, they made their way through town to the Egret Pointe Harvest Festival. Within the big car the sisters had to admit being charmed by the town, with its little shops and ice-cream parlor. They asked Bill to slow down long enough to catch a glimpse of the windows at Lacy Nothings, which were now filled with baskets of autumn vegetables, small piles of colored leaves, and mini rakes among the blue, green, and violet lacy bras, thongs, teddies, and nightgowns. Finally they arrived at the festival, and Bill parked the limo in an adjacent field next to Ashley's sports car.

With Ashley leading them they walked among the awninged tables and booths where a variety of handmade and homemade goods were on display for sale. Soon Ryan's brothers-in-law found themselves loaded down with all manner of purchases being made by their wives. Deirdre and Kathleen were expecting new grandchildren, and there was a booth offering handmade baby garments both sewn and knitted.

"Ohh, I love watermelon pickles," Magdalena said, and promptly bought six jars, along with three more of corn relish, and several jars of jam.

Coming into an open space, they saw a gentleman seated above a vat of something green, a crowd gathered before him.

"What on earth is that?" Bride wanted to know.

"It's the Dr. Sam Dunk," Ashley told her. "Dr. Sam is the chief of staff up at the hospital. Everyone just loves him. His family have been the town doctors since we were founded. You get three balls and three tries for two dollars. If you hit it just right he goes into a vat of Jell-O. All the money is for the hospital. He's really a very good sport about it, and the Dr. Sam Dunk always earns a lot of money. Anyone want to try?"

Her new brothers-in-law all bought their three balls, but none of them could hit the target properly. Even Ryan tried. And then Ashley sauntered up, waving her two dollars, and the crowd began to chuckle.

"Here comes trouble," Dr. Sam called from his perch above the Jell-O. "Hello, Ashley. I suppose you're going to try to dunk me, like you do every year?"

"And you're going down like you do every year," Ashley taunted him. Twice she made a big issue of winding up for the pitch, and twice she missed, but Ryan could tell she was missing deliberately, and he could see Dr. Sam knew it. The third ball hit the target square-on, and the physician was dumped into the green Jell-O, to the cheers of the onlookers and the clanging of a bell. "See you next year, Dr. Sam," Ashley said as she moved off with her party.

"Pretty good pitching," her brother-in-law Kevin said. "Was it a lucky pitch?"

"Nope," Ashley said with a grin. "Actually, I could have dunked him every time, but Dr. Sam and I have a deal that I'll do it only once each year. I used to pitch on the girls' high school softball team."

"Is the author here, Ashley?" Elisabetta asked eagerly.

Ashley looked around, and finally she spied Emily Devlin in her author persona of Emilie Shann. She was seated at a card table beneath an awning, but the pile of books before her was down to three. Ashley led her party over to the table. "Hey, Emily!"

"Ashley." Emily Devlin looked up, smiling, from behind her table.

Ashley spied a basket beside Emily's chair. "Oh, here's your little baby!" She squealed, genuinely excited. The baby gave her a toothless grin.

Emily smiled happily and, bending down, lifted the infant up. It had a headful of dark hair. "Meet Sean Michael Devlin," she said. "Born the twenty-ninth of June."

Ashley sighed, and all the women with her cooed and commented on what a lovely little boy he was. "These are my sisters-in-law," Ashley said. Then she pointed. "Bride Franklin, Kathleen McGuire, Magdelena Butler, Deirdre Napoli, and Elisabetta Sweeney, who is a huge fan of yours, Em. Will you sign the new book for her?"

"Sure I will," Emily said with a smile at Elisabetta. "How do you like the sexier books?" she asked her.

"I *love* them!" Elisabetta gushed. "I mean, I always loved your books, Ms. Shann, but last year's *The Defiant Duchess* was incredible. Soooo romantic! I hadn't gotten the new one yet." She looked down at the books left on the table. "*The Playful Prince*," she said. "I'm going to like it, aren't I? Is it as sexy?"

"Sexier," Emily promised Elisabetta.

"She has an excellent role model for her heroes," a tall, dark, and very handsome gentleman said, coming up to the table. He bent and kissed Emily. "Time to take the heir and go home, darling," he told her. "Hi, Ashley."

"Hi, Mick. This is Emily's husband and editor, Michael Devlin," Ashley introduced him to her guests. "Mick, this is my husband, Ryan Mulcahy."

The two men shook hands, and Michael Devlin said, "I've been meaning to get in touch with you. I'd like to do a coffee table book on restorations. Can I call you?"

"I'll be back in my office Tuesday," Ryan said.

Michael Devlin nodded and, bending, picked up his son. "I'll meet you at the car," he said to Emily.

"Gotten that van yet?" Ashley teased him.

"The basket fits in the back of the Healy very nicely, thank you," Michael Devlin said with a chuckle. "But I expect we're headed that way." Then, with a smile, he nodded at them and walked off carrying his son.

Emily signed Elisabetta's book, but Ashley would not let her sister-in-law pay for it. "A little remembrance of your day," she said, smiling. "Em, I'll take the other two books. Just put your name in them. I'll give them to Nina and Brandy."

The sun was sinking low on the horizon now. Ashley led her party back to their limo. It followed her back to the house, where Byrnes was waiting with tea, finger sandwiches, and small cookies. It was getting chilly as the day came to a close. And finally Ryan's sisters and their husbands took their leave. They were surprised that their mother was remaining behind.

"So Lina and I can visit," Ashley said sweetly. "It was wonderful meeting you all. I hope you'll come up over the holidays." She and Ryan waved them off as the limo drove away down the hilly drive. Then they joined Lina in the comfortable den, where Byrnes had already lit a fire.

"So, my children, it is love, is it?" she said with a smile. She was seated in a wing chair by the fire, a cashmere lap robe over her knees. Her beautiful Ferragamo shoes were set neatly by the chair. Angelina Mulcahy was seventy-three, but her dark hair, slender figure, and beautiful skin made her appear younger.

Ryan bent to kiss his mother. "Yeah," he answered her. "It's love. Go figure."

Angelina turned to Ashley.

"Love," the younger woman confirmed unabashedly. "I never thought it could happen to me."

"You loved the others," Lina said, "didn't you?"

"Not like I love your son," Ashley told her mother-in-law.

Angelina nodded. "Then I am content," she said. "Perhaps I should have returned home with my daughters." Her warm brown eyes twinkled.

"We're putting you in a room at the end of the hall from us," Ashley teased her.

Angelina laughed heartily, shaking her finger at her new daughter-in-law.

Ryan grinned, very pleased to see how well the two women got along. He poured them all small glasses of wine from a tray on the table. They toasted each other and sat talking quietly until Byrnes arrived, pushing a trolley.

"I thought you would enjoy eating by the fire tonight after your busy day," he said.

"What smells so good?" Ashley asked him.

"Corn chowder and toasted cheese bread," Byrnes said, handing them each a napkin. Then he began to ladle out soup into earthenware mugs. When Byrnes had handed them their mugs and spoons, he uncovered a plate of buttered cheese toast. "There are baked apples and a pot of tea below," he said, pointing to the second level of the trolley, which was electrified. "When you're ready I'll come back and take the cart." Then he was gone.

"You are very fortunate," Lina said.

"I know," Ashley agreed.

"The toast is delicious," Lina complimented.

"Mrs. B. makes real cheese bread," Ashley said.

They ate their supper, and then Ashley got out a Monopoly set.

"I haven't played since the children were young," Lina said. And then she proved herself to be a most formidable player, beating them both, taking all their money, and easily winning several games.

"You haven't lost your touch, Ma," Ryan said. "She used to beat us regularly."

"You could have warned me," Ashley said, smiling.

"I think it is time that I retired," Lina told them both. "It has been a long day." She slipped into her shoes and stood up. After kissing them both, the older woman left them in the comfortable den. Byrnes returned and removed the cart with its dishes.

"Good night, Mr. and Mrs. Mulcahy," he said.

They bade him good night. Ashley now sat in her husband's lap, and began kissing him little kisses on his mouth. His hand slipped beneath her sweater to unhook her bra. He grasped a soft, warm breast and began fondling it tenderly. Ashley kissed him more deeply now, and one kiss blended into another until it was impossible to tell where the kisses both began and ended. His thumb was now rubbing her nipple. He pushed her sweater up higher and, dipping his head, took the nipple in his mouth.

"Oh, that's nice," Ashley murmured as he began to suck on it.

His hand now unzipped her slacks and slid into her panties, down, down, to her plump pussy. "All day I've wanted to fuck you," he said low in her ear. "All day long while my sisters carped and nattered and gushed, I thought about fucking you." The tip of his tongue encircled the shape of her ear. "Did you know that's what I was thinking? Did it make you hot to think about my big cock pushing into you, Ash?"

"You're so bad, Ryan," she murmured against his mouth. "And yes, I knew. You had half a hard-on all day. I hope your sisters didn't notice." She nibbled on his lower lip. "Tell me how badly you want me. Tell me what you're going to do to me, darling."

"First," he began, "I'm going to find your naughty little clit, baby." His finger slipped between the lips of her labia, stroking, seeking. And then he found it.

"Ohh," Ashley said. "Oh, that's so nice, darling. Yes. Don't stop!" She squirmed her bottom into his lap, grinding deeply as she did. The delicious tingling tension was beginning to build within her. She was very wet, and he was going to bring her to a clitoral climax fairly quickly. She sighed and moaned low when he did. Then she said to him, "Do it again, Ryan. That was so good!"

"You're a greedy little witch," he said. "And I'm getting hotter than a firecracker, baby." He began to play with her clit again, and within minutes she was climaxing again.

He thrust two fingers hard into her cunt, moving them back and forth quickly.

"Oh, yes, darling!" Ashley gasped. "Do it! Do it to me! No! Don't stop!" she complained at him when he withdrew his fingers.

"You're having all the fun, baby," he said to her. "I need to have a little bit of fun too. Ever get screwed on the floor before a fire?" Ryan asked as he gently dumped her out of his lap. "I want to do it now. And I want to do it there," he told her, pointing to the floor before the fireplace.

"What if someone comes in?" Ashley said.

"Who's going to come in?" he countered. "The door is closed. My mother has gone upstairs. The Byrneses are in their apartment over the kitchen. This is the perfect time and place. Come on, Ash. Let's get out of our clothes and do it right here and now." Ryan kicked his elegant loafers off his feet. He pulled his sweater over his head and tossed it on the couch. Undoing his belt, he unbuttoned and unzipped his pants. Then he stepped out of them, pushing them aside with a bare foot. "Come on, baby," he crooned at her as he slid his silk jockey shorts over his narrow hips, and the wad in those shorts was suddenly revealed to be a massive erection.

She wasn't certain she was breathing at that point. He really had the most wickedly delicious body. She reached out to caress his big cock, but he moved away.

"Not until you get out of your clothes," he told her, shaking a finger at her.

Ashley had taken her leather boots off earlier. Now she pulled off her sweater, her slacks, and her bra. She cupped her breasts in her hands, as if offering them to him.

"Get rid of the panties, baby, or we can't play," he said.

"You take them off," she teased him.

Ryan reached out, but Ashley shook her head.

"With your teeth," she told him.

"You are a very bad girl," he said, but, kneeling, he pulled the scrap of silk and lace off with his teeth.

"I need to be spanked," Ashley told him, stepping away from her last garment. As he stood she grabbed one of his hands and began to suck his fingers one by one in a very provocative manner. "Bad girls," she said as she sucked, "are always better for a good spanking, Ryan, and I've been a bad girl."

"Get over here," he said roughly, sitting back down in the chair and pulling her over his knee. "Yeah, you really do need a spanking, baby." His big hand fell on her plump buttocks, and she squealed. Jesus, she really knew how to turn him on. This was a whole new side of his wife. He smacked her several times until her cute butt was beginning to get pink. "Are you going to be a good girl now?" he said.

"No!" she told him.

His hand came down a few more times, and the pink deepened. "You're a very disobedient girl," he scolded her as he spanked her. "Now are you going to be a good girl, Ashley?" He gave her a final whack with his big open palm.

She didn't answer him at first, and then she said, "Maybe."

He laughed. "Okay, that's good enough for now, baby."

She scrambled off of his lap. "You really know how to spank a girl," she told him. "I like being spanked now and again." She knelt before him and took his dick in her hand. "Have you ever been spanked, Ryan? I mean by a lover?" She kissed the tip of his penis, and then began to lick about the head of it.

"No," he answered her. "Do you want to spank me, Ash?"

"Sometime. Not tonight," she said.

"Have you ever spanked a man?" he wondered.

"Not in this life." She giggled. Well, The Channel wasn't really this life, was it? The Channel was a fantasy world. "But I've always wanted to, Ryan. I hear a good spanking can make a man's cock hard for a very long time." She took him into her mouth and began to suck.

"I could have never found a woman like you on my own," he told her. "You've got a libido as hot as mine, Ashley. Ohh, baby, that's nice, but don't make me come. I want to fuck you hard and deep before that." His big hand stroked her dark head gently. "The lawyers were just considering how to save our inheritances when they matched us up. They could not have known how good a match it was going to be, could they?" He closed his eyes and briefly enjoyed her mouth on him. She sucked him gently, teasingly, not enough to bring him on, but he wanted to put it in her. "Enough," he said. "On your back, wife, and spread yourself for me now." He slid between her thighs as she quickly complied with his command.

Her tongue ran over her lips. *"Do it!"* she hissed at him. "I am so hot for you, Ryan. I'm going to explode if you don't get that big cock of yours into me now. Ohhh, yes, darling! Just like that. Hard! Deep! And fast!" Her eyes closed as he filled her and began to fuck her just as she asked of him. Her legs wrapped about him, allowing him deeper, and she moaned with pleasure as he touched that wicked little spot that always started her toward the edge. But this time he would touch it once or twice, and then avoid it for several more strokes of his big dick. Her heels drummed against his back, and he laughed softly.

"Don't like being teased?" he taunted her. "Funny, I like teasing you." He touched the magic spot again several more times before drawing away, and Ashley whimpered beneath him. He felt her nails begin to dig into his shoulders.

"Oh, Ryan." She gasped. "Don't. Make me come, darling! *Make me come!*"

"Not yet," he told her. "You're too greedy, Ashley. You want to savor this."

"No, damn it, I want to come!" she yelled.

He put a hand over her mouth. "We don't want to draw attention to what we're doing, do we?" He laughed. She bit his hand, and he pulled it back with a yelp. "Okay, you little bitch," he growled at her. "You want to come? Then I'll make you come!" And he honed in on her G-spot, fucking and fucking and fucking her until she climaxed with a small scream of pure pleasure.

"Oh, God, that was so good." Ashley sighed gustily.

"Was it?" he purred in her ear. "And in just a little while you're going to do it again, baby, because while you're satisfied, I'm sure as hell not."

And then she realized that he was still in her. And he was still very, very hard. "I'm sorry," she said softly. "I didn't mean to be so greedy."

"Yes, you did," he responded. "But you're going to pay for it, wife." And he began to move on her again, this time with long, slow strokes of his cock, and Ashley was soon moaning, her head thrashing as he began to bring the passion in her out again. She had never felt so overcome with such undiluted lust as she did now. Her legs, which had fallen away from his torso when she had last come, now encircled him again. And he was going deeper and harder, harder and deeper. Her nails raked down his long back, and he stopped briefly to catch her hands up and put them above her head, where he might control her better. "You like this, don't you?" he whispered in her ear.

"Yes! *Yes!*" she whispered back. "Kiss me, Ryan!"

His lips eagerly found hers, and his tongue slipped into the hot cavern of her mouth, thrusting in time with his penis. Ashley sucked on the tongue, clutching it even as the muscles in her vagina were suddenly contracting about the massive cock fucking her. He groaned, and she pushed her hips up to meet his downward thrust. They would come together this time, and when they did it was in an explosion of beating hearts, a roaring in the ears, and a flood of their juices mingling hotly together.

"Oh, my God," Ashley finally managed to gasp as she pushed him off of her. "I have never in my life had such incredible sex. Are we alive?"

"I think so." He groaned and, reaching out, took her hand in his, bringing it to his lips to kiss. "You are an incredible woman, and I am so glad we found each other. I love you, Ashley," he said. "I never thought to say that to a woman and mean it, but I love you, baby."

"I love you too," she admitted softly. "I never believed in fate before, Ryan, but I sure as hell believe in fate now. Only something like fate could have brought us together. It would appear that we are perfect for each other."

They lay silently and quietly together on the rug before the fire for some minutes, and Ashley thought afterward that perhaps they even dozed off for a short time. Finally he said, "We'd better go upstairs, baby. I'm falling asleep with all that terrific exercise." They didn't bother to dress, because they knew that no one was about. Lina would be fast sleep in a guest room, and the Byrneses were at the other end of the house completely. Gathering their clothing, they hurried up the wide staircase, down the broad upstairs hall, and into their own bedroom suite, where they fell into bed, exhausted from their passion.

Ryan awoke earlier than the woman by his side. After showering and dressing, he kissed his sleeping wife and went downstairs to the kitchen to put on the coffee. To his surprise his mother joined him almost immediately. She had obviously been out walking.

"You're up," he said to her. "Good morning. Juice? We have orange, pineapple, and tomato."

"Pineapple," Lina said. "I can have orange any day."

He poured it for her, handing her the glass.

"You are happy," she said. It was a statement, not a question.

"I owe you one, *mamma mia*," he said. "I love her."

"You might not have," Lina reminded him.

"Ashley says it's fate," Ryan told his mother.

Angelina Mulcahy smiled. "She believes in fate?"

"She didn't, she says, until now," Ryan answered.

"Fate is what brought your father and me together," she told him.

"You were happy," he said.

"We were content," Angelina Mulcahy said candidly. "And no matter that he was Irish and I was Italian; we had much in common. A religion, a work ethic. But I never loved Finbar Mulcahy. I was fond of him, yes. But I never loved him."

"But you had seven kids!" Ryan exclaimed.

"We both liked sex," she said bluntly. "I know that isn't something a mother should say to her son, but that's the truth of it. Your father and I enjoyed a healthy sexual relationship. That was another thing we had in common. That and we wanted a family. We never meant to have seven kids, but your father wanted a son, and I kept having girls. And then after you were born we tried for another boy and got Francesca. That's when we decided the pope be damned, and your dad started using condoms until I got through the change. Do you know how lucky you are, Ryan? You actually have fallen in love. It's a blessing, *mio figlio.*"

"I never knew just how much until now, Ma," he told her. "Want some breakfast? I make pretty good scrambled eggs. I learned from an expert."

Angelina smiled. "Where is Ashley?"

"I'm letting her sleep," he said. "Eggs?"

His mother laughed. "Yes, please," she said. Then she grew serious. "Tell me, Ryan, does she love you? And will you give me grandchildren?"

"She loves me," he responded, "and she says as soon as she gets these two new shops open and going, she'll throw away her birth control pills. Haven't you got enough grandchildren, Ma?" he teased her.

"I have grandchildren," Angelina said. "But no Mulcahy grandchildren."

"Ashley wants kids. Don't worry about it," he told her.

"The couple? They don't work on Sundays?" Lina wanted to know.

"Sundays and Wednesdays are their days off," Ryan said as he took eggs from the fridge and began breaking them into a bowl. "Hey, how long has it been since you and I had breakfast together, Ma?"

She smiled. "Give me the bacon, Ryan, and I'll start to fry it up."

Together mother and son fixed breakfast: scrambled eggs and perfectly cooked crisp bacon to be served with a plate of Mrs. B.'s mini cranberry-apple muffins that had been left in the pantry for them. When it was just about ready Lina filled a plate and gave it to Ryan.

"Take Ashley some breakfast before we eat. You have obviously worn her out."

"She can keep up with me." He grinned.

"Much too much information," Lina told her son.

"After what you told me?" he said, laughing.

"I told you nothing that you did not already know, Ryan. If your father and I had not liked sex, you and your six sisters would not be here. You were not, after all, delivered by the stork, now, were you?"

He picked up the plate she handed him, along with a cup of coffee laced with half-and-half. "I won't be long," he said with a grin.

"If you are I will know what you are doing, won't I?" Lina teased.

Laughing, Ryan hurried up the back staircase to take his wife her breakfast. Both his wife and mother were to be reckoned with. He was glad that they were friends.

Chapter Nine

They were happy together. Ryan was working out a system of cameras that would allow his whole office and workshops to be viewed from his computer at home. He had decided to go into town only once a month for a day. If there was an emergency he would, of course, be available. And he was always available for clients. He had hired Bill away from the car service that had brought his family out to Egret Pointe in mid-October. And he had traded his sports car for a Town Car tricked out with every device he might need. Bill, a bachelor, was offered an apartment above the garages, where a chauffeur used to live when the house had employed a full staff. It even had its own small kitchen, but Bill could eat with the Byrneses, which he preferred to do most nights. He had the weekends off, as Ryan didn't need him then.

Ashley had brought her new employees out to Egret Pointe, and with Nina's help was training them. *Lacy Nothings* on the Upper East Side and in its suburban mall location would be ready to open on time. On the thirtieth of October, Suzette and Mrs. Babcock, along with their new staffs, departed Egret Pointe. Their stores would be ready for business on November first. Ashley was relieved to have everything going so smoothly. The new catalog, shot in August and mailed in late September, was already bringing in more early orders than she had anticipated.

She and Ryan had taken to eating together in the den now. The porch was closed up for the winter, and the formal dining room was just too big for a single couple. Byrnes set up a table in the den's bay window, where they could watch the moon come up over the bay while they ate in the evening.

"I have to go to Venice next week," Ryan told her one night.

"For how long?" Ashley asked him.

"Just a few days. An old friend, the Contessa di Viscontini, has found a wonderful seventeenth-century wardrobe in a small town over the Austrian border. It's alleged to have belonged to a doge who was her ancestor. She's had it brought to her villa in Venice, but she wants R&R to restore it and make any repairs that are necessary. I don't trust anyone else to oversee the packing of this piece. If it's authentic then it's too valuable to leave in clumsy hands. So I'll go to Venice and see to it myself," Ryan said.

"I'll go with you," Ashley suggested. "The new stores are open as of last weekend, and Nina can handle the shop here, with Brandy coming in Saturday and after school. We haven't had a real honeymoon. I can't think of a more romantic place to have one than in Venice, and I've got the time now. Once the Christmas rush begins I'll be too busy, and as I recall I did promise to throw away my birth control pills once the new stores were up and running. What if I get pregnant? I can't take a honeymoon then."

"November isn't the prettiest month to go to Venice," he said.

"Venice will still be Venice no matter the weather. The Piazza San Marco and the Campanile will still be there whatever time of year it is," Ashley reasoned.

"Venice is one of my favorite cities," he said. "I want you to see it first at its best, not in a month that's apt to be cold and rainy."

"What if it sinks into the sea before I finally get there?" Ashley wanted to know.

Ryan laughed. "Okay, I give up," he told her. "You can come to Venice with me. I suppose you're right. Venice will be Venice no matter what. And better with you. And we'll be staying at the contessa's villa. You'll like Bianca. She's a very cool lady."

"Wouldn't a hotel be better?" Ashley wondered.

"Nope, and besides, Bianca would never let us," he replied.

"How do you know a Venetian contessa?" Ashley asked her husband.

"The summer I was sixteen, Dad took Mom, Deirdre, Frankie, and me to Venice. There was a great craftsman there, Paolo Venutti. My father wanted to learn his technique, and he took only one student each summer. Dad was on his waiting list, and that summer's student canceled. Venutti called Dad, and the next thing I knew we were on a plane. Venutti arranged for us to rent the Conde di Viscontini's guesthouse. He was old and sick, but he needed the income the rental would bring in, and they didn't entertain any longer. His wife was much younger, I guess in her late thirties or early forties then. She welcomed us. She showed Ma where the best markets were, and how to get around the city easily. She found friends for Deirdre, who was twenty then, and really pissed she had to come with us, but my folks weren't leaving her home alone, and the other sisters were all married. None of them wanted the responsibility for her. I don't blame them. Dee was a pretty wild kid then."

"How old was Frankie?" Ashley wanted to know.

"Fourteen, and the contessa found a few friends for her too. They spent more time at the Lido than anywhere else that summer. There was always an older woman, someone's relative, with them to keep them out of trouble." He laughed.

"And what did you do in Venice that summer?" She smiled at the thought of Ryan at sixteen.

"I explored the whole city. I even took Ma with me now and again. Sometimes I went with Frankie to the Lido. And the contessa taught me to speak Italian. In return I taught her English. It was a great summer, as I recall. I hated to come back."

"You've been back since?"

"Three times. The first time was two years later, when Bianca's husband died. My father felt the family should be represented, and so I was sent. The conde's funeral barge, all decked in black, traversed the length of the Grand Canal and back again. I paid my respects and those of my family, and was on the plane again for home. And I've been back twice since, but the contessa was never there when I visited. I haven't seen her in years. Venutti used to do all her restoring, but I imagine he's dead now. I'm surprised she remembered us, but then R&R's reputation is the best."

"Will you take me for a gondola ride in the moonlight?" Ashley asked her husband. "And can we listen to a band concert on the Piazza San Marco?"

"I don't think they do outdoor concerts in November," he told her. "Next time we'll go in summer. But even now there will be lots for you to see while I'm working, and yes, I'll take you for a gondola ride, if I can find a gondola, but I can't guarantee a moon." Ryan chuckled.

"What do you mean, if you can find a gondola? I thought Venice was full of gondolas," Ashley said. "If I go to Venice I have to ride in a gondola. You can't say you've been to Venice if you haven't had a trip in a gondola."

"The gondolas hibernate nowadays," he said. "And it is late in the year. But if the weather is good and there are still some tourists in Venice, then there will be a few gondolas to be had, and we'll go for our ride," he promised her.

"Is there an airport in Venice?" Ashley wanted to know.

"There are two, north of the city. When I went as a kid we flew to Rome, visited some of Ma's relatives, and then took the train into Venice. I remember Frankie and me leaning out of the open window of the first-class carriage Dad had booked, and taking pictures as we came into the city across the lagoon. When we came out of the station we took the *vaporetto*, which is like a bus, to Piazza Viscontini, and then, lugging our suitcases, we walked the rest of the way," he recalled.

"So how are we going? And do I have to carry my suitcase?" she asked him.

"There's a direct Delta flight from the city to Venice. It's a nine-hour flight. Book us two first-class tickets as soon as you can get us on the plane," Ryan said.

They departed Kennedy two nights later. They had checked one bag each onto the plane. Ashley carried only her handbag on board, and Ryan brought nothing on the plane but a small book on Venetian furniture. They took off their shoes, which were carefully inspected, walked through a metal detector, put their footwear back on, and picked up the book and the handbag. They were then allowed to board. She was glad she didn't have to do a lot of flying these days. It was getting to be more and more of a hassle.

Ashley had been surprised that there were first-class seats available, but it was an odd time of year to be going away for pleasure. And Thursday night wasn't exactly a night for business travel. Their plane was a new one, with seats that turned into single beds. After dinner she and Ryan turned in, falling asleep holding hands. The steward woke them an hour before landing. Looking outside the windows, Ashley noted that it was a beautiful day. A stewardess brought them breakfast: scrambled eggs, croissants, and *café au lait*. They landed right on time.

Aeroporto Marco Polo was six miles north of the city. Claiming their bags, they boarded the shuttle bus that would take them to the dock. Ryan had booked a private powerboat to take them to their destination in the city. When they reached the boats they saw a young man holding up a sign that read, MULCAHY, and they headed for him.

"Signore Mulcahy?" the man asked as they reached him.

"*Si*, Ryan Mulcahy *e* Signora Mulcahy," Ryan said.

"I speak English, signore. I'm Pietro. Let me take your bags." Reaching for them, the boat captain quickly stored them. Then he helped Ashley into his vessel, followed by Ryan. "I like to practice my English, signore, if you don't mind. It helps me with the tourists in the summer," Pietro told them. "I know the signore speaks Italian, for the contessa has said so."

"You know where we're going then?" Ryan inquired.

"Palazzo di Viscontini, signore, *si!*"

"I take it this isn't a *vaporetto*," Ashley said, smiling at her husband.

"No. This is first class," Ryan replied with a grin. "The weather is good?" he asked the boat's captain.

"You have brought the good weather with you, signore," Pietro replied. "They say for the next week we will have sun. Unusual for November."

Out in the open water the boat sped its way across the lagoon. Ashley could see the city ahead of her. It looked like something out of a fairy tale, all gold, blue, and with terra cotta roofs. "Where are the gondolas?" she asked Pietro.

"There will be a few still out," he answered her. "Most have been put away for the winter. Not many tourists come to Venice in the winter months, signora."

As they drew closer to the city, Ashley was delighted to see a variety of boat traffic suddenly surrounding them as Pietro slowed down to keep pace with what was definitely a traffic pattern. Ryan pointed out a *vaporetto* which was the Venetian method of public transportation. Ashley could see it was crowded with rush-hour traffic. *What a fun way to commute if you had to commute,* she thought. There were other powerboats such as the one they were in. There were barges carrying all manner of goods, but the one that fascinated her was unloading fresh vegetables and fruit at what was obviously a marketplace. They stopped once to allow a boat that was marked as an ambulance to speed by. Everything seemed to use the water here. Finally their boat slowed and turned down a narrow canal. Beyond the buildings on its corner there were trees and gardens on either side of the waterway.

"Canal Viscontini," Pietro said. "It is very special. Even the great palazzos on the Grand Canal do not have this, signora. In the great days the two buildings that we have just passed served as warehouses for the di Viscontini. Like all the *seigneury* families, their wealth came from trade. To have such a private garden in the midst of the city is unheard-of, and the contessa could gain a great deal of money if she would sell."

"But she will not," Ryan said with a small smile.

"Ah, you know the contessa well, then," Pietro said.

"I stayed with my family in her guesthouse one summer when I was a boy," Ryan said. "She taught me Italian, and I taught her English. Look there, Ash. It's the guesthouse." He pointed to a charming mini villa in the middle of the contessa's gardens. "And look ahead of you. Here is the palazzo. God, I don't think it has changed at all."

"Very little changes in Venezia, signore," Pietro remarked as the powerboat came to a stop beside a stone quay. He tied the vessel to an iron ring in the stone and, climbing out, reached down to help Ashley, and then Ryan. "I will bring your bags," he said.

The door to the palazzo had opened, and a woman came forward to greet them. "Ryan?" She was a beautiful, small woman with flawless skin and red-blond hair cut in a short, fashionable bob. "Ryan! I cannot believe it is you! *Dio mio*, you are taller than Finbar himself, aren't you?" She reached up as he bent and kissed both of her cheeks. "Welcome back to Venice, *cara*!" Then the contessa turned and smiled. "You are Ashley, Ryan's bride. I am so glad that you have come. While Ryan fusses with my wardrobe and scolds me about dry rot, you and I shall sightsee. You have never been to Venice, have you? I recognize the look on your face. It is the look that everyone gets who comes for the first time." She kissed Ashley's cheeks. "Welcome! Now come into the house with me, and we'll get you both settled. Have you eaten?" She linked her arms in theirs.

"On the plane, yes, thank you," Ashley said. A palazzo! She was staying in a palace. It was so beautiful. As the boat had come up the little canal she had studied the elegant building ahead of her. It was of red brick that had been worn by wind and weather until it was a rich rose color. It was three stories high, with colonnades and arches. The wide stone quay that they walked across was dotted with great terra-cotta pots filled with rosebushes and ivy. It had obviously not been that cold in Venice yet, for some of the bushes were still in bloom.

They entered the house, and the contessa led them into a beautiful white-and-gold salon. A servant was immediately there, offering them tiny cups of espresso and small pastries. "You were such a boy when I last saw you, Ryan," the contessa said. She turned to Ashley. "But he was quite charming." She laughed. "He thought himself very sophisticated. He roamed all over the city by himself, investigating everything. Considering that he was an American I was very impressed. Never once did he ask me where he might obtain a hamburger."

"What did he look like at sixteen?" Ashley wanted to know.

"Not so tall, but with those same expressive brown eyes and a headful of dark hair," the contessa said. "I thought of him as a young Heathcliff. And he had beautiful manners, which I appreciated." She smiled again. "You must both call me Bianca," she said. "Do you remember that that is my name, Ryan?"

"Yes, I do," Ryan said. He turned to Ashley. "Ma was furious when she heard me address the contessa by her first name. She thought I was being fresh." He chuckled. "Tell me, Bianca, where is the wardrobe?"

"Ah, you are barely off the plane and you wish to work? You are indeed your father's son, Ryan. Old Venutti always said that Finbar Mulcahy was the best student apprentice that he ever taught. He died several years ago."

"Is that why you called me?" Ryan had suspected it.

"Your reputation is exceptional," the contessa told him. "This is a rare piece with a wonderful provenance. I want only the best man to restore it. You are that man. But I am being rude. Let me have one of the servants escort you to your room. Then come back, and I will take you to see the wardrobe. *Si?*"

"*Si*," he agreed.

Ashley and Ryan followed upstairs the serving man who answered the contessa's call, and they were shown to a large, airy bedroom. Ryan assured the servant that he could find his way back downstairs again, and then they were alone. Ashley went over to the windows of the room and pushed open and back the long shutters. There was a wrought-iron railing at each window, and to her surprise the view over the garden and the rooftops beyond was of the Grand Canal. "It's beautiful!" She gasped. "It's like being in another world, Ryan!" Turning, she hugged him. "Thank you for letting me come!"

"I'm glad you're with me, baby," he told her. Then, turning her from the windows, he said, "Look at that bed. Is that not the most baroque piece of furniture you've ever seen? It is a bed made for lovers, Ashley." He flopped down on the bed, and then he grinned. "Come here," he said.

"You've got to go to work, remember?" she admonished him.

"I know, but I want you to see something." He beckoned her over.

Ashley joined him on the big bed. "What?" she said.

"Look up," he said.

The bed had a wooden canopy, and it was painted with cupids, naked full-breasted maidens, and well-endowed gentlemen cavorting about an oval mirror that had been set in the very center of the canopy.

"Oh, my God!" Ashley exclaimed, feeling a blush rising.

"Indeed," Ryan said, chuckling.

"I cannot make love with you in this bed with that mirror hanging over us," she said. "It's...it's...it's...obscene!"

"It's fun," he replied. "You'll like it, Ash. It'll be a real turn-on seeing me fucking you, and when I watch you riding me I'm going to love it. I can't wait until tonight, baby. Just seeing us here side by side is getting me all excited."

Ashley jumped up from the bed. "Don't you dare go downstairs to look at her wardrobe with a hard-on," she scolded him.

He chuckled wickedly. "I missed you last night."

"I was sleeping right next to you," she said.

"I didn't have a chance to initiate you into the Mile-high Club," he teased her. "We'll have to do that on the way home next week."

"You're terrible! Don't you ever think of anything else but sex?" she asked.

"Yeah, I do think of other stuff, like the business, but I seem to be married to a very sexy woman, and I can't seem to get enough of her." He got up.

"Go downstairs and think dry rot," she told him.

"What will you do while I'm gone?" he asked.

"Unpack," she answered. "Now get out of here, Ryan!"

He left her with a grin, and Ashley couldn't help but grin too. She spent the next hour unpacking their two bags, carefully hanging up garments in a baroque wardrobe. Other garments she placed carefully in the drawers of the wardrobe. Then she tucked the two suitcases beneath the big bed. Their bedroom had a bathroom, and Ashley inspected it. It was all black-and-white marble and tile. There was a bidet and a commode, a sink, a shower, and an old-fashioned tub. Everything was spotless, and nothing showed any wear. Ashley laughed to herself, thinking back to the first time she had seen a bidet. It had been that Paris trip when Ben had joined them. He had her convinced it was for washing her feet until a shriek from the chambermaid, followed by her explanation of what a bidet was really for, cleared it all up. Ben and Grandfather had both laughed until they were crying at her outrage and embarrassment.

Ashley felt the tears come. She really missed her brother and her grandfather. She wished they had gotten to meet Ryan, but then, if Ben were alive there would have been no necessity to get married, and she might never have met Ryan Finbar Mulcahy. Was it a good trade? she wondered. But why couldn't she have had both, her brother and her husband? She had not brought her birth control pills with her. If she had a little boy she was going to name him after Ben. Benjamin Kimbrough Mulcahy. Then she would have both Ryan and Ben in her life again.

The manservant came to escort her back downstairs. She followed him.

"It's got some dry rot, Bianca," she heard Ryan saying to the contessa as she entered the smaller salon to which she had been escorted. "But it's in surprisingly good condition, considering its age and its travels. How the hell did it end up in Austria?"

"About three hundred years ago a di Viscontini virgin was married to some Austrian nobleman. I suppose it was part of her dowry. It had originally been made for a doge who was faintly related to the family. How it came into our possession I have no idea. One of my friends was in a small antique shop in Austria a few months ago. He found the girl's name on the inside of a drawer. Lucrezia di Viscontini was her name. It was too good a piece to have belonged to some peasant girl, so she called me. I checked the family records, and sure enough a Lucrezia di Viscontini was married to Count Otto Von Brunner back in 1653. The wardrobe was listed among her dowry possessions."

"Amazing!" Ryan, said running his hand over the door of the wardrobe. "Okay, Bianca, how much restoration do you want done? The piece is walnut, and it's filthy. Do you consider dirt antique value, or do you want it cleaned back to its original state? There are two schools on that. Some people think removing the grime takes away the antique value. Others don't."

"I want the piece to look the way it did originally, and I do not believe the filth of several centuries adds anything to it," the contessa said. "Clean it up, Ryan, and do whatever else needs to be done to bring it back to its original condition."

He nodded. "You're also missing a hinge and some hardware. I'm going to take them all off the wardrobe and see what I can match here in Venice. If I can't match the missing stuff here, then I have a man back in the States who can. He'll make molds of the originals, and then cast new hinges and hardware."

"You are very thorough," she told him.

"My father always said it wasn't worth doing if you didn't do it right," Ryan answered her. He turned at the sound of Ashley's footfall. "Here's my girl."

"And it is time for luncheon, and then siesta," the contessa said. "Come along." She led them from the room where the wardrobe stood, and into a small dining room.

A servant seated the contessa while Ryan held out Ashley's chair before seating himself. Immediately the food was brought. First small plates of *bigoli*, a whole-wheat pasta, were served with a light tomato sauce. This was followed by a lemon chicken with steamed zucchini. Finally a bowl of fresh fruit was brought. There were red grapes, slices of green and yellow melon, and small brown pears.

"I like to serve the *bigoli* with a salsa of onion, oil, and anchovies, but I did not know if you would enjoy it," the contessa said. "Americans are more used to a tomato-based sauce."

"I like fish," Ashley said, "but I will admit that anchovies are not a favorite of mine. The pasta was lovely, and your sauce wonderful."

"We eat dinner late in Venice," the contessa said. "Eight or nine o'clock. I hope you will not be hungry before then. Now, I am going to let you rest for the remainder of today, but tomorrow, while Ryan works with the carpenters to build the container in which to ship my wardrobe, I should like to show you my Venice."

"That is so kind," Ashley replied. "I do not wish to be a bother."

"You are no bother," the contessa insisted. "This is my home. I was born and raised in Venice. I love showing it off."

"Then I accept," Ashley said with a smile.

"*Bene!*" the contessa responded. "And now I shall go and take my siesta."

They left the dining room, and Ryan and Ashley returned upstairs to their bedroom.

"I think I could take a nap," Ashley admitted. "I think the jet lag is beginning to catch up with me." She kicked off her shoes and yawned. Then, slipping off her travel clothes, she pulled on a silk robe over her nakedness.

"I want to go back downstairs and check out that piece again," he said. He had watched her undress swiftly, and enjoyed the glimpses of her lush body.

"Go ahead," she told him, and lay down on the bed as the door closed behind him. She tried to avoid looking up, but it was impossible. She giggled when she did. Ashley wasn't certain whether she could allow her passions free rein in a bed with a mirrored canopy. She suspected she was going to find out, however. Ashley yawned again. She hadn't realized how tired she really was, and then she fell asleep. When Ryan came back an hour or more later, he found his wife sleeping soundly. He smiled down at her. She looked so cute all curled up, a ray of afternoon sunlight touching her bare feet, which stuck out from beneath her silk robe. He stripped off his clothes. It wasn't even four yet, and dinner would not be served until after eight. Lying down, he spooned up against her, one hand reaching around to clasp a breast beneath her robe. He fondled the breast, teasing at the nipple, kissing the nape of her neck.

"Ummmm," she murmured.

"I want to make love to you," he said softly. "Here on a beautiful Venetian afternoon. Now." He pressed up against her tightly.

"There's a mirror over us," she replied low. "I don't think I can do it in a mirror."

"You don't have to look," Ryan said. He pinched her nipple. "You always close your eyes anyway when we get to a certain point."

"I won't be able to look away," she said.

"Stay on your side then," he suggested, pushing up the silk to bare her buttocks. "I know what we can do," Ryan said. "Get over on your tummy, Ash."

The bed shifted beneath them as she complied.

"Now bring your legs up beneath you, and stretch your torso and arms forward so that your butt is elevated. Yeah, that's good."

Ashley felt the mattress shift again as Ryan knelt behind her. He ran his hands over her rounded bottom slowly, seductively, and she shivered.

"Can't see the mirror now, can you?" he asked.

Ashley had to admit she couldn't see the mirror even if she turned her head. She felt him reaching beneath her to find and play with her clit. She squirmed as he began to arouse her lusts. Twice she squealed with pleasure. Then she felt him positioning himself, and his thick long cock slid into her vagina. "Oh, God, yes!" she sighed. "Why is it, Ryan, that you feel so good?"

"Because my dick was fashioned just for that tight cunt of yours, baby." He groaned. Then, fastening his big hands about her firm hips, he thrust hard, deep. "Damn!" he moaned. "You feel so good. You're tight and hot, Ash. I could stay inside you forever, but right now I just want to fuck you." He began to drive himself in and out of her with hard, fast strokes. Looking up, he almost came then and there. The antique mirror gave a golden hue to their bodies, and seeing himself, his cock deep inside her, her round ass raised up, was more exciting than anything he had ever watched before.

"Make me come, Ryan!" she sobbed. "Make me come!"

He realized that he had slowed his pace, so fascinated was he by the tableau in the mirror. He increased his rhythm, struggling to hold his own climax in check until she was near hers. And then he felt her tightening about him, and the spasms came. He let himself go and flooded her with his cum.

"Ohh." Ashley sighed deeply. "That was soo good, darling."

"Yeah, it was," he agreed. He fell back on the bed and pulled her onto his smooth chest. "Do you want to know how we looked in that mirror? It was the sexiest thing I've ever seen, Ash. The mirror is so old that it gives our bodies a golden look."

"But you could see what you were doing without looking up," she said.

"But I wanted to look up, and what I saw in the mirror was even more exciting than what I could see right before me," Ryan told her. "I had one hell of a time holding back."

"You were wonderful," Ashley purred. She nibbled at his shoulder. "And you taste good too." She licked his skin with leisurely strokes of her tongue.

"Behave yourself," he said sternly. "You're going to make me hot again, and I can't let you exhaust me, baby. I have to begin work tomorrow."

"So," she replied, "having satisfied your lust, you're going to toss me aside now?"

"I will never toss you aside, but you've already had a little nap while I worked downstairs. Now I need a nap so that when we go down to dinner the contessa doesn't think we've been doing nothing but fucking all siesta," he told her.

"If she didn't think we would be making love," Ashley reasoned, "she wouldn't have given us a bed with a mirror in its canopy."

"I imagine the other bedrooms are even more sensual. It's the nature of a sixteenth-century Venetian palazzo to be devoted to the pleasures of the senses," he said. "You should see the bedroom ceilings in the guesthouse before we go back. My poor mother was horrified. She had the servants stretch sheets across them so we wouldn't be able to see them and be led astray." He laughed. "But I figured a way to loosen the sheets to look at the ceiling in my bedroom at night, and then cover it again in the morning. I was one horny sixteen-year-old."

Ashley giggled. "And you're one horny thirty-nine-year-old," she told him, snuggling now into the curve of his arm. "Good thing I love you, Ryan."

He smiled into her hair. "Good thing I love you too," he told her.

They slept, awakening to see the sky beyond their windows darkening with evening. After bathing and dressing, they joined the contessa in a small salon for an aperitif before dinner. And after dinner they sat again in the salon talking, until Bianca di Viscontini arose and excused herself.

"I am not," she said, "as young as I once was." And she smiled. "I now must seek my bed before midnight, but Ryan, feel free to take your lovely wife and explore some of Venice's nightlife,"

"Not tonight, Bianca. We are both still tired from our flight, and tomorrow I wish to begin the construction of the crate. Your workmen will be here early, I know," he said.

When they returned to their bedroom they discovered the bed had been remade and turned down for the night.

When Ashley awoke the following morning Ryan was already gone from their bed. Sleepy still, she turned over and fell back into slumber, awakening only when the sound of their bedroom door clicked open. Ashley turned over as a woman in a maid's uniform came in with a tray.

"*Buon giorno,* signora," the servant said. She set the tray down on a small table and, going to the bed, plumped the pillows so Ashley might sit up. Then, fetching the tray, she set it on Ashley's lap. *"Ecco la prima colazione."*

"Parla lei inglese?" Ashley asked.

"*Si,* signora," the maid answered.

"Where is my husband?"

"He is in the salon with the workmen."

"*Grazie,*" Ashley said, and the maid left the room with a nod of her head.

On the tray Ashley found a plate with a small portion of scrambled eggs, a slice of melon, a croissant, butter, and a cup of cappuccino. To her surprise she discovered she was hungry, and ate it all, savoring the cappuccino, which Ryan had explained to her Italians drank in the morning, and not any time of day. When she had finished her meal she got up, showered, and got dressed. She chose a pair of beige slacks in a mix of light wool and silk, and a cream-colored wool turtleneck. Her watch said ten thirty. She had really slept in. Ashley brushed her hair and put on some lipstick and gold earrings before heading downstairs.

Hesitating at the bottom of the stairs, she was rescued from her predicament by the contessa's butler, who, seeing her, said, "The contessa is awaiting you in the blue salon, signora. I will show you." And he did.

"Good morning," Ashley greeted her hostess. "I apologize for keeping you waiting. I seem to have overslept."

"No, no," Bianca di Viscontini told her. "I am only just down myself. I have the habit of breakfast in bed at nine thirty each morning. It is a privilege I allow myself now that I am to be sixty. I am amazed to realize I have lived six decades," she said with a laugh. "My poor husband died when he was sixty-three, but then, he had been ill for so many years. It was why we had no children. Do you want children? I can see Ryan as a father." And Bianca di Viscontini smiled.

"Yes, we want children," Ashley answered. "Soon. I am not a young girl."

"You are beautiful, and perfect for him. You do not take him too seriously, or defer to him, as his mama and sisters were always doing. As the only boy he was very much spoiled, I fear," the contessa said. "Did Elvira bring you your breakfast?"

"Yes, it was wonderful. Usually Byrnes brings me coffee in the morning, but to have such a lovely little meal and a cappuccino was quite a treat. When will you be sixty? You don't look like a woman of sixty."

"December third," the contessa said. "I think sixty today is very different from when my own mother was sixty."

"You are December born? I am the ninth," Ashley told the contessa.

"Then we two Sagittarians should get on famously," Bianca said. "Are you ready to do a little sightseeing?"

"I am!" Ashley agreed.

"Come along then," Bianca di Viscontini said and she led her guest outside and across the broad cobbled street to the quay where a gondola awaited them, "I think you will enjoy the flavor of the city better if we travel by gondola rather than a powerboat," she told Ashley as they stepped down into the vessel and seated themselves.

"*Buon giorno,* contessa," the gondolier said as they entered his boat. Then as soon as he saw they were comfortably seated, he pushed away from the quay, and began to row down the small canal.

Ashley could feel the pull of the current as their gondola entered the Grand Canal, and she looked at the city about her. "This is so beautiful," she said. "The colors, the way the sunlight hits them. It really is an artist's city."

"It is even more brilliant in the summer, when the sun is higher," Bianca said. "For now the color is muted, more like the canvas of a French Impressionist painter. But it doesn't matter what time of year it is. I love this city!"

"I can certainly understand why," Ashley responded.

"I will take you first to the Piazza San Marco," Bianca said. "We are not far from it. But first you should know a little bit of our history, of how Venice came into being. At first it was just a few small joined towns built about the lagoon, perhaps late in the fifth century, perhaps a bit earlier. Rome was in its decline. The barbarians had fallen upon its civilization and were devouring it. At first the refugees from the violence would return to their destroyed homes, but eventually many made up their minds not to stay. They sought a place that would be difficult and unappealing to the Goths, the Huns, and the others who followed them to attack. I will not bore you with an in-depth history. We pledged our loyalties to the emperor in Constantinople. While Europe struggled in the barbaric time known as the Dark Ages, we organized and grew within the safety of the Eastern empire. We were known as Byzantium's favorite daughter, and the truth is we were a Byzantine city, yet different from other Byzantine cities. The city as we know it today, with its walls, its plazas, towers, and palazzos, emerged from the mud banks and waters of the lagoon. Sometimes we were protected by the armies of Byzantium. Sometimes we sent our mercenaries to fight for Byzantium." She stopped in her recitation. "Ah, here we are at the Piazza San Marco." The gondola slipped into a mooring, and the gondolier jumped out to help his passengers. "You will wait for us, Antonio," the contessa said in quick Italian.

"The American is very pretty," the gondolier replied in the same language.

"She is a married woman," the contessa replied.

"I like a woman with experience," he said with a grin.

"Behave yourself, you bad boy," the contessa scolded him. She turned to Ashley. "Are the columns flanking the piazza not glorious? That one is topped by the winged lion of Saint Mark, the spiritual guardian of Venice. The other is crowned with Saint Theodore, who was once considered our spiritual guardian. Long ago they hanged criminals from those columns, a poor use of such beauty to pair it with such ugliness as an execution."

The two women made their way across the piazza through large flocks of pigeons strutting about, cadging for food, and toward the great domed cathedral of Saint Mark.

"There have always been great festivals held in the piazza and before the cathedral," the contessa said. "The Fourth Crusade set out from here."

They entered the basilica of Saint Mark, and Ashley was rendered breathless by its beauty. "There is something very Eastern here," she said.

You are clever to have realized that," the contessa said. "Byzantium was very Oriental in its way, and Venice has traded with the Eastern lands for centuries. One of our doges asked that every ship trading with Egypt, Syria, Turkey, and the like return with *objets d'art* that could be used to beautify our city. The lion of St. Mark's, with his agate eyes, came from Syria. It is actually a chimera. And see the screen behind the high altar? We call it the Pala d'Oro. It was beaten into its great form by goldsmiths in Byzantium, and beautifully decorated by the finest jewelers in Byzantium. It seems to radiate light, doesn't it?" the contessa said.

After they had seen the great church, the contessa pointed out the Doge's Palace, which stood on one side of the piazza. Next the contessa led Ashley from the great piazza across a stone bridge into a charming small square. The square had several tiny shops, and a little café with tables outside beneath a striped awning. It was there they stopped to have a light lunch before walking back to their gondola to return to the palazzo for the siesta hour.

"Tomorrow at eleven," the contessa told the gondolier.

Ashley thanked the contessa for the morning, and went to see how Ryan was doing. She found him sitting with the workmen eating bread, sausage, and cheese, and sharing a bottle of Chianti. A huge half-finished crate was now taking up part of the salon, empty of furniture but for the wardrobe. "Wow, you got a lot done this morning," she said. "You should get it finished by day's end."

"Almost finished," he told her. "Remember, siesta. The men will eat, and then stretch out to sleep for an hour or more. Did you have a good morning?"

"Wonderful, starting with breakfast in bed," Ashley told him. "I could get used to this Venetian way of life, Ryan."

"Are you going upstairs now?"

"Uh-huh. Are you?" she teased him.

He sighed. "I'll take my siesta here," he said. "That way I'll be ready to go back to work when the men are. I want the crate finished by tomorrow morning. It's going to take another full day to pack it, and then I want to be here when FedEx picks it up the day after. Then we'll head home, baby."

"I'll go take my siesta alone then," she said with a smile at him, and with a wave of her hand she left him.

"*Sposato?*" one of the workmen asked.

"*Si,*" Ryan replied.

"*Ella e bella ragazza,*" the workman said, nodding approvingly.

"*Mille grazie,*" Ryan told him with a smile.

The following day the contessa took Ashley to see the great church of San Giorgio Maggiore, and they visited the public gardens, a swath of green on the Bacino di San Marco. But then to Ashley's surprise the gondola headed back up the Grand Canal, bypassing the little canal that led to the palazzo.

"There is a woman I want you to visit," the contessa said with a smile as their vessel turned into a small canal and docked itself. "It is not far, and I see you are wise enough to wear sensible shoes."

Mystified, but nonetheless curious, Ashley followed her hostess into another of Venice's small, pretty squares, where

Bianca led her into a charming little shop. Ashley's green eyes lit up when she saw the exquisite lingerie displayed.

"This is the shop of Valentina Sforza," the contessa explained. "She has a mulberry garden outside of the city where she raises silkworms. She has a coterie of village women who harvest the cocoons and then spin the threads into fabric. From that fabric she makes, as you can see, the most beautiful one-of-a-kind garments. I thought that perhaps you might be interested in her work."

Ashley was already examining the negligees and other intimate garments on display throughout the shop. They were beautiful, and the workmanship was the absolute best. "Yes," she said, suddenly all business. "I am most interested in this woman's work, Bianca. I should like to speak to her."

"As she does not speak English, and your Italian is charming, but scant, I will translate for you," the contessa said. "May I present to you Signora Valentina Sforza."

"Tell her I am delighted to meet her, and that never have I seen such exquisite work," Ashley replied.

Bianca spoke quickly to the dark-haired older woman who had been behind a counter since their arrival. The woman was dressed all in black. She chattered back to the contessa, who then said, "The signora thanks you. She wants to know if you wish to purchase something."

"Tell her I have three shops in the United States. We carry only the finest intimate garments for women. I want to know if she can supply me with her work."

Bianca spoke again. Signora Sforza spoke. The contessa then turned back to Ashley. "Signora Sforza says because her garments are handmade from her carefully raised silk, she is unable to supply in quantity like some factory."

Ashley smiled archly. The bargaining had begun. "Please tell Signora Sforza that I am not interested in quantity. I seek only quality. I would require six garments three times a year, to be delivered in November, January, and May. I will set up an account here in Venice with FedEx or DHL that will be my responsibility. Does she have a computer and e-mail?"

The contessa translated. "Yes, she has e-mail."

"Good," Ashley replied. "Then she will be able to communicate with me. My husband's Italian is good, and he can translate her messages to me, and tell me what to write to her. Now, can she deliver what I require?"

The contessa spoke. Signora Sforza spoke, and then Bianca turned to Ashley. "When would this arrangement begin?" she asked.

"I will, with her permission, pick out six garments today, and pay for them. She will prepare them for shipping, and I will send someone for them. I will expect the next six garments in January. Can she have them ready then?"

The contessa spoke earnestly to Signora Sforza. The conversation was longer than the previous ones had been, and Ashley wished she were able to understand. Finally the contessa said, "She wants to know where her creations will be sold."

"Tell her I have three shops, but her garments will be sold only in New York, where the rich and famous will clamor for them."

"She wants her label in them," the contessa said.

"Tell her no. I will pay whatever she asks within reason, but if her label is in the garment, people would know where they came from, and would trade with her directly. I must keep her exclusive to Lacy Nothings. If she prefers not to sell to me I will buy something for myself and let the matter go." Ashley turned away and began examining a nightgown. Her heart was hammering. She really wanted the signora's work, but she wasn't going to introduce it into the States, only to have Neiman Marcus steal the designer away from her. "You might tell her a large store will attempt to copy her work," Ashley said, "and then we will both lose."

The two older women exchanged more talk, and finally the contessa said, "She will agree to this arrangement for two years. After that your agreement must be renewed. Can you live with that?"

"*Si*," Ashley said with a smile, holding out her hand to Signora Sforza. "*Mille grazie*, Valentina."

The designer smiled and nodded. Then she said something to Bianca, who laughed.

"She says her creations will be very expensive," the contessa told Ashley.

Ashley nodded. "Let me pick what I want, and then she will tell me."

Returning to the palazzo, she thanked the contessa. "The New York store will have people going wild over the signora's work," Ashley told the older woman. "Very wealthy men at Christmas who can't spend the holiday with their mistresses will snap up these negligees." She chuckled. "And they will pay the price I charge."

"What will you charge?" the contessa asked curiously.

"I don't know yet," Ashley said. "I must work out what it costs me to purchase them. Not just the signora's price, but the cost of shipping and gift wrapping them, for they will have to be wrapped beautifully. The presentation is every bit as important as is the gift inside the box, especially when you are disappointing a woman."

"She overcharged you," the contessa said.

"I know," Ashley replied. "But it is actually reasonable by American standards. Thank you so much for introducing me to her work. It really is quite beautiful and very unique.

I'm just sorry I can't carry it in Egret Pointe, but my trade there would not go the cost, nor would the mall shop."

They sat to have afternoon tea in the contessa's small garden.

"I must go to Milano tomorrow," Bianca di Viscontini informed Ashley. "I shall not see you again. I hope you will not mind being on your own in the palazzo. Antonio and his gondola will be at your disposal, but beware of him," she said with a smile. "He would like to seduce you. All these young gondoliers live to seduce an American lady."

Ashley laughed. "I'll take Ryan with me. They have already begun loading the wardrobe into the crate this afternoon. Why are you going to Milan?"

"I have the final fittings on my winter wardrobe," the contessa told her. "I saw several wonderful outfits at the autumn shows last spring. Now that I am a wealthy widow I find that gossip and fashion fill my world."

"I will miss your company," Ashley said. "You have been such a wonderful hostess to us, but I shall not mind staying in your palazzo for a day or two more and pretending it is mine, and that I am a princess."

Bianca di Viscontini smiled warmly. "I am so glad you have enjoyed your visit."

They had a wonderful dinner that evening, but Ashley awoke after they had gone to bed to find Ryan was not by her side. Hearing voices on the terrace below, she got out of bed and, going to the window, looked down. She could see the shadowed forms of two people stretched out together on a chaise. They were speaking Italian, but she recognized the voices of both her husband and the contessa. What was Ryan doing with Bianca di Viscontini so late at night? She stood next to the window's balcony railing, watching for some minutes. Then finally, to her relief, the couple on the chaise got up, embraced, and then went back inside the palazzo. Ashley got back into bed quickly, and shortly she heard the bedroom door open, and her husband slipped into bed beside her.

She pretended to be asleep, as she had obviously been when he had left her. And why had he left her? And why was he lying on a double chaise with the contessa? She didn't know how to ask him without revealing that she had been spying on him. Then she chided herself for being silly. They were old friends. The contessa was twenty years older than her husband. Tomorrow Bianca di Viscontini would be gone to Milan, and the palazzo was theirs, and she was going to look up into that mirror over them while Ryan made love to her, Ashley decided. But still her curiosity nagged her. Maybe one day she would ask her husband why he had gotten up in the middle of the night to speak with another woman. But not this day. Or tomorrow, or the tomorrow after that. But one day.

Chapter Ten

It was raining when they left Venice. November weather had finally set in. There were a total of only five people in the first-class section of the plane. Ashley slept most of the trip, as did Ryan. They had had a sexual marathon that last day and night in the palazzo, because the weather was already getting lousy. And Ashley dreamed quite vividly during the flight. Dreamed of their naked bodies, all golden, reflected darkly in the mirror in the canopy above their bed. She had never seen—even imagined—anything so wickedly erotic as the images of the two of them vigorously fucking. She had never had so many orgasms in a night as she had had last night.

The first one had come, surprising her with its suddenness, when she watched her husband, his dark head between her pale thighs, kissing, nibbling, sucking, and licking her. The view was a completely different one from just gazing down her torso at him. Mesmerized by the portrait of him even as she felt his mouth and tongue on her clit, she went over the edge in an explosion of sensation that left her gasping for breath. And the night had continued on in that vein. At one point she had taken him in her mouth and milked him dry, his salty, creamy cum spurting down her throat, and he had groaned with his pleasure as he watched her in the mirror.

"Wake up, baby." Ryan's voice pierced her consciousness. "We're going to be landing shortly."

Ashley slowly opened her eyes. "How shortly?" she asked him.

"About forty minutes," he said.

The dream lingered, and frankly she was hot. She really needed to be screwed right now. "You promised me something," she murmured against his ear. Then she got up and headed for the first-class restroom, glancing over her shoulder once as she went to make meaningful eye contact with him.

Ryan couldn't help but grin when he realized to what she was referring. He waited a moment, and then followed her. The compartment was a bit larger than the one in tourist or business, but it was still small. He squeezed into it, throwing the lock shut, pulling her against him as she unzipped his trousers and slipped her hand in to fondle him. The thought of what she had in mind had already begun to have its effect, and it didn't take long for his penis to stiffen and lengthen. "You are a very bad girl," he said softly as he backed her up against a bulkhead, his hands pushing up her skirt to her waist, discovering she wasn't wearing any panties. "Very bad." He chuckled as his hand cupped her mound, and he found that she was wet. Very wet.

"I was dreaming of last night," Ashley said, her lips against his lips. "You woke me up just as I was sucking you off," she told him.

His hands cupped her buttocks. She wrapped her legs about his middle as he raised her up just enough so that he could push into her wet, hot vagina. Sinking to the hilt, he whispered in her ear, "I love it when you're bad, baby." Then he began to fuck her with quick, sharp strokes until they both quickly climaxed and collapsed weakly against each other. "Welcome to the Mile-high Club, Ash," he said softly, kissing her mouth.

"You are probably the best husband in the world," Ashley said with a deep sigh. She pulled her skirt down. "I really was dreaming about us last night, and when you woke me I was so hot. Now I'll make it home." She turned and washed her hands in the tiny sink, then dried them. "I'll go first," she told him, and slipped from the small compartment, walking back down the wide aisle to her seat. Reaching into her bag she pulled out a small pair of silk briefs, and, since there was no one around them, Ashley slipped them on as Ryan reached their seat.

He grinned. "You weren't wearing those when we got on the plane?"

"Hey, you said you were going to initiate me into the Mile-high Club," Ashley answered. "I thought it better not to wear them until after we had our little rendezvous."

He laughed, genuinely amused. If he had let nature take its course, could he have found a better wife, a life partner, a mate, than Ashley? He didn't think so. And it had been so easy to fall in love with her. He had told Bianca that very thing a couple of nights ago. Restless, he had gotten up and wandered downstairs to the main salon. He had seen Bianca out on the tiled terrace smoking, and had joined her. They really hadn't had a moment alone to talk privately, and they had a lot of catching up to do.

It had been twenty-three years since he had last seen her. He was surprised to see how well she had aged. Hardly at all. Of course, her elderly husband was dead now many years, and he was curious as to why she had never remarried. She had laughed that husky laugh of hers that he still found sexy, and said she enjoyed her freedom.

"I am wealthy. I have my interests, and am on several committees regarding the preservation and well-being of Venezia, *cara*. When it amuses me I take a lover, but never for too long. And I am very discreet. I am content as I near sixty. My family understands, and I do not have to be alone if I do not choose to be."

"I never had an opportunity to thank you," Ryan said quietly.

"Thank me? For what, *cara*?" the contessa asked him.

Ryan smiled. "For taking a boy and turning him into a man that summer. Whatever I've learned about pleasing a woman, Bianca, I learned from you when I was sixteen. I couldn't have had a better tutor. Thank you, *cara*."

She laughed. "It was very bad of me. I should not have seduced you, Ryan. Your poor mother. I will never forget the look on her face when she confronted me with it. It was very wrong of your sister to tell her. Our affair would have ended quite naturally when you returned to America in September. I was so sorry your mother felt she had to take you and your sisters home immediately, but at least your father remained to finish his course those last two weeks. He moved in with Venutti, you know."

"I didn't," Ryan said.

"Have you thought of me over the years?" the contessa asked him.

"I have, Bianca, with gratitude. That summer is a bittersweet memory," Ryan told her, and he took her hand and kissed it. "To have loved you once made me realize the treasure that I have in my Ashley. You were my first love. She is, will be, my last love."

"She is a charming and intelligent girl, *cara*. I hope you will tell her about our summer one day. Perhaps you should have told her about it before you came."

"It is in the past, Bianca," Ryan said. Yes, it was in the past, he thought. The door had closed on it years ago.

"We'll be landing shortly, Mr. and Mrs. Mulcahy," the steward said. "You might want to fasten your safety belts. Weather is fair in New York, and the temperature is currently fifty degrees. Will you have anything to declare?"

"No," Ryan said. "It was a business trip."

"Then you should zip right through customs," the steward replied.

"Bill will be meeting us," Ashley reminded her husband. "And how about those nightgowns in my luggage?"

"Declare them if you want," Ryan said, "but they're women's clothing, and it's your bag, and we'll get through faster if we don't."

"There is a decidedly larcenous streak in you, Ryan Mulcahy," she told him.

They landed smoothly, collected their two bags, and breezed through customs. Bill was awaiting them immediately on the other side of the barrier with a porter, who carried the bags to the car to be loaded into the trunk. Seeing all the people around them vying for taxies, Ashley appreciated the convenience that money could buy. Bill piloted them home without incident, and as they came up the driveway in the dusk of early evening, Ashley realized how glad she was to be home.

The camera system had been installed and perfected at Ryan's business while they had been in Venice. And Frankie had turned a large room and a small adjoining room at the top of the house into an office for her brother while they had been gone.

The next day Ashley returned to Lacy Nothings, and Ryan went upstairs to his new offices to check on the workshop in the city.

Driving down to the shop, Ashley enjoyed the last of the autumn color. In the back of her Solstice were the six negligees she had purchased from Valentina in Venice. She wanted Nina to see them before she sent them into the New York shop. Nina was already in the shop waiting for her. The two women embraced.

"Was it wonderful?" Nina wanted to know.

"It was perfect. The contessa is lovely. She showed me all the high points of Venice herself while Ryan worked to get her piece of furniture packed and ready for shipping. The palazzo was incredible. We could see the whole city and the Grand Canal from our bedroom. And, Nina! The bed was seventeenth-century, with a mirror in the canopy! Oh, the food was good too, but a little too much seafood for my taste."

"A mirror in the top of the bed?" Nina chuckled. "I'll have to program that into one of my fantasies for The Channel. Maybe I'll go to Venice and take Casanova for a lover. I think I'll be a sexy sixteen-year-old virgin for him."

Ashley giggled. "You know, I had such a good time I didn't even miss The Channel. I'm probably not going to need it now. Ryan and I are getting along terrifically. And wait 'til you see what I brought back from Venice for the New York shop. I found a source. She has silkworms, a mulberry orchard, peasant women who actually spin the silk, and she designs the most gorgeous negligees. I bought six."

"We can't sell them?" Nina said.

"They are going to be outrageously expensive, and I believe the city shop is the only one in which we'll carry them. Valentina will ship me six garments, three times a year. Everything is handmade. She just can't do any more, and she has her own shop. We'll have them for Christmas,

Valentine's, and the June brides." She set the embroidered satin lingerie case on the shop counter and opened it up.

"Wow!" Nina said, looking down at the ice blue silk nightgown on top. Carefully she examined it, noting the almost invisible stitches. "It's only two pieces," she said. "It's amazing. And it's so simple, but my God, it's sophisticated and elegant. I agree. This is strictly for the city shop. We couldn't sell this in Egret Pointe." She looked at the other five garments. Then she said, "You want me to ship these to Suzette?"

"Yes, but first we have to remove Valentina's labels and sew in our own. I told her not to put her labels in when she sends us the shipments from now on," Ashley said.

Nina nodded. "You're right. We don't want anyone learning our source for these gorgeous negligees. They are going to make the city shop's reputation. Suzette knows some important people. Some actress is going to end up wearing one of these."

"It's getting near Thanksgiving," Ashley said. "Has the town committee decided exactly what the windows theme is to be this year?"

"Winter Wonderland," Nina answered. "The bulletin came last week."

"Ohh, then I had better get started working on a design," Ashley replied.

The days that followed seemed to fly by. The wardrobe arrived from Venice, and Ryan went into the city for a few days to supervise the unpacking and start his craftsmen on the restoration. They spent a quiet Thanksgiving, inviting Lina, Frankie, her son, and Nina to dinner. December came, and on the ninth the florist delivered a Waterford crystal vase of lavender roses with a card reading, *Happy Birthday,* cara *Ashley, Bianca.*

"Oh, I feel terrible," Ashley said. "Her birthday was on the third."

"Don't," Ryan said. "It's her way to remember things like that. She did not expect you to remember her birthday."

"The local florist is in shock that someone would have a Waterford vase delivered to him in which to put flowers," Ashley said.

That night as they sat down to the birthday dinner Mrs. B. had cooked for Ashley, Ryan said, "You haven't asked what I got you for your birthday."

"No, I haven't," she said, smiling.

He handed her a jeweler's box, and, opening it, Ashley saw a beautiful round canary yellow diamond set in Irish red gold. "I never got you an engagement ring," he said quietly. "I had the ring made for you in Venice and sent home for Byrnes to secrete. I didn't want you to find it before I gave it to you."

"Oh, Ryan," Ashley said softly as she took the ring from the velvet and slipped it on her finger. "It's beautiful. I've heard of yellow diamonds, but never before seen one."

"I thought it suited you," he answered. "Happy birthday, baby."

"Thank you, darling," she replied, leaning over and kissing his lips.

That weekend they began decorating the house for the holidays. Byrnes went off to the local nursery and returned with garlands of princess pine, which were then wrapped about the columns on the portico, and strung between them with lights. A enormous wreath of pine, pinecones, red berries, and white heather was hung on the front door. Electric candles were set in every window of the house, and on the twentieth Ryan and Ashley went back to the nursery to choose trees for the living room, the dining room, and the small parlor of their bedroom suite. A ten-footer had already been delivered and set up in the center of the round foyer. It was decorated with red plaid bows, papier-mâché lacquered red apples, and white lights. The one in the dining room had green and burgundy silk bows, and multicolored glass balls in ruby, sapphire, emerald, amethyst, gold, and silver. It had tiny white lights. The tree in the living room was done with Victorian ornaments, many of them authentic and beautifully preserved. It had multicolored tiny fairy lights.

The tree they had chosen for the parlor in their bedroom suite was set on a round table that was covered with a dark green velvet cloth. The table was placed near the fireplace. The tree was decorated with painted glass balls that depicted the various activities in Santa's workshop, and little red velvet bows. Its lights were multicolored.

"This is where we will put our gifts for us," Ashley said softly. "I have a very special gift for you on our first Christmas together, Ryan." And she smiled mischievously at him. "And I've found some boy toys that you'll like too," she teased.

"What do I buy the woman who has everything?" he asked candidly.

"I like beautiful and unusual things. And soft things. And you can always add to my Santa collection," she told him.

"The one in the dining room on the sideboard?" he asked her. "That's one fantastic accumulation of Saint Nicks."

Ashley laughed. "My grandmother started it for my father when he was a little boy. My mother added several pieces in the years that they were married. I began adding to it after my brother was killed," she told him. "I'm always looking. Ohh, Ryan! It's going to be the best Christmas ever! The house hasn't been so full in ages, and Christmas is when a house should be filled with family and laughter."

"Did you have to invite them *all?*" he asked in a pained tone.

"Ryan, Christmas Day will be our four-month anniversary. I know your older sisters are difficult, but surely by now they have accepted the fact that we are married. That what began as a marriage of convenience for us both has by some miracle turned into a love match. They backed off their attempts to sue you, didn't they?"

"Only because Ray and their lawyers told them to forget about it. They didn't have a leg to stand on. Dad's will just said I had to marry by forty, and I did. I won't be forty until spring. And Ma made some pretty dire threats. Remember, she's got a lot of money herself to leave one day, and the harpies are greedy."

"They just need to get to know me better," Ashley said. "Didn't they all accept our invitation for Christmas?"

"You asked them for two nights, Ash. They're dying to see how you live. Frankie has been enjoying torturing them. Having the harpies here is going to be pure hell on wheels." Ryan groaned.

"It will be fine," Ashley assured her husband.

He looked dubious, but there was nothing he could do to prevent his older sisters and their husbands from descending on them en masse for the holiday. For one thing, Mrs. Byrnes had been cooking up a storm. And Byrnes had been polishing more silver than Ryan had ever imagined even existed. And the daily housekeeper had, with Ashley's permission, been bringing two other women with her for ten days now. All the bedrooms were turned out: rugs, draperies, and hangings vacuumed, furniture dusted, the beds made with lavender-scented linens, feather beds, and lovely, puffy goose-down comforters. On the day their guests were arriving, small vases of red carnations and green pine were put in each of the bedrooms. By the time the extra-long limousine pulled up to disgorge his relations, Ryan was almost resigned. It was Christmas Eve, and the house smelled of pine and cinnamon. He was in love with his wife, and he couldn't have imagined a year ago at this time how happy he would be. "Welcome to Kimbrough Hall!" he boomed jovially, standing on the portico. He embraced his mother.

They came up to him in birth order, as they had always done. Bride and Peter Franklin; Elisabetta and Paul Sweeney; Kathleen and Kevin McGuire; Magdalena and Frank Butler; Deirdre and Robert Napoli; Frankie and her son, Michael O'Connor. He greeted them each, and they moved on to Ashley, who stood next to her husband.

"Quite the lord of the manor, aren't we?" Bride said sharply.

"As a matter of fact, he is now," Ashley replied, smiling. "I'm so glad you could all come. Let's go in. It's cold. Byrnes will take your coats." She turned to speak to their own chauffeur, who was standing nearby. "Bill, will you help the limo driver with the luggage, please? Thank you." She led her guests inside, where Byrnes was waiting.

"Boy, you sure fell into it, didn't you?" the limo driver who knew Bill said.

Bill grinned. "It's like the old days my granddad used to tell me about, when he worked for a family. I even got my own digs above the garage."

The limo driver whistled. Then he said, "Let's get these bags inside. I got a long trip back to town, and the wife will have my head if I'm not back in time for church tonight." He opened the trunk of the car, and together the two men began getting the bags into the house, where Byrnes was waiting for them. Helping them, he led them upstairs, showing them the bedrooms where the bags were to be deposited. Then, coming back down, he handed the limo driver a plain white envelope.

"Merry Christmas from Mr. and Mrs. Mulcahy," he said. "There'll be another envelope when you come to pick them up on the twenty-sixth. Drive carefully." Byrnes opened the front door and ushered the driver out.

To Ryan's surprise the evening went smoothly. They sat down to a supper of shrimp cocktail, followed by small plates of pasta with a simple marinara sauce, followed by Dover sole broiled in butter with lemon, a marvelous casserole of carrots made with cheese and cream, tiny potato puffs, and a green salad. Dessert was a plain caramel custard in individual cups topped with raspberries.

Angelina Mulcahy smiled, well pleased. Her new daughter-in-law, while not a Roman Catholic, had known that December twenty-fourth was a fast day, although she hardly thought the lovely feast placed before them would qualify as a fast. She noted that her daughters and their spouses were eating to the point of silence. "Is there a church we may attend tonight?" Lina asked Ashley.

"St. Anne's," Ashley told her. "Ryan can take five in his car, and Bill will take the rest in the limo I rented for the weekend. The mass begins at eleven. That's why we've eaten early. I thought you all might like a little nap before church."

"Will you be going with us?" Kathleen asked pointedly.

Ashley shook her head. "I'll be at St. Luke's. I'm an Anglican. I'm driving myself. And before you ask, I don't intend to convert to Roman Catholicism. If this were a perfect world there would be no differences in religion to divide us, but it isn't a perfect world, and I prefer my own church." She smiled at Ryan's family.

"Will you ever get married in the Church?" Bride wanted to know.

"Yes," Ashley said, but added nothing more.

"And your children? That is, if you have any," Elisabetta said. "How will you raise them, I'd like to know?"

"I'm sure you would." Ryan stepped into the conversation, which was beginning to lean toward confrontational. "We'll cross that bridge when we come to it. Now, girls, I think that is enough questions for tonight." He saw his eldest sister, Bride, smile just ever so slightly, and thought, *My God, I think she's actually beginning to warm up.*

At ten thirty the cars were ready, and they were transported to St. Anne's. Ashley honked and waved at them as she passed them by, pulling up at the pretty stone church across the street. Both churches let out at approximately the same time, and Ryan asked Frankie to drive his car home while he joined his wife. They led the way back to Kimbrough Hall. There they found whiskeyed eggnog and hot mulled cider, along with very thin slices of an almost black and extremely rich fruitcake awaiting them.

"This is fruitcake?" Angelina was surprised.

"It's how the Irish make it," Ashley told her mother-in-law. "It's my great-great-grandmother's recipe. It's one of the few things I actually make every year."

"It doesn't taste at all like those disgusting light fruitcake bricks we had to sell in Catholic school," Frankie noted. "Remember, we used to kid about using them to build a house." She laughed. "All those yucky candied cherries, and big pieces of nuts."

Everyone departed for bed. The tree in the living room was now surrounded by gifts, as each of the sisters had brought presents. Ashley walked through the house, smiling to herself. She had a really big surprise tomorrow for her husband. She stood for a moment in the living room, darkened now but for the dying fire in the fireplace. It was well after midnight, and there was absolute magic in the air. She could feel it. Going upstairs, she noted it was silent behind all the bedroom doors. She entered their bedroom suite to find Ryan standing naked, a large red bow about his very distended cock.

Ashley giggled. "You're kidding," she said.

"You don't like my present?" he said.

"I want to know how you got it that way without me," she replied.

He grinned. "I've got a talented hand and a great imagination."

"Well, I suppose I should try it on for size," she said as she began to pull off her turtleneck. "It looks like it might be a good fit, darling." She unfastened her lacy bra and tossed it aside. Then she kicked off the slippers she always wore in the house when she wasn't barefooted, unzipped her slacks, pulled them off, pulled down her silk briefs, and stepped out of them. She was quite naked now. Reaching out, she undid the bow adorning his long, thick penis, let it drop, and then, wrapping her hand about him, she led him into their bedroom.

Pushing him down on the bed, she climbed atop him, her butt toward his head, and, leaning down, captured his dick between her two full breasts, moving it up and down.

"Ohh, baby," he murmured as he hardened seriously. His hands reached out to squeeze her cute ass cheeks.

"You like?" she asked him. Her tongue snaked out to lick at the tip of his cock.

"Yesss!" he hissed. "I like."

She took the tip of him between her lips and rotated her tongue about him. "Mmmm," she said. Then she bent lower and sucked him deep into her mouth and throat, but she was careful with him, because she didn't want him to come in her mouth this time. For a moment or more she sucked him, and then released him, gasping as she did when Ryan pushed a finger deep into her ass. "Ohh, my!" He had never done that before. She squeezed her butt cheeks together hard.

He chuckled and rotated the finger. "You like?" he parroted her query of a few moments before.

"I'm not sure," she admitted.

"We'll get a nice little dildo and play sometime. I think we should expand our horizons, don't you?" he said softly as he withdrew the single finger.

"Oh, God, am I boring you?" Ashley asked, turning around to face him.

"You will never bore me, baby," Ryan told her. Then he rolled her over and thrust himself into her wet pussy. "This is where I belong!"

Ashley wrapped herself around him and let him fuck her until she was weak with pleasure. He took her high, and she scratched and bit and screamed as he groaned and finally, as they climaxed together, shouted. Afterward she giggled as they lay together, replete and satisfied.

"Good thing we're way down the hall from everyone else," she said. "The harpies would sure as hell be jealous."

He chuckled. "Fuck 'em!" he said, and she laughed.

"That was your first Christmas gift," she told him.

"Yours too," he responded, pulling her into his arms, and then yanking the down quilt over them.

They fell asleep, waking several hours later to the smell of coffee in their sitting room. Byrnes had crept quietly in, as he did almost every morning, to bring it. Getting up, they pulled on robes and went out to find the tray decorated with a sprig of holly and containing a plate of cinnamon rolls and butter as well. They fell upon the food, realizing that their exertions several hours previous had given them an appetite.

"Can we open our presents?" Ryan asked boyishly, and she nodded.

Together, like two kids, they took turns pulling off Christmas paper and opening the boxes beneath their small tree. They had decided beforehand to limit their gifts to two each. Ashley's boxes contained a red cashmere turtleneck sweater and a beautiful gold chain, at the end of which was a ruby heart. It was the necklace that caused her to cry. She had gotten Ryan a beautiful antique gold and bejeweled miniature triptych she had found in Venice with Bianca's help, and a leather desk set for his new office. He was delighted with both.

"We hung our stockings for Santa," Ashley reminded him. "I see there's something in yours. You'd better go check it."

"I thought we said two gifts. I forgot about the stocking. Stocking gifts don't figure in the total, do they?" He looked a little distressed.

"You'll remember next year. Go see what Santa left you," she encouraged him.

"Probably a lump of coal." He grinned. Reaching in, he pulled out a narrow rectangular box all beautifully gift wrapped. Carefully he pulled the paper off of it. *Probably a new watch,* he thought. Lifting the box lid and then the tissue, he stared down, confused, at the plastic rectangle with the pink plus sign. "What is it?" he asked her.

"A pregnancy test kit I took the other day," she said softly.

Ryan's mouth dropped open. He stared down at the pink plus, and then he looked up at Ashley. A smile suddenly split his handsome face. "We're going to have a baby?" he said in a husky voice.

"We're going to have a baby," Ashley told him, smiling back.

"When?"

"Sometime next August," she told him. "I think it was that mirror in the canopy above the bed in Venice that did it," Ashley teased him.

"We gotta get married," he said. "Right away!"

"We are married," she reminded him.

"Not in the eyes of the Church," he told her nervously.

"If it will make you happy, then fine," Ashley agreed. "But it has to be with your priest *and* mine, Ryan."

"No argument," he replied. "But right after the holiday, okay?"

"Fine," she told him. "I'd like to tell your family today after dinner."

He nodded. "Ma will be so pleased, especially since we're going to get married now."

"We are married, you dumb Eyetie-Mick!" she insisted. "It's legal."

"Yeah, yeah, okay, but not without the Church's blessing. Bear with me on this one. I can't help the way I was raised," Ryan said.

Ashley laughed. "I like the way you was raised," she teased him.

They finished their coffee, dressed, and went downstairs to greet their guests.

Byrnes had laid out a breakfast buffet on the library table in the living room. After a good night's sleep and a lot of rather excellent food, the five elder Mulcahy sisters were leaning toward acceptance of their new sister-in-law. Outrageous promises from their husbands had helped to cool their disappointment over losing the monies they had hoped to gain from selling R&R. They exchanged gifts with one another, their youngest sister, nephew, mother, brother, and Ashley.

"They're actually laughing," Frankie's son, Michael, whispered to his mother. "I never saw your sisters laugh so much."

"Scary, isn't it?" Frankie murmured back.

"Behave yourselves, the pair of you," Angelina scolded softly.

"Sorry, *Nonna*," Michael replied.

At four o'clock in the afternoon Christmas dinner was served.

"I wasn't certain what your traditions were," Ashley apologized, "and so I asked Mrs. B. to do prime rib, which my family has always served, a ham, and a turkey." She noted that most of her guests took a little of everything, and realized that she had just begun a new tradition. There were potatoes done about the beef, a sweet-potato casserole, and mashed potatoes, along with French-cut green beans, mashed turnips, creamed onions, and a fruit salad. There were freshly baked rolls, butter, and cranberry and horse-radish sauce.

"Where do you get such fresh beans?" Magdalena wanted to know.

"We have a small greenhouse where we grow them, along with peas, lettuces, radishes, carrots, spinach, and baby beets in the winter. We tried growing tomatoes, but it's a small greenhouse, and we haven't room to heat it enough. We pick the beans young."

"It's like being in your own little private world," Kathleen put in. "Is there any crime out here?"

"A little," Ashley said. "Egret Pointe isn't paradise, but it's as close as you can get to it, I think. Most of the crime is kid stuff, and when you live in a small town like this you get found out pretty fast. Everybody knows who you are, who your parents and family are, and what you did."

"Drugs?" Kevin McGuire asked.

"The kids get what they want, but they aren't getting it in the village. It's probably at the nearby mall," Ashley said.

When they had finished dinner, which concluded with Ashley's homemade plum pudding, mince and apple pies, and an ice-cream bombe created from chocolate, vanilla, and raspberry sherbert, along with coffee and tea, they returned to the living room, where the tree's glow reflected itself in the window, and the fire crackled. Ashley went to the library table, now set with a tray of liqueurs, and offered her guests an after-dinner drink.

"That's a beautiful engagement ring you're wearing," Bride noted.

"Ryan had it made for me in Venice when we were there last month," Ashley said proudly. "He gave it to me on my birthday. And I got this necklace for Christmas." She held up the gold chain with the ruby heart.

"Did you like Venice?" Elisabetta asked.

"Very much," Ashley responded. "We stayed with the Contessa di Viscontini in her palazzo. It's gorgeous, and she was so nice to us. Ryan is restoring a family piece that she found in an Austrian village shop."

"I think you're very broad-minded," Deirdre said softly.

"Why on earth would you say that?" Ashley asked her.

"Staying with your husband's former mistress," Deirdre replied. "I'm afraid I couldn't be that sophisticated, Ashley." She smiled a small smile.

The room had grown deathly silent, but before Ashley could even consider what she could possibly say to her sister-in-law, Ryan was on his feet.

"Bianca di Viscontini was never my mistress," he shouted. "Jesus, Dee, I was sixteen the last time I saw her. I haven't seen or spoken with her in twenty-three years!"

"You fucked her, Ryan," Deirdre said calmly. "All summer long that year."

"Deirdre Mary Mulcahy!" Angelina exclaimed. "I don't want to hear language like that coming out of your mouth ever again. How dare you! And in front of your nephew to boot. Apologize to Ryan and his wife at once!"

"Why? Are you going to pretend it didn't happen, Ma?" Deirdre asked.

"The contessa seduced your brother that summer. She should not have done such a thing, but sometimes women do things they should not. She apologized, and sooner or later your brother was going to gain carnal knowledge. If the truth be known, and God only knows I never thought I should say this aloud, but if your brother was to know a woman—and I knew he wasn't going to be a priest—I am just as glad it was Bianca di Viscontini who initiated him. Italian women know how to love and be loved. But she was hardly Ryan's mistress, and as soon as you came and told me what was going on we left Venice." Angelina's color was high with a mixture of distress and anger.

Ryan was obviously furious. "Why the hell did you bring this up now?" he demanded of his sister. "Is it impossible for the Mulcahy sisters to get through a family gathering without starting a riot?"

"I told you that one day I would get back at you for Carlo," Deirdre said.

"Uncle Ryan had a mistress when he was sixteen?" young Michael O'Connor said admiringly. "How cool is that? Just wait 'til I tell the guys in my dorm."

Frankie began to giggle, and even the withering look her mother sent her couldn't stop her laughter.

"Who the hell is Carlo?" Ryan wanted to know. "And what the hell did I do to him? You are off your nut, Dee. You need serious help."

"You don't even remember, do you?" Deirdre said dramatically. "Carlo Fabiano was the love of my life, and you told Dad some filthy lies about him. If you hadn't I wouldn't have told Ma about you and the contessa. We wouldn't have left Venice! Maybe I would have never left Venice."

"Are you talking about the slimeball you dated that summer? The one who had bets all over Venice with his friends on how long it would take him to get into your pants?" Ryan snapped at his older sister, astounded. "I saved your stupid butt, sis."

"I didn't believe that story you told Dad then, and I don't believe it now. Carlo loved me. He wanted to marry me," Deirdre said angrily.

"You were to be a notch on his bedpost, *stupida*," Ryan told her. "He had no intention of marrying you. Dad questioned him about that. Know what he said? He said he had to finish university first, and then he was going to law school. And his own father told Dad that the family was arranging a marriage for Carlo with a distant cousin when he finished his education. She was an heiress, and guess what? It all happened just the way we were told. The little prick is a big-shot lawyer in Milano, and is married to his fat, rich cousin. You only escaped with your virtue intact because one of the young men who knew Carlo and had met you thought Carlo was no gentleman, but that you were a proper virgin and needed to be protected. So he told me. And I told Dad. You don't have to thank me, Deirdre," Ryan finished sarcastically.

Deirdre's husband had listened to the exchange, surprised. "How soon after this love of your life did you marry me?" he asked her sarcastically.

Ashley had finally regained her composure. She was furious at Deirdre, and angrier at Ryan. "Robert," she said, addressing her brother-in-law, "I would prefer that you continue this discussion with your wife when you get home. Deirdre, if you don't shut your mouth this instant, I will throttle you myself. I will not have discord in *my* home, and especially at Christmas, which is supposed to be a season of peace."

"Wow," Michael O'Connor said softly. "Uncle Ryan got laid at sixteen."

Angelina threw up her hands in exasperation, but the boy's continued fascination with Ryan's teenage behavior caused enough laughter to break the tension in the room.

"Gimme a little more of that Madeira sherry," Kevin McGuire said. "You keep a good table, Ashley. It's been a wonderful Christmas for us because of you."

Ashley smiled. "Thanks," she said. "It's certainly been the most interesting holiday I can ever remember in this house."

"Who is the distinguished gentleman whose portrait is hanging over the fireplace?" Kathleen asked.

"That's my grandfather, Edward Livingston Kimbrough," she answered. "There are other ancestor portraits hanging all over the house. The one in the front hall is the Kimbrough who built the hall."

The rest of the evening continued on with light conversation, but the tension still lingered below the surface. Finally the guests began feigning yawns and deciding it was time for bed. Frankie practically took her son by his ear upstairs, because she could see he was dying to hang around and question his uncle, but Angelina remained until all of her daughters and their husbands had gone.

"Well, I think I'm ready for bed too," Ashley said.

"Wait," her mother-in-law said quietly. "I want to speak with you."

"Lina, there is nothing to say. It's over and done with. I'm just sorry that Deirdre nursed her anger for so long. She has hurt her husband very much. How soon after your return from Venice did they marry?"

"She had just become engaged to Robert before we left for Venice," Angelina replied. "The wedding was planned for the following spring, and it was celebrated then. I never knew she felt this way. She did not really love him, of course. Carlo Fabiano was suave and charming. Deirdre was very sheltered, and had never met anyone like him. They were never alone, that we knew of, but rather traveled in a group of other young people. We knew his reputation, but assumed she was safe, and in the end she was."

Ashley nodded.

"I told you the truth." Ryan suddenly broke into the conversation. "I hadn't seen or communicated with Bianca in over twenty years."

"We will speak upstairs," Ashley said quietly.

"*Cara*—" her mother-in-law began, but Ashley held up her hand.

"This is between your son and me, Lina."

And her tone told Angelina Mulcahy that Ashley was not to be trifled with in this matter. The older woman watched as the younger left the room. Then she turned to her son. "You should have stayed at a hotel," she said. "What in the name of God possessed you to accept the contessa's invitation? Are you so insensitive then? That is the Irish male in you, Ryan." She stood up. "I am going to bed, and you had better straighten this out with Ashley immediately." She departed the living room.

He sat alone for several minutes. Then, standing up, Ryan Mulcahy went upstairs to meet his fate. He found his wife awaiting him in their sitting room. "Baby, listen—" he began, but she put up a hand like a traffic cop.

"Sit down, Ryan," she told him.

"You can't be angry at me for something that happened when I was sixteen," he protested, obeying her directive.

"Of course I'm not angry at you for losing your virginity to the contessa," she told him. "I'm angry at you because you didn't trust me enough to tell me before we went to Venice. What a little ninny Bianca must have thought I was, Ryan."

"I'm sorry. You're right," he agreed. "But to be honest with you, I never even considered that summer again after it happened."

"It was thoughtless, Ryan," Ashley said. "I know our marriage began as one of convenience in order for both of us to save our assets, but you've said you love me, and I certainly love you. You know everything there is to know about me. I made no secret of my past with you. Marriage is based upon trust, among other things. That you didn't trust me enough to share that bit of information with me makes me reconsider whether we really have a marriage, or at least the chance of a real marriage."

"I swear to you I never thought of Bianca in all the years since that summer," he protested. "I do love you!" He stood up. It was impossible to feel the way he felt right now and remain seated, but she did stay seated. And calm. Frighteningly calm.

"That isn't the point, you moron!" Ashley shouted at him. "You brought me into the house of the woman who taught you all about sex, and you didn't warn me beforehand. Why the hell couldn't you tell me, Ryan? Why couldn't you allow the decision to stay in a palazzo or a hotel be mine?"

"It would have been inconvenient to stay in a hotel," he said. "I needed to be where the wardrobe was. It's my business! And how the devil was I supposed to tell you? 'Oh, by the way, baby, our hostess relieved me of my virginity when I was sixteen, but don't let it bother you. She's a real nice gal.'"

"Don't you dare hide behind your business, Ryan! All you had to do was explain to me about that summer. I would have understood. Do you think I'm so unsophisticated that I would have had a hissy fit, and refused to stay with the contessa? Hell, the woman is over twenty years older than you are, even if she does still look good, and after all, I am your wife. If you were still in love with Bianca di Viscontini you would have married her. But you should have told me, and you didn't. How can I ever trust you again, Ryan? How do I know what else you are keeping from me?"

"Baby, listen to me."

"Do you have something I could possibly want to hear, Ryan? I don't think so. At least not now. The couch in your office opens into a bed. Go sleep there tonight."

Suddenly his voice was cold. "I will not sleep in my office while my mother and the rest of my family are in the house," he snapped. "You can make whatever arrangement you want tomorrow when they are gone, but not tonight."

"Very well," Ashley agreed. "Tomorrow I will return to my old bedroom. You can have this. And, Ryan, you are not to tell anyone that I am pregnant. I had intended announcing our *happy* news tonight, until your sister decided to drop her bombshell."

"Yeah," he said. "It would have been a bit anticlimactic, wouldn't it?"

"I'm going to bed," she replied, and she slept as far away from him as she could that night, taking the bolster that usually lay at the head of their bed and running it lengthwise like a barrier between them. But the real barrier was the fact that he was a fool, Ryan knew.

The next morning they joined their guests for the breakfast buffet before the limousine arrived to transport them all home. The chatter was light and inconsequential. And afterward Ryan's eldest sister, the formidable Bride, took Ashley aside.

"I want to apologize for my sister," she began. "Okay, so we all were counting our chickens before they hatched, and Ryan's marriage took us by surprise. Especially as neither of you made any bones about the fact that it was to save yourselves, and not true love. But we're not fools. Well, maybe Dee is. We can see that you and Ryan do love each other at this point, and we don't want to see either of you unhappy because Dee can't get over her past. She hurt a lot of people last night. I'm sorry. The rest of us feel terrible about what she did. I hope you won't hold it against us. This was really a wonderful Christmas, and to be honest, we haven't had such a nice time in years. Any of us."

"Apology accepted," Ashley said. "And don't worry, Bride. I'm not going to throw your brother out. But he is going to get a very hard lesson in sensitivity training. I do love the big lug."

Bride smiled warmly. "Geez," she said. "You really are the right wife for him, Ashley. He needs someone who won't put up with his crap. We're with you all the way." And Bride Mulcahy Franklin actually hugged her sister-in-law.

"What's that all about?" Ryan murmured to Frankie.

"I think your wife has just joined the enemy," Frankie replied with a grin. "Serves you right too, dummy."

"No lectures, kid," he growled at her. "You don't want me poking into why you buy sexy apparel from Lacy Nothings now, do you?"

"You'll know soon enough," Frankie said mysteriously.

"Hey, Uncle Ryan, could I talk to you a minute?" Frankie's son asked.

Ryan looked to his youngest sister.

"Oh, go ahead," she said. "He'll never let you be until he does. Make it quick, Michael. The car is here, and we've got to go."

Ashley bade each of her guests good-bye, and Deirdre burst into tears as she faced her hostess.

"I'm so sorry," she sobbed. "It's the change. It makes me do cruel, stupid things."

"It's okay, Dee," Ashley assured the woman, but she thought, *I'll probably never really like you for what you did last night.*

"I don't know why I said what I said," Deirdre sobbed. "Robert is mad as hell at me now, and I don't blame him. I really am sorry." Then she joined the rest of them in the limousine.

Ashley almost felt sorry for her as her sisters moved away from the weeping Deirdre, and she heard Bride tell her sibling to belt up and stop howling.

"Can you ever forgive him?" Angelina asked before she too entered the car.

"Of course," Ashley murmured low. "But not until I've taught him a lesson about trust. You trusted your husband, didn't you? And he you?"

Her mother-in-law nodded. "Trust is every bit as important as love and sex," she answered. "Don't be too hard on him, *cara*. Men have many virtues, but usually common sense isn't among them. And men, for all their sizes and ages, never really grow up. They are all boys at heart, no matter how old they get. Trust me on that one." She kissed Ashley's cheek. "You will go into church before the baby is born, won't you? It would make me very happy if you did."

Ashley colored. "Did Ryan tell you? I'll kill him!"

Angelina shook her head in the negative. "*Cara*," she said, "I've borne seven children. I know the signs. I won't say anything until you are ready to make your announcement, and then I shall be totally surprised with the rest of them."

Ashley laughed softly. "I can see I won't get much past you, Lina. I was going to tell everyone last night, but then Deirdre started babbling."

"Of course, and then afterward you could say nothing."

"I'll call you," Ashley said, and then she ushered her mother-in-law into the car. She stood with Ryan as the stretch limousine drove down the hill and out of sight.

"Come in out of the cold," he said to her.

Wordlessly Ashley reentered the house. "I think," she told her husband, "that you'd better stay in town for a few days. I'm sure R&R could use your presence."

"Are you kicking me out?" he wanted to know.

"Only for a few days," she said. "Go tomorrow."

"I don't want to go," he said stubbornly, following her upstairs into their little sitting room. "I want to straighten this out right now."

"Ryan, there is nothing to straighten out. I do not hold a youthful indiscretion against you any more than you hold Carson, Chandler, and Derek against me. But as I told you last night, I would have liked to have known about Bianca before I accepted her hospitality. Did she know I didn't know?"

"Yes. A few nights before we left Venice we talked. She told me I should have told you, but that, not having done so, I had best remedy the error sooner than later," Ryan said.

"You spoke on the terrace below our bedroom. I saw you," Ashley responded.

"You never said anything," he replied, surprised.

"No, I didn't. I assumed you would speak of it eventually, and I certainly didn't suspect you of any infidelity," Ashley said. "I didn't believe you were that kind of man. Now I'm not so certain about that."

"I am not that kind of man," he said.

"If you say so," Ashley responded dryly.

Ryan gritted his teeth. Why the hell was she making this so difficult? So he hadn't told her that Bianca banged him when he was sixteen. So what? "I'm not going anywhere," he repeated.

"I'll sleep in my old room then," Ashley told him.

"Go ahead," he said. "You'll miss me, baby. You will."

"I'll survive," Ashley answered him sharply. "You would be surprised at how well I can survive without your exalted presence, darling." But she hated sleeping alone now. And she wasn't interested in uninhibited sex on The Channel either. What she really wanted was to talk with her brother. He'd been dead for so long, but she still missed him. Ben always knew how to help her. Ashley had always used The Channel for sex, but now she wondered if she couldn't use it to bring her brother back. Oh, she knew he wouldn't really be there, but she needed someone of her own to talk to, not someone on Ryan's side, no matter how nice they were.

Ben, she said to herself, *I want you back. I have to talk with you. Let's meet down on the beach. Remember that October day when we just sat and talked? That's what I want now. For us to sit and talk.* She pressed the button that let the wall covering the flat screen television open. She pressed the on button on the channel changer, programmed in The Channel, and then she hit the A button, and enter. And there she was on the beach below the bluff on which Kimbrough Hall stood. And there was her brother, Ben, coming toward her. She ran into his arms. Though he would be over forty now, he looked as he always had.

"Hey, kiddo, what's the matter?" he asked, his blue eyes sympathetic. He led her to the bench by the water's edge. "Tell your big brother, and I'll try to make it all right."

"Oh, Benji, why did you have to get killed in that damned war?" she asked him.

"Hey, kiddo, that was my fate, but you didn't fantasize me just to ask that. What's the problem?"

Ashley started to cry, and between sobs she told him.

Ben listened quietly, and then when she had concluded her tale of woe he said, "Kiddo, you know you can't hold it against him that he was either too dumb or too scared shitless to tell you about the contessa. You've married one of the good guys."

"But I don't think he would ever have told me about her if his damned sister hadn't shot her mouth off," Ashley said.

"Have you told him about The Channel?" Ben asked her.

Ashley's jaw dropped, but then she quickly said, "That's different!"

"Nope, it isn't, kiddo," Ben told her. "Look, everyone has something in his or her life that for whatever reason they don't want to share. It doesn't mean they're thoughtless or being dishonest. It just means they don't want to share it. You going to tell Ryan about The Channel, Ashley?"

"Of course not! It's a women's thing. No woman who gets The Channel talks about it to a man," she replied. "It's an unwritten rule."

"I rest my case, kiddo," Ben said. "Look, Ashley, we never know what's going to come at us in life. I never expected to die in Desert Storm. Frankie never expected to lose her husband in the attack on the Twin Towers. You don't want to waste a moment of the time you're given. So Ryan *neglected* to tell you about the contessa. Maybe he was never going to tell you about her. Call it a sin of omission." He smiled at her. "Hey, kiddo, you love him. Now don't waste any more time being pissed at him. I can tell you that you've scared him to death, Ashley. He won't make the same mistake again." Ben laughed, and his eyes crinkled just the way she remembered them doing.

"I miss you so much," Ashley said. "You're right about Ryan. He's smart in so many ways, but where women are concerned he's just a big dumb jock. And I do love him. I really got lucky, Benji, didn't I?"

"Yeah, kiddo, you did," her brother said wistfully, with a smile.

"We're having a baby," Ashley confided.

"Yeah, I know," Ben replied.

"I think I got pregnant that last night in Venice," she told him.

"Nope," he said, a twinkle in his blue eyes. "But it was before you got back to Egret Pointe, kiddo."

"Not that last night, but before we got back?" And then Ashley blushed a deep pink color, remembering their trip.

"Yeah." Ben chuckled. "It was then." He put his arm around her and gave her a loving squeeze. "Well, I've got to be going now, kiddo."

"Can we talk again?" Ashley asked him.

He shook his head. "You're not on The Channel this time, little sister. You're dreaming," he explained. "I wouldn't be here otherwise. The folks who run The Channel aren't on my boss's invite list. But the place is harmless for most women. They don't linger that long as a rule."

"But I distinctly remember turning on the television and programming you in as a new fantasy," Ashley insisted.

"Did you, Ashley? Maybe you were just too tired and upset to realize what you were doing." He stood up, and she did too. Then Ben Kimbrough bent down and kissed his younger sister gently. "So long, kiddo. Oh, Granddad and our folks say hello."

And before Ashley could say another word her brother began walking down the beach, disappearing into a mist that had suddenly come in off of the water. "Ben," she said softly, but he was gone, and the mist was surrounding her too. To her great surprise she awoke. The flat-screen television was still hidden behind its wall. The remote lay on the nightstand next to her bed. Beyond her bedroom windows the day was gray, and she could see that snow had begun to fall.

Ashley slowly got out of bed. *Ben!* She had spoken to her brother. She had! She smiled. And as always his advice had been good. It was good now. She was going to take it, because she didn't want to end up like Deirdre, foolish and bitter. Glancing at the clock on the mantel, she saw it was about to strike six a.m. Ashley opened the door to her old bedroom and hurried down the hall to where Ryan lay sleeping in their own bed. Entering the room, she slipped into bed beside him, and at once his arm encircled her.

"Am I forgiven then for being a coward and a jerk?" he asked her.

"Only if you make mad, passionate love to me," Ashley told him.

"Thanks, baby, and I do apologize," he said. "How did I ever get so lucky?"

"I don't know," she said, "but I think we both got lucky. Now cut the talk, darling, and let's have a little more action, please."

He laughed happily. "Anything you say, baby. Anything you want," he promised her, grinning.

"Now, will you look at that?" Ashley said. "You've finally got it, darling. You finally understand how it works in a modern marriage. I am the mistress. You are the slave. Now pleasure me, my darling, and then we have to decide when to go into the church so this child of ours will be one hundred percent legal and legitimate."

He kissed her a kiss that Ashley could have sworn curled her toes, and she felt him harden against her. "Yes, mistress," Ryan Finbar Mulcahy said to his wife, his hands beginning to roam over her body.

Ashley purred with her total satisfaction as both outside and inside the storm built and increased in its intensity. She had to remember tomorrow to cancel her subscription to The Channel. It was unlikely she would ever need it again.

Epilogue

Benjamin Kimbrough Mulcahy was born on the nineteenth day of August, a week before his parents' first anniversary. Everyone remarked on his bright blue eyes, which several months later at his baptism were still an unrelenting blue.

"The blue of his namesake," Ashley said quietly.

The baby was baptized in St. Anne's, the same church where his parents had spoken their vows some months before. It was Thanksgiving weekend, and the hall was filled to capacity with Angelina and her family. Michael O'Connor, now a freshman at Princeton, stood as godfather to his cousin. His mother, Frankie, was the baby's godmother.

Back at the house afterward, Angelina noticed a pair of very rococo antique silver candlesticks on the dining room table. "I have not seen those before," she said to her daughter-in-law. "They're beautiful, and quite valuable, unless I miss my guess."

"They belong to your grandson," Ashley said. "A gift."

"From whom?" And then, carefully inspecting the candlesticks, she smiled. "Bianca di Viscontini?" she said, recognizing the Italian workmanship of the candlesticks.

Ashley nodded. "We sent her a birth announcement and told her that Venice could still claim to be the most romantic city in the world."

Angelina laughed. "Well," she noted as she looked at her newest grandson, "certainly no one in this family can deny that."

And Ashley replied softly, "Romance, Lina, can be wherever you make it." Yes, everyone could believe that little Benji had been conceived in Venice, even Ryan. But Ashley knew better. She knew because her brother had told her, and Ben had never lied to her. Her son had been conceived aboard a jetliner over the Atlantic, or possibly Montauk Point. She had joked to herself about calling him Mile High, or Skylar. He had been created from the love she and Ryan had for each other, and from the delicious sudden pleasures that they always seemed to find with each other.

Her husband came up, slipping an arm about her waist. "Ready for another?" he teased Ashley, and turning, she whispered something in his ear. Ryan Finbar Mulcahy actually blushed and chuckled. "Anytime, baby," he said. *"Anytime!"*

Grandfather Kimbrough had been right after all, Ashley thought with a smile. There really was a happily ever after.

About the Author

Bertrice Small (1937–2015), was an American *New York Times* and *USA Today* bestselling author of over fifty historical, contemporary, fantasy and erotic romance novels. She lived on Long Island, New York. Her first novel, *The Kadin*, was published in 1978. She was a member of The Authors Guild and Romance Writers of America, and in 2004 received a Lifetime Achievement Award from *Romantic Times* for her contributions to the romance genre.

About the Publisher

This book is published on behalf of the author by the Ethan Ellenberg Literary Agency.
https://ethanellenberg.com
Email: agent@ethanellenberg.com

www.ingramcontent.com/pod-product-compliance
Lightning Source LLC
LaVergne TN
LVHW012059070526
838200LV00074BA/3665